COMRADES... OR MAN AND WIFE?

"Monsieur le Comte?"

Lamotte turned his head with a snap. His mouth fell open in shock to see Sophie, her soft brown hair in ringlets about her face and looking like a dream in a dress of rich green, holding out her hand to him.

"You are rather lacking in gallantry, Monsieur le Comte, to ignore us so pointedly."

He blinked twice to make sure he was not seeing visions. "I did not know it was you. You look . . . different."

"I am the same Sophie Delamanse I always was—only in a dress."

He could not get over how feminine and fragile she looked—how unlike a soldier. He had an overpowering urge to take her in his arms and hold her close, to protect her from the world outside. "It suits you."

She gestured first to one and then the other of the women accompanying her. "My friends, Mademoiselle Ruthgard and Mademoiselle Dardagny. They have come to see me wed."

Lamotte bowed perfunctorily to them both, but his eyes were captivated by Sophie. His wife-to-be was beautiful—truly beautiful. He had not thought a dress could make so much difference. In her gown of emerald green, her blue eyes shining, she was the woman he had dreamed of marrying. She was the Sophie he had always imagined her to be. . . .

Dear Romance Readers,

In July of 1999, we launched the Ballad line with four new series, and each month we present both new and continuing stories set everywhere from medieval England to the American West—the kind of passionate, romantic stories you love best, written by the most gifted authors. At the back of each book, we tell you when you can find subsequent books in the series that have captured your heart.

This month, rising star Cheryl Bolen offers the third installment of her atmospheric *Brides of Bath* series. What will happen when a man driven by honor loses his heart to **A Fallen Woman**? Next, the always talented Tracy Cozzens explores **A Dangerous Fancy** in the next entry of her *American Heiresses* series as a proper young woman, who has caught the eye of the Prince of Wales himself, discovers that a roguish nobleman might be her unlikely savior—and the kind of man who could win her love.

The fabulous Pat Pritchard continues her *Gamblers* series with the second of her incredibly sexy heroes. A U.S. Marshal posing as a hardened card player has no time for romance—until he meets a woman who makes him feel like the **King of Hearts.** Finally, promising newcomer Kate Silver whisks us back to the glittering French court of Louis XIV in her brand-new series . . . *And One for All*. When a Musketeer in the King's Guard learns that his comrade may not be all "he" seems, he must promise to keep her secret, **On My Lady's Honor**—unless passion sweeps them both away. Enjoy!

Kate Duffy
Editorial Director

... *And One for All*

ON MY LADY'S HONOR

Kate Silver

ZEBRA BOOKS
Kensington Publishing Corp.
http://www.kensingtonbooks.com

ZEBRA BOOKS are published by

Kensington Publishing Corp.
850 Third Avenue
New York, NY 10022

Copyright © 2002 by Catherine Sneyd

All rights reserved. No part of this book may be reproduced in any form or by any means without the prior written consent of the Publisher, excepting brief quotes used in reviews.

If you purchased this book without a cover you should be aware that this book is stolen property. It was reported as "unsold and destroyed" to the Publisher and neither the Author nor the Publisher has received any payment for this "stripped book."

All Kensington titles, imprints and distributed lines are available at special quantity discounts for bulk purchases for sales promotion, premiums, fund-raising, educational or institutional use.

Special book excerpts or customized printings can also be created to fit specific needs. For details, write or phone the office of the Kensington Special Sales Manager: Kensington Publishing Corp., 850 Third Avenue, New York, NY 10022. Attn. Special Sales Department. Phone: 1-800-221-2647.

Zebra and the Z logo Reg. U.S. Pat. & TM Off.

First Printing: August, 2002
10 9 8 7 6 5 4 3 2 1

Printed in the United States of America

Prologue

The Camargue, in the south of France
Autumn 1669

"Oh, Gerard, I will miss you so." Sophie Delamanse stood in the courtyard, shivering in the early morning darkness, and held tight to her twin brother's thickly gloved hand. She fought to control the tears that threatened to spill over onto her cheeks.

Well-bred young ladies don't make a vulgar display of their emotions, she repeated to herself to keep the tears at bay. That had always been one of the hardest lessons for her to learn. Just last eve her mother had scolded her for her long face and now here she was crying again.

"You'll break my fingers with your death grip, you silly cabbage," Gerard said, as he drew her toward him in a bear hug. Under the cover of their embrace, he whispered in her ear, his words muffled in her woolen hood, "Now that I am a soldier, I doubt I should confess as much, but I'll miss you, too."

She clung tightly to her twin. They had never been separated for longer than a day since their birth. The mere thought of his absence made her feel as though an essential part of her was gone. How would she manage when he was over a week's journey away from her, living among strangers? "Look after yourself, Gerard."

The bay gelding beside them stamped his feet and gave a snort of impatience, his breath misting around his head. The jingling of his harness carried clearly through the still, crisp morning air. "Look after Seafoam, too. Feed him plenty of corn and don't ride him into the ground." She blinked furiously to hold back her tears. "Be brave."

"I will be the bravest musketeer in the King's Guard," he promised her. "I shall make you all proud of me."

Her sorrow at losing him should be tempered by pleasure at his advancement in the King's service, she told herself. She would not spoil his last moments alone with her by indulging her grief.

With some effort, she held him at arm's length and gave him a saucy smile. "I already am. How could I not be proud of you, in your fine waistcoat and jacket and leather boots polished to a shine? You look as fine as a peacock strutting around the Queen's garden."

Gerard lost his manly dignity for long enough to poke his tongue out at his sister. "When I am the best swordsman in the King's Guard, you will not dare to be so disrespectful, or I shall cut off a dozen of your precious curls with a flick of my sword."

Sophie smiled through the tears that would slip out, however she tried to restrain them. "You will do no such thing, younger brother . . ."

"Younger by a scant ten minutes," he reminded her, in a repeat of the game they had played ever since they could talk.

She ignored his interruption. ". . . for I will equal

you in swordmanship when you come home next summer."

He looked at her with a measure of respect. "I believe you could, too, if you put your mind to it. You have a strong will for a woman, and the courage to match."

Sophie glowed under her brother's praise. He did not give compliments lightly. Kind words from him were precious, and had to be savored. "A duel, then? Next summer? The loser to pay a forfeit of the winner's choosing?"

"Sophie, you are a madcap and I love you dearly." He brushed the corner of his eyes with his sleeve. Were he not a man, she would swear he was weeping. "The sun will soon rise, and I must needs be on my way before dawn. Come with me and I shall make my farewells to Mother and Father."

She took his hands in hers one last time and gave them a squeeze. "Go on up alone. I will say my last good-bye to you now."

He bowed his head in acknowledgement of the pain he saw reflected in her eyes. "Good-bye, Sophie. God bless you." And he was gone.

Sophie returned to her chamber and stood at her casement window, gazing down into the courtyard below her. The sky was just lightening with the first touches of pink when her brother strode back again. He swung his leg over Seafoam's back and cantered off into the lane, the flaps of his greatcoat flying behind him like a banner.

At the gate he wheeled Seafoam around and stopped for a moment, the gelding's hooves kicking up the dry dust of the lane around his knees. His eyes sought the flicker of the lighted candle she had placed in her casement window. He raised his whip in a final salute before turning his head once more toward the road ahead, to Paris and the new life he would carve out for himself as a soldier and a courtier.

To his new life—without her.

One

Twelve months later

Sophie glared at the piece of sewing in her hands as rebellious thoughts ran through her head. Gerard would not notice whether she greeted him in a new gown she had stitched herself or not. He had been absent for a full twelve months in Paris, and her anxiety to see him again almost overwhelmed her. She did not understand why she must have a new gown for the occasion. She had a baker's dozen of gowns already that she scarcely ever wore. Her mother's insistence on needless stitchery was wearying.

She made three more stitches, so small and fine they could barely be seen. Gerard was lucky to have been born a boy. His future lay in adventure and excitement, guarding the young King from his enemies and keeping the peace in the turbulent streets of Paris. How she envied the life he was able to lead, while she, his elder by ten long minutes, was doomed by an accident of birth to a life of interminable sewing.

She shifted uncomfortably on the hard wooden bench. From the open casement window, she could see the tops of the trees swaying in a gentle breeze. How she longed to gallop furiously through the fields in these last few days of golden sunshine before the clouds obscured the sun and the snows of winter started to fall. There would be no such fast riding when the ground was covered with snow. A false step in the snow would break a horse's leg and ruin the beast for good.

Ouch. A moment's inattention, and she had pricked her finger. A large drop of red blood welled from the tip and threatened to drip on to the precious blue silk bundled in her lap.

With a muttered curse, she flung her unfinished gown to one side and popped her injured finger in her mouth.

"Wrap a scrap of linen around it," her ever vigilant mother suggested, her own needle never pausing, "so you do not ruin your gown."

She had not the patience for another stitch. "May I not exercise my mare? She has not been out of the stables all day and she will be getting restless."

Her mother smiled, more with resignation than with mirth. "Like her rider, perhaps?"

"Or practice my archery while the light is still good enough to see the targets well?"

"Fine stitches need good light, too. Besides, I fear the marsh is not a healthy place to be at this time of the season." Her mother's normally placid face bore a look of unusual worry. "There is news of an aguish fever in the village on the far side. The parish priest believes the swamp mist to be the cause and would have us all keep away from it for our safety. I would not have us all fall sick of an ague while Gerard is here."

Sophie made an exasperated noise. Plague take the fever. Would her mother not have mercy and release her? "My legs are cramped from sitting so long in one place together and my arms ache."

Her mother laid her sewing aside for the moment in her lap and looked at her with a small sigh. "I will never make a competent needlewoman out of you, I fear. You have little diligence or patience."

Sophie bowed her head under the mild rebuke. She knew how well deserved it was when it came to needlework. If only her mother could see how well she had practiced her archery, though, she would not accuse her of being lacking in diligence. Her knife throwing was improving, too. She could hit her target eight times out of ten now when her throwing arm was in good form.

"I suppose you may leave your new gown for the moment to rest your weary limbs . . ."

She sprang to her feet. "Ah, mother, I promise I will go nowhere near the marshes, even though it is good hunting there, and I could bring back a brace of fat ducks for the table before dusk fell."

". . . but not to practice your archery."

She sank back down on the stool again, her eagerness to leave less fierce now that she was forbidden her favorite pursuit. Still, if she could not hunt, she could walk or ride. . . .

"If you will not sew, go and help the cook with making gooseberry preserves. It is time enough you learned a woman's duties. Your father is concerned your education has been sadly neglected of late."

"I can speak a smattering of English," Sophie protested, seeing her afternoon spent in the sunshine disappearing into the mists, "and read Italian very well. Besides which I can write and cipher, too."

Her mother sighed. "You know little of running a household and supervising servants, which will be more use to you as a noblewoman than all the books in Italy. Your husband will not care whether you can speak that slippery English tongue or not, but he will mind if his apartments are not kept warm and clean, with good, hot dinners served to him betimes, and the bed linen fresh and sweet-smelling."

"I have no husband who needs such care."

"Not yet. But your father would speak to you tonight on that very matter."

A husband? She felt a wealth of excitement and apprehension mingle in the pit of her belly. Her father had never mentioned the possibility to her before.

Despite Sophie's less than subtle probing, and even her outright pleas for more information, her mother would give nothing else away.

Her father must have made a match for her, Sophie decided, as she made her way to the kitchen to help the cook.

She said a silent prayer as she stirred the pots of simmering gooseberries that he had chosen Jean-Luc for her. Jean-Luc was young and handsome, with light brown hair that fell straight about his shoulders and a happy smile never far from his face. He could ride like leaves on the wind and outshoot her three times out of five. His father owned the manor house to the adjoining village and was well respected in the county, and Jean-Luc was his eldest son and heir.

Though Jean-Luc's family was not as wealthy as her own, she hoped with all her heart he would still be an acceptable match in her father's eyes. None of the other likely candidates in the neighborhood were half so appealing: they were too old and dull or too wild and vicious. If she was to get married, she would choose Jean-Luc above all others.

Her father was in rare good humor that night when

Sophie peeked through the half-open door to his private apartments, visions of Jean-Luc running through her mind.

He beckoned her in with a smile. "Come in, Sophie, and pull a chair up to the fire. I have business matters of some importance to impart to you."

He never discussed such matters with her. Sophie now regretted all the deliciously sweet-tart gooseberry preserve she had gobbled that afternoon with the cook. With one grave look from her father, it suddenly lay uncomfortably heavy on her stomach, in a curdled foment of sugary acid. What if her intended was not Jean-Luc after all, but the old Marquis de la Renta? He was at least fifteen years older than she and talked interminably of poetry.

"Your mother tells me you have been attending well to your education today."

She swallowed nervously to keep the gooseberry preserve down in her stomach. "I have been helping the cook with the preserving, sir. We have enough now for the coming winter and into spring as well."

"Good, good," he said abstractedly, hardly seeming to have heard her. He steepled his fingers together and regarded her with a serious eye. "Your brother Gerard will be returning home in little over a week. You will be glad to see him, I've no doubt."

She nodded. "Yes, sir. I have missed him."

"As have we all." He held his hands out to the fire. "His good friend, the young Count Lamotte, will be joining us shortly after Gerard arrives."

He looked at her as if he expected an answer to this remark.

"Yes, sir." Gerard had written to her of his friend, Ricard, Count Lamotte. He had been a musketeer in the King's Guard for three years and had quickly become her brother's bosom friend. She was not overjoyed to hear the count would be visiting them. She had been looking forward to having her brother all to herself again after so many months of separation.

"Lamotte is a healthy young man of good family," her father continued, "and in high favor with the king. His estates are reputed to be well managed, and by Gerard's reports he is neither a gambler nor a wastrel, but a man of honor whose word can be relied upon." He paused. "He is of the age to take a wife."

The conversation had suddenly taken a menacing turn. Sophie shivered. "A wife?"

"Lamotte's uncle and I have come to a satisfactory arrangement about your dowry and the settlement that would be made upon you in the event of the young count's death." He chuckled deep in his throat. "The old man is shrewd, I'll warrant you, but we hammered out a fair enough deal in the end. You'll take a good enough stack of gold and other stuffs with you into the union, and if the count dies before you, you'll be treated as you deserve."

Her head was whirling in confusion. She was not to marry Jean-Luc, nor even one of her neighbors at all, but a man she had never met? "The two of you have decided I will marry the count? Without his consent? Or mine?"

"Lamotte has consented to the match, and I have accepted on your behalf. You will be betrothed when he arrives, and wed as soon as the banns have been called. When he returns to Paris, it has been agreed you shall be sent to manage his household in Burgundy. Paris, and the court of Louis XIV in particular, is no place for a young, country-bred woman."

She shook her head in an attempt to clear her thoughts. "I thought I would wed Jean-Luc," she said, speaking to more to herself than to her father. The full import of her father's news overwhelmed her powers of rational thought.

"I had been considering an overture from Jean-Luc's father, it is true," her father answered. "But the count has far more exciting prospects. You will be much better off as his wife than as the wife of a simple country squire."

Sheer panic assailed her, and she swallowed twice before she could manage to utter a single word. "I am to wed the count and be sent away from here? Far away from you and mother and Gerard and the village and everything I know?" Her voice rose dangerously high as she sought to keep back her tears.

Her father placed his hands, palms upward, on the table, as if offering her up an explanation for his decision. "Your mother misliked that you would live so far away in Burgundy, but every woman must some day leave her parents' household and cleave to that of her husband."

Burgundy, she murmured to herself. The word rolled off her tongue with a strange flavor. She had never been farther than the village in all her life before, and now she was to travel across France to live a new life as a married woman—wed to a man she had never met.

When she had thought about marriage at all, which was seldom, she had imagined herself married to Jean-Luc. She had hoped one day he would ask for her hand and allow her to settle into a comfortable life close to her family.

But to be wed to a stranger! She could not, *would* not bear it.

Gerard. She clutched onto the thought of her

brother like a lifeline. He was returning home in a sennight. He would save her.

Surely her twin would see how repugnant this marriage was to her soul. Their father would listen to his son's objections where he would ignore those of a mere daughter. She must win him over to her cause before it was too late. "Does Gerard know yet of my betrothal?"

"Indeed. He was the first to propose the match."

The words hit her ears with the force of a hammer striking an anvil. Gerard, her beloved twin, had betrothed her to a man she had never met? He knew how much she wanted adventure in her life, how she envied him his life in Paris. He even knew how fond she was of Jean-Luc. He could not be responsible for having her sent away to some faraway county to manage the household of an absent stranger. He had never breathed a word of this marriage to her. She shook her head in denial. "No, I cannot believe it."

The gooseberry preserves roiled around in her insides once more, and her stomach finally revolted. "Excuse me, sir," was all she managed to stammer as she stumbled, white-faced, out of the door.

She barely made it to the privy before she sank to the floor and was violently ill. Retching convulsions racked her body until at last her stomach was emptied of everything but bile.

She did not sleep that night, her mind turning over and over with a sense of utter rejection and betrayal. As the first fingers of daylight began to appear over the horizon, she finally gave up on her attempt to rest.

The stableboy was snoring in the corner in a bundle of hay when she crept quietly into the stables. She saddled Firedancer as quietly as she could, unwilling to disturb the young lad's rest.

The early autumn air on her face made her shiver, and she wrapped her heavy coat around her more tightly. She felt strangely light-headed—from lack of sleep, she supposed. She hadn't broken her fast that morning either, but the memory of the gooseberries was still too recent for her to feel hungry.

She could leave now, she supposed, if she had anywhere to run. She could not go to Jean-Luc and ask for his help. Marriages were made by fathers, never by the parties involved themselves. Jean-Luc was as powerless as she in this matter.

For a brief moment she flirted with the idea of riding to Paris and throwing herself on the mercy of the king, begging him to forbid the marriage, until the practicalities of such a flight intruded into her despair. She had no food either for her or for Firedancer and no money with which to buy any. She did not even know the right road to take to get to Paris. And even if, by some miracle, she were able to get to Paris without losing her way or dying of starvation or being robbed and murdered by brigands on the road, the king might not be there. More probably he would refuse to see her, or, most likely of all, he would tell her to cease her disobedience and to honor her father's wishes in the matter.

Running away was impossible.

Refusing to marry the count would dishonor her father, but marrying him was unthinkable.

She'd reached the outer marshes now. This was her favorite place in the whole world, the spot that was hers and hers alone. She came here whenever she needed time to herself, to think or just to daydream. Never had she needed the consolation this place held for her more than this morning.

As she approached the water, the croaking of the

nearby frogs stopped, and she heard the tiny plops as they jumped into the water, disturbed by her nearness. A group of flamingos, their pale pink feathers showing clearly against the green-brown marsh, stalked through the water in the distance, their long, thin legs picking delicately through the mud.

Firedancer was soon tied to a tree at the edge, grazing on the lush grass that surrounded him. With blades of green poking out of the sides of his mouth, he snorted and tossed his head, enjoying his reprieve from the early morning exercise.

Sophie sat down on a hillock of dry ground by the edge of the marsh, her bow within easy reach. She could not run away, but at least she could still hunt.

A flock of geese passed overhead, but they were too far away for her to shoot. Jean-Luc would have shot at them anyway—and wasted his arrow, like as not.

She wondered if Count Lamotte ever hunted, or if he believed women should spend their lives on dull household chores. God preserve her from a husband like that. She would almost rather have the Marquis de la Renta and his interminable poetry. At least he considered hunting a healthful pursuit, as he was overfond of telling her.

Cicadas chirruped sadly, their rasping song reminding her that summer was nearly done and the dark, cold days of winter were not far away. The lowing of nearby cattle resonated through the stillness.

Her patience was soon rewarded with the sight of a pair of ducks just come from their nest of grasses at the edge of the water. With the ease and grace of long practice, she fitted an arrow to her bow and let it fly with a soft thwang. The drake was dead before he registered the presence of a predator. The duck flew squawking into the misty morning, only to be brought down a few seconds later with a second arrow.

A brace of ducks already. Usually she would be satisfied with her morning's work, but today she did not want to return. Her home was no refuge against the dangers that faced her.

She gutted her kill, wrinkling her nose at the stench of the innards. The by now familiar pang that Gerard was not there to laugh at her squeamishness tugged at her heart. She flung the bloody mess into the water and wiped her knife and hands on the grass to clean them.

She had to face up to the reality of her future, she chided herself, as she flung herself down on the ground in the early sun.

She was heartsick that she could not marry Jean-Luc. She had loved him so well and for so long. Her heart wrenched in two to have to give up all thoughts of wedding him.

Still, her husband-to-be was a musketeer—a Parisian, as Gerard was now. If Gerard liked the count, he could not be all bad. He would not be violent or a drunkard, at any rate. Gerard had no time for such men. She only hoped she and the count would achieve at least a small measure of liking for one another. She could not bear to be married to a man she disliked and who would be sure to despise her in return.

Gerard would be bound to visit her once she was married to his closest companion. If she played her cards well maybe Gerard, or even Lamotte himself, would one day take her to Paris with him. She had always longed to go to Paris.

Doubtless Burgundy would have its own charm, too, even though it was far from Paris. At any rate, her marriage would give her a new world, one she was certain she could order in some measure to please herself.

Her father had handed her adventure on a plate, she thought wearily, even if she had been too shocked at first to recognize it. Once she was over the suddenness of the proposal, her fate did not seem so bad. She would try not to pine overmuch for Jean-Luc, whom she could never have now. She would do her duty to her parents as she had been brought up to do, acquiesce to this marriage to the count with a good grace, and prepare herself for adventure. Indeed, she had no other choice.

Her decision once made, and with the sun warming her tired limbs as she lay in the grasses at the edge of the marsh, she fell into a deep, troubled sleep.

The sun was high in the sky when she awoke again. Midges swarmed around her, attacking every scrap of bare skin they could find. She brushed them away with a lazy hand, but there were too many of them.

Her sleep had not refreshed her, but had left her with a pounding head and a body that felt tired and aching all over. She felt worse than she had before she went to sleep. Moreover, she was dying of thirst, and she had no water bottle with her.

Chiding herself for her foolishness, she brushed the midges off the brace of ducks she had killed early that morning, picked them up by their webbed feet, and tossed them over the pommel of the saddle. Firedancer snorted at the smell of dried blood, but he allowed her to climb on his back and wearily point his head toward home.

The gelding was in no hurry. Despite her thirst, which had grown almost unbearable by now, she had not the strength to hurry him on his way. He ambled slowly through the fields and down the rutted path,

Sophie concentrating all that remained of her energy on keeping herself upright on his back.

Mists threatened to engulf her vision while the bright sunlight of the clear autumn day overwhelmed her eyes, which were made doubly sensitive by the pain that throbbed behind her temples. Her arms barely had the strength to hold the reins, and her legs hung limply along the gelding's side, too weak to hold her in her seat as she flopped about with every step he took.

Nightmarish apparitions appeared in the air around her, tormenting her with the empty promise of the water she longed for and filling the air with maniacal laughter before dissolving back into nothing. She didn't know if she was awake or dreaming.

By the time she reached the courtyard, she was hanging on to the merest thread of remaining sense by the sheer force of her will.

The courtyard was thronged with people rushing hither and thither, and the noise of it assaulted her ears like a blow to the temple.

Her brother—at least she thought it was her brother, but wasn't he still in Paris?—strode toward her from among the crowds of people, his arms held out wide.

Sophie gazed uncomprehendingly at the apparition in front of her, expecting it, too, to dissolve before her eyes, as had all the others. "Water," she croaked from between her cracked lips, when the form in front of her stayed strangely solid. "Give me water."

His arms reached out to lift her down from her horse, but she could not make any move toward him. "Water," she begged once more, as her sight grew black and she felt herself slip and fall.

She could not tell whether it was her body or her

mind that was tumbling down. All she knew was that the pit engulfing her was cold and dark, and the bottom was a long, long way away.

The next few weeks were a blur. Now and then she awoke with a raging thirst, calling out for drink until a blessed figure would come and drip some precious drops of life-giving liquid down her throat and smooth her brow with a cool, wet rag scented with lavender. Sometimes the figure was her mother, sometimes her brother, and sometimes her childhood nurse, dead of a dropsy more than three seasons ago.

At times she was so hot she knew she had died and gone to hell, where devils were roasting her over hot coals for all eternity.

Then the cold would ambush her, freezing her limbs until she could feel the ice forming on her toes, on her knees, on her belly, immobilizing her with the caress of its deadly fingers.

Always the pain was there, lurking just out of reach in the recesses of her head or engaged in a full-frontal assault on her entire body. Then she would shake and cry and beg to be released from torment, until the pain receded once more into the mini death of her deep, trancelike sleep.

Then one morning when she awoke the pain was gone, the curtains around her four-poster bed were drawn back to let in the fresh morning air, the sun shone through a chink in her windowpane, and she knew she was no longer asleep in a feverish nightmare. Her arms felt strangely heavy when she tried to move them and the light still hurt her eyes, but her mind was clear.

With some effort she turned her head on the pillow. Her brother was standing by the window, his figure silhouetted against the light. She blinked quickly to make sure she was not seeing chimeras still. The figure didn't disappear. "Gerard?" Her voice came out as a hoarse croak.

He strode over to her side. "Sophie? You are awake?"

She held out her arms to him, but she was too weak to lift them off the coverlet to embrace him. With Gerard home, she felt whole again. "I'm so glad to see you."

He took her hands in his. "And I you. I feared I had come too late, that your sickness had taken you out of my reach before I could see you once more. I am beyond happy that you are better."

She smiled into his deep blue eyes, which so closely mirrored her own. He would always be first in her heart. "I am better now that you are here with me."

"You must be hungry. See if you can sit up a little, and I will feed you some soup."

She was ravenous. Soup sounded heavenly. It seemed an age had passed before Gerard returned with a couple of bowls of warm broth.

She lifted herself up in the bed a little and he placed a large bolster under her head so she could swallow without choking.

He spooned a sup of broth into her mouth. It was thin and weak, but she gulped it down greedily. After a couple of mouthfuls her shrunken stomach felt full and she turned her head away from the spoon. Her weakness shamed her. "I cannot eat any more. Thank you."

She had lost track of time in her fevered state. When had she been to the marshes and fallen asleep in the sun there? Was it yesterday, or much longer ago? "Have I been ill for long?"

Gerard took a mouthful from his own bowl of broth. "The day I arrived home you were sick and raving with fever, and you fell off your horse into my arms without even knowing I was there. I have been home for three weeks now. My leave is well nigh gone already."

Surely not. She could not have been ill for the entire time he was here. There was so much she wanted to tell him and show him. Her skill with the bow, for one, not to mention the colt captured from one of the herds of wild horses that roamed freely throughout the Camargue that she was taming and had already trained to eat apples out of her hand. "Must you leave again so soon?"

He gave a slight grimace as he swallowed. "I will stay here with you until you are recovered."

She suddenly felt ashamed of her selfish desires. She was only his sister, and should not stand in the way of his advancement. "Your captain will not mind that you overstay your leave?"

A bitter laugh escaped him as he lay the empty bowl to one side. "I doubt my captain would thank me for bringing the sickness back to Paris with me. Were I even to get within ten miles of the city walls, I have no doubt he would shoot me on the spot and have my body hauled away into the country for burial."

"The sickness?" He had spoken the word with such a dread certainty and deadly acceptance that a cold shiver of apprehension passed down her spine. "What sickness?"

He made the sign of the cross to ward off evil. "No one can get in or out of the Camargue. We have been shut off by soldiers from Saint-Marie-de-la-Mer, and villagers from outside the boundaries would kill us did we try to escape anyway. They would rather murder innocent strangers than run the risk of being infected by them. For none of us are innocent. God has sent us the plague."

Two

The plague. The word itself was enough to strike a deathly fear into her heart. Like the locusts in olden days, the plague was a curse from heaven sent by a wrathful God to punish the wrongdoing of his creatures. Few escaped the avenging hands of a wrathful God. "The Black Death?" she whispered.

"Even so."

She felt the horror of it strike her heart. "I have had the plague?"

"You were one of the lucky ones, my dear sister. You were struck down and yet you still live. Before this very hour, I had not even dared to hope you would be spared."

No wonder he looked so drawn and pale. "The plague is in this house?"

He nodded. "Most of the servants have been struck with fever. The few who remained have fled to the hills to save their skins—if they can."

She could barely breathe with the fear of it all. "And the village?"

"The village has been struck, as well." He shook his head gravely. "The news from there is not good."

"Our parents?" She could not frame the question as she wanted to, fearing to hear the answer.

"Father has been well up until now, but yesterday

he took to his bed with a slight fever. He has a strong constitution. He may pull through as you have done."

"And mother?"

He was silent for a moment. "She is . . . not well."

Not her mother. She could not lose her mother in this way. "How sick is she?"

A shake of his head with frustration. "I am not a physician."

She could not let the question rest. "What does the apothecary in the village say?"

"The apothecary was one of the first to die."

"What of a doctor from town?" Surely a doctor would be able to cure their mother. "Have you not sent for a doctor from town?"

He shrugged his shoulders. "It is no use. There are none to come. Half of them are arrant cowards and have refused to visit their patients for fear of catching the plague."

She was almost afraid to speak now. "And the other half?"

"The other half are dead or dying."

"The priest? Has he at least been with her to offer her comfort?" She whispered the words, grasping at the merest straw of hope, not wanting to hear of yet more bad news. The priest had always been devout in his faith and would not abandon a dying soul of his flock.

He put his head in his hands. "I buried him yesterday." His voice shook with distress. "I loved Father Capin dearly."

Sophie let her eyes close with a groan. Maybe it would have been better if the plague had taken her, too—if she had never awakened to this hellish day, with the world she knew disintegrating around her.

"You have had a rude awakening, sister," Gerard

said, coming out of his grief to lay a cool hand on her forehead. "I am sorry. I did not mean to give you the bad news all at once. Sleep again now, and I shall be with you when you awake again."

She would never sleep again. Her head whirled with images of pain and death—images from her most feverish nightmares: carts stacked with bodies being tipped into common burial pits, smoking funeral pyres spilling ill-smelling smoke that reeked of human corruption and burning flesh, and every stinking, rotten, worm-ridden corpse bore the face of one of her loved ones.

Her body was weak from her long illness, and despite the horrors invading her mind, she soon sank into a restless slumber.

She was alone when she woke again, and her belly was rumbling with emptiness. Judging by the patch of darkening sky she could see from her window, it was early evening.

The house was as quiet as a tomb. There were no footsteps, no voices, not even the barking of a dog to indicate there was any living soul there besides herself.

She called out in a voice weak from illness, but no one answered. Silence reigned supreme. Gerard had promised he would be there when she woke up again, and she trusted him with her life. She waited for some minutes to see if her brother would return as he had promised, but he did not come.

The stillness in the air had an eerie quality about it, a sense of tenseness and foreboding. Finally she could bear it no longer. She pushed herself up on the bed until she was sitting upright. A black mist appeared before her eyes as the blood rushed from her head, but she willed herself not to faint. When she began to feel stronger, she swung her legs over the side of the bed until her feet touched the floor. The cold seeped through the bare wood into the soles of her feet, but this minor discomfort only fueled her determination to set herself above it.

Her legs trembled with the exertion of holding her upright, but slowly she shuffled her way to the door, hanging on to the bedposts, the wall, anything to help hold her on her feet.

With shaking steps, she made her way to her mother's apartments. She pushed open the door and took two steps in, and then wished she hadn't.

The curtains around her mother's bed were closed and a smell of corruption and death lingered in the air. She made herself shuffle over to the bed and draw back the curtains. Her mother lay among the rumpled sheets, her eyes open wide in a sightless mockery, her face blackened with dark spots and tinged the green-gray color of death. The Black Death had claimed her for his own.

With a shaking hand, Sophie brushed her mother's eyelids shut. She could do no more for her body, but must pray that her soul find peace in death.

Her father's apartments were as quiet as her mother's. She knew what she would find when she opened the door, but she forced herself to do it anyway.

Her father had died in his chair, his face twisted with pain and covered with the same spots that marked her mother.

With a quick prayer that God in his mercy grant him grace, she shut the door again.

The door to her brother's chamber was slightly ajar. As she approached it, she heard a voice calling out to her. She quickened her step as much as she was able.

If her brother was yet well, they could work together to survive this tragedy that had felled the rest of their family.

"Gerard?" she called as she tapped at the door.

He mumbled unintelligibly back at her through the partly opened door.

She pushed it open and went in. Gerard was lying fully clothed on his bed, and to her horror she saw his face was dripping with the sweat of a desperate fever. She rushed to his side, not knowing what else she could do but soothe him with her presence and let him know she was near him.

He opened his eyes and seemed to focus on her face. "I will get up and make you some more soup soon, Sophie," he muttered. "I just had to lie down for a bit first. I don't feel so well. My head hurts."

His head was burning. Sophie looked around wildly for a rag, but there was nothing she could use. With a strength born of desperation, she tore the ruffle from her cotton nightgown, dipped it in the pitcher of water by her brother's bed and used it to sponge the sweat from her brother's forehead.

He relaxed a trifle under her ministrations. "That feels so good," he mumbled. "I am so hot."

"You have made yourself sick with nursing me," she said. "Lie back and you will soon recover."

"Mother and father . . ." he began, his voice trailing off into nothingness.

She knew what he wanted to say and would spare him the pain of giving it voice. "I know," she said simply.

He shut his eyes in anguish. "I tried my best, but it was not good enough. I could not save them."

"No man on earth could have saved them. God had marked them for his own."

ON MY LADY'S HONOR

"I did my best, but they went so quickly in the end. There was nothing I could do."

She laid her hand on his burning forehead, sharing his anguish. "Hush now, and try to rest."

He tossed and turned with a feverish agitation. "When I die, you will be left all alone."

"Do not be foolish," she reproved him. He was her beloved brother, her twin. She could not live without him. He could not be so sick as all that. "You are ill with exhaustion. Nothing else ails you."

He gave a wan smile as he drew his right arm from under the bedclothes and pushed the sleeve up to his elbow. "You cannot fool me, sister, and you will not be able to fool yourself for much longer. You had best be prepared for the inevitable."

She stared at the black spots on his arms with a horror verging on madness. Not Gerard. Not her brother. God had taken her mother and her father. Could he not spare her brother?

"I have the plague. I have seen many others die of it these last weeks and I do not flatter myself I will survive where so many others have not. I will be dead before the morn."

She would not let him go so easily. She would fight Death for the life of her brother. She clutched at him with frantic fingers. "You must not die. I will not let you die."

He loosened the death-grip of her fingers and took her hand in his. "I have made my peace with the world and I am content to leave it. It is time for me to join God's kingdom. My one regret is that I will not be here to take care of you. You will have to look out for yourself. Promise me you will take good care of yourself."

"I promise."

"I had thought to see you married this summer. I would have danced at your wedding with a good grace."

She shook her head with impatience. "I care naught for being wed."

"Count Lamotte is a good man. He would be a good husband for you, Sophie, or I never would have proposed the match. I loved him like a brother, and knew you would love him as I did."

She bit her tongue. She would not quarrel with her brother when he was so ill.

"You will need someone to look after you when I am gone. If the king takes any notice of his wealthy new ward, it will only be to marry you off to the highest bidder, or to some new favorite who has more charm than wealth. Promise me you will consider Lamotte's suit."

How could she think of marriage when her parents were both dead and her brother was dying? "You must think only of getting better, not of such foolish things as my marriage. I can look after myself. Besides, you will not die."

"Promise me." His voice was urgent.

However unreasonable she considered it, she could not refuse a sick man's request—not when that man was the brother she loved better than she loved herself. "I promise."

She was promising only to consider Lamotte's suit, she told herself to quiet her uneasy conscience. If she could not have Jean-Luc, she had no intention of marrying anyone, but she would give Lamotte's suit fair consideration if ever an appropriate time came to do so.

Her words brought her brother ease. He heaved a faint sigh of relief and closed his eyes as a spasm of pain crossed his forehead. "You have put my last care to rest."

Fear clutched at her heart as she looked at her brother's drawn face. He was preparing himself for death. "I carry ill luck around with me. He may not want to wed me now."

He gave a hoarse, hacking cough. "He swore on his mother's soul that if aught happened to me, he would care for you. I sent word to him when I first arrived, telling him we had the plague in the house. I know him, Sophie, and he is no oathbreaker. I can die in peace knowing he will come to your aid as soon as he can be here."

Sophie laid a finger over his mouth. The strain of talking was weakening him before her eyes. "Hush now, and rest."

He closed his eyes again and, exhausted with the effort of conversation, soon sank into an uneasy slumber.

Sophie sat in the armchair by his bed keeping watch over him, dozing fitfully when her eyes would no longer remain open. She did not leave his side, forgetting her own hunger and thirst in the pain of watching, in terrified helplessness, as her brother's life slowly ebbed away.

When his face beaded over with sweat, she laved his forehead with water to cool down the raging heat of his body and prayed for the Virgin Mary in her grace to heal him. When he cried out in his sleep, tossing and turning in the grip of a fearful nightmare, she stroked his hand and murmured soft words of peace and love into his ear until he calmed down once more.

Toward morning, when she heard the death rattle in his throat and watched his breath fade away until there was nothing left, she brushed his eyelids over his staring, sightless eyes and held his hand until the warm flesh grew cold and stiff in death.

She could not cry for him. She was beyond tears. She had gone far beyond grief, to a place where utter desolation became a new normality.

The gray of dawn was creeping over the horizon. She stood at the window, irresolute. One step was all it would take. One step, and her body would lie broken on the cobblestones of the courtyard, her soul winging its way to paradise with her twin.

Of its own volition, her hand crept to the casement and began to open it. Through the crack, fresh morning air crept in to dispel the putrid miasma of death.

She hesitated. Death would mean an end to her pain, but was she brave enough to face death, so unprepared as she was to meet her Maker?

Besides, she was thirsty, and her hunger was beginning to return tenfold. She dropped the casement again. Before she made any such choice to join her family in death, she would slake her thirst and fill her belly.

The kitchen was empty and the fire in the grate long since gone out. There were no servants and no sign of life. Sophie had not expected to find any, but she felt her heart sink even lower nonetheless. There was no welcoming life or heat to greet her, only ashes long grown cold. The kitchen, like the rest of the house, smelled only of decay and death.

A quick rummage around the kitchen afforded her some small beer, a hunk of cheese, some crisp, green apples, and a crock full of gooseberry preserves. With her booty tucked securely under her arm, she tottered back to her bedroom. She had no desire to explore the house further. Her reserves of courage and endurance were gone, and she feared to find more unpleasant surprises.

After a nibble of cheese and a sip or two of small beer, her stomach revolted and she did not want to eat anymore. She had seen too much of death to be concerned with mere food.

Still, she forced herself to plow through the provisions she had gathered. There was little point in dying of starvation and weakness now that she had survived the plague. She ate and drank halfheartedly through much of her plunder before falling deeply asleep, a half-eaten apple core grasped tightly in her fist.

Late in the afternoon, she woke for a while to eat the remainder of her supplies and drink the rest of the small beer, until exhaustion claimed her again.

A new day had dawned before she woke once more. Her body felt stronger than before, her mind more clear.

Desolation and sadness had replaced her utter despair of the previous morning. No longer did she want to end her life. Her natural will to survive was stronger than her desire to die. Her duty lay in burying her loved ones with all the respect they deserved, in saying masses for their souls so they might be released the sooner from Purgatory, and in honoring their memory in every word and deed.

As she had feared by the oppressive silence, the house was deserted by all but bodies. Her brother had simply been the last to die.

She screamed when she stumbled across the bloated carcass that had once been Piers, the scullery lad. No more would he sneak extra rations from behind the cook's back, disarming those who would reprove him with a cheeky grin. He had died as he had lived, hiding away from his duties in a dark corner, a stolen pastry clutched tightly in his hand.

By the time she found the head gardener slumped against the orchard wall, flies crawling in and out of his open mouth, she was inured to death, and had no room left for more horror or disgust.

Behind the herb garden she found what she had been half looking for all the while—a partially filled-in grave. The length and breadth of it left no room to doubt the seriousness of the plague that had descended upon the manor house.

She had no wish to disturb the light covering of soil that lay over the human remains, to uncover the ghastly remainder of people she once knew and loved. She could only add her mite to the pile.

Carting dead bodies for burial was heavy work, and she was not yet back to full strength after her long weeks of illness. Still, she persevered, dragging one body after another to the edge and tipping them into the shallowing pit, unwilling to spend another night in a charnel house. She refused to cry over each familiar face as she tipped the rotting corpses one after the other into the hole. She had no energy to waste on tears.

Her family she left until last. She could not mete out such an undignified end in a common grave to her mother and father and brother. The shovel was heavy and awkward, but the ground was soft enough, and after an afternoon's labor, she had dug three graves deep enough to keep their bodies safe from scavengers.

"Farewell," she whispered into the wind, as she lay them gently side by side in the ground. "May we meet again in Heaven."

With the last of her strength, she shoveled a covering of dirt on their bodies.

The sun had set before she returned to the house once more. She was filthy, covered from head to toe in mud and filth and the stench of corruption.

The water from the well was sweet, with no taint in it. She stripped naked in the courtyard and hauled bucket after bucket of water up from the well, tipping each one over her in turn to wash away the horror of the day.

Only when all of her felt clean again, from her head of dripping wet hair to her bare feet on the cobbles, and she had overpowered the smell of death with that of sweet lavender and rosemary, did she go inside once more.

She lay exhausted on the bed, unable to sleep, thinking back to the last day of normality before her world had turned into a living hell.

How trivial her concerns of a few weeks ago seemed to her now. She would gladly marry the count a thousand times over to have her old life back again, but no marriage would bring the dead back to life again. How foolish did her thoughts of rebellion seem, another whole life ago, that morning in the marshes.

The marshes.

Her blood suddenly ran cold, and fear and guilt assailed her.

Her mother had warned her against going into the marshes for fear of the swamp fever that had hit the next village. She had disobeyed her mother, and God had punished her by sending the fever to her house.

Faint with despair, she racked her brains with the effort of remembrance. She had been well when she went to the marshes. She had returned sick. The household had been in good health until she went to the marshes. When she returned to herself again, they were all dead or had fled.

She could not escape the feeling of dread that washed over her. With her willfulness, she had murdered all those she had ever loved.

If only Count Lamotte had not wanted to marry her, this tragedy would never have come about. Had she not had this marriage sprung upon her, she would not have disobeyed her mother, she would not have caught the plague from sleeping down by the marshes, and her family would yet live.

She half hoped Lamotte had not escaped the destruction that had fallen on her family. It would be no more than he deserved. She would have traded his life a thousand times over for one extra day for her brother. Why could not God have taken him in Gerard's place?

She had no intention of marrying the count now. Indeed, she would never wed at all unless she ever found a man worthy of her esteem in every way. She had no need of a man to take care of her. Henceforth, she would depend on no one but herself.

Her family was gone. She was the only remaining survivor. For the rest of her life she would study how to atone for her fatal act of disobedience, seeking only to uphold the honor of the family she had destroyed.

Two weeks earlier

Lamotte tucked the precious bottles wrapped in thick rags into his shirt, where they would lie in safety against his skin. He had paid a king's ransom and more for them. A charm to keep the plague away was worth more than its weight in gold in times like this, when rumors of sickness in the outlying counties were reaching even the ears of self-absorbed Parisians. The king's physician himself had prepared the medicine he now carried so carefully with him.

Within the hour he had left the city, carrying little but a small amount of food and a clean shirt in his saddlebags. His horse would carry him farther and faster if it was more lightly loaded. Gerard had need of him, and of what he carried with him. He would not tarry on the way.

For the first few days, the wayside inns were welcoming, offering him a warm fire and hot food to fill his belly. He traveled far and fast, stopping only when his horse began to stumble with weariness and the road was too dark to see.

As he got further into the provinces, people looked at his travel-worn clothes and flagging horse suspiciously. Even his gold was little use to him here. More than once he was turned away from an inn late at night and had to sleep out under the stars, his clothes wet with the dew and his belly rumbling with hunger.

Rumors of sickness were rife. Once he passed by an quiet farmhouse and thought to exchange a few sous for a loaf of bread and a glass of fresh milk. He knocked on the door, but no one answered.

The door had not been latched securely, and it came open with the force of his knocking. Such a stench of putrefaction and death came from the opening that he immediately turned tail and fled. He was too late to help the dead who rested within, and he had no desire to feast his eyes on the ghastly spectacle that lay behind the door. He could imagine it only too well.

How he hoped Gerard's family had been spared the worst. Gerard's letter had told him little, only that his sister, Sophie, was sick. Sophie, his best friend's twin sister, and the woman he had contracted to marry.

He fingered the miniature he carried in his breast pocket next to his heart. Gentleness and femininity shone out of her clear blue eyes, so like her brother's in color—though, as befitted a woman, lacking his martial spark. Her soft brown hair hung in pretty ringlets about her white neck as she gave a half smile at the painter who captured her spirit on the canvas.

She looked all softness and beauty—everything he admired in a woman and valued in a wife—and he was half in love with her already. He ached to be her savior and protector, shielding her from all that would destroy the delicate blossom of her innocence. He could not bear to lose her to Death before he had even begun to know her. If the medicine he carried next to his heart could save her, he would count himself a lucky man.

He was barely three day's ride away from his journey's end when he came upon the mob of peasants on the road. Hatless and shirtless most of them were, and dressed in little better than rags, but their faces all bore the same look of grim determination and desperation.

The foremost of them shook a pitchfork in his direction. "Halt," he called in a guttural voice when Lamotte had approached close enough to hear.

Lamotte pulled up his horse and laid his hand on the hilt of his sword, though he didn't draw it out of its scabbard. The villagers were unarmed, unless one could count wicked-looking scythes and pitchforks as weapons, and he was no coward to draw his sword on unarmed men. "What do you want?"

The leader held his pitchfork braced on the ground with the sharpened points turned out toward him in a threatening manner. "Don't come any closer. Turn your horse around and go back the way you've come. You may not pass."

"Why not? I have done no wrong."

A babble of angry voices came back to him.

"We have no sickness in our village."

"We don't like strangers around here."

"Get back to the pit of hell you've come from."

"Get off with ye. We won't have no truck with you, ye plague-ridden devil."

He would not turn his horse around and lose a day's riding because of the ill-founded fears of a mob of peasants. Even now, his own sweet Sophie might be dying for want of his medicine. "I come from Paris. There is no plague there. I do not have the sickness."

"Then go back to where you've come from and leave us be."

A general murmur of assent greeted these words.

"I cannot go back. My betrothed wife is ill and I must bring her the medicines that will save her. I must go on."

The crowd shuffled its feet uneasily, not knowing what to make of his claim. Then a man from the back spoke up. "There ain't no medicines made by man that can save one who has the plague. It's a curse sent from God to punish the wicked."

"His wife deserves to die."

"And he along with her."

He did not like the turn the mutterings were taking, or the angry looks directed his way. He set his spurs to his horse, intending to break his way through the crowd by sheer force.

His horse was too weary from the days of traveling to respond quickly. Before the pair of them could get through the mob, the villagers were upon him.

He saw the pitchfork being swung in his direction,

but he could not escape it. A sensation of fire burst into his side as the outermost tine tore through his flesh. His horse screamed in pain, his powerful hooves lashing out at their attackers.

Many hands reached out to pull him out of his saddle. He hit the ground with a thud on his newly injured side. The world in front of him faded to gray and then went black, and he knew nothing more.

Six months later

Sophie Delamanse rode slowly through the busy streets, taking in each new wonder with the wide open eyes of a stranger to the city. The street vendors calling their wares, the swaggering young bullies parading their strength, the merchants going about their business, all the hurly-burly of the most important city in all of France—she marveled at the cacophony of sights and sounds and smells that was Paris.

The crowds at once disturbed and elated her. She had lived alone in the deserted manor house in the Camargue all winter until she had become accustomed to the fearsome silence of solitude. In Paris, she need never be alone again.

A woman of the street called out to her from a dirty alley. She blushed and turned her head away before suddenly thinking better of her shyness and returning the woman's saucy greeting with a polite tip of her plumed hat. She was a man now, the reincarnation of her brother, Gerard, who lay still in his shallow grave in the marshy swamps of the Camargue. She must remember her new self in all her dealings and bring honor to her brother's name and to all her family. She would remember her love for her brother and her hatred for all those who had wronged them both, and they would make her strong.

During the long, cold months of winter she had brooded constantly on her brother's death. Her guilt and despair had nigh destroyed her until she turned her pain and her guilt outward and focused her loathing on the enemy she could hate without destroying herself in the process—Count Lamotte.

For the first few weeks after her recovery she had waited for him to appear. He had promised her brother he would care for her. Where, then, was he when she had most need of him?

Had he come to her then and saved her from the horror of spending the winter alone in a house of death, she would have welcomed him with open arms. She would nigh have welcomed the devil himself, if he had come to rescue her.

Lamotte was her betrothed, she told herself over and over again as she huddled in front of the tiny fire she kept in the kitchen grate, eating her meager rations and trying to stop her teeth from chattering with cold. Surely when he heard of her plight, he would ride to her rescue. Gerard had had faith in him. She did not want to believe the count was so afeared of the plague he would break a solemn oath to her brother.

The weeks passed by at a snail's pace, until snow covered the ground, making travel impossible and utterly destroying her hope that he might come to her. She grew stronger in her solitude, but gradually she also grew more and more embittered against the man who might have saved her from this solitude but had not.

Lamotte had not come to claim her. As the snows of winter started to melt, she had to face the miserable truth—that, like a sniveling coward, he had stayed away to save his own skin, leaving his comrade in arms and his betrothed wife to die a miserable death.

Were he ever to renew his suit, she would treat him with the derision he deserved as a false friend and a traitor to loyalty and honor. Lamotte: coward, traitor, and false friend. How she wished to make him suffer as her family had suffered. How she hated him for being alive when all she loved were dead.

Lamotte. The very name sounded evil on her tongue. She could never wed him. She would sooner murder him and cut out his heart and throw it to the wolves.

Spring arrived at last, and with it the knowledge that another such winter would drive her mad. With spring came the news that Jean-Luc was dead, along with his father and much of their household. She had no grieving left in her, but she said a rosary for their souls so they might rest in peace the sooner.

A handful of villagers had survived the plague. The most trustworthy of the survivors she made her steward, while she put into action the plan she had dreamed up at her lonely fireside. As Sophie, she had nothing left to live for. She would become a ward of Louis XIV and sign her destiny over to the whim of the king. She determined to remain Sophie no longer. Instead, she would become her brother.

As Gerard, she would take control of her life. As Gerard, she would win the honor that should have been his. As Gerard she would live, and as Gerard she would die.

Well she knew that she was a weaker, paler version of the proud musketeer who had left Paris seven months ago to attend the betrothal and wedding of his twin sister. That would easily be explained away by the weeks of illness she had suffered and the months of recuperation she had had to undergo before she, in the guise of her brother, had recovered sufficiently to be deemed fit for active service once more.

She only hoped those who had known Gerard intimately would not be able to detect the slight softening of her features and the unusual smoothness of her chin, untouched by any razor. With her hair cut short to curl around the nape of her neck, and wearing Gerard's breeches and boots, she was an exact copy of her twin. She would defy even her mother to tell them apart from more than ten feet away.

Neither would she be discovered a woman by lack of skill in the martial arts. She had spent her last few months wisely, practicing with Gerard's sword until her arm ached with weariness and riding Seafoam until it seemed as though she and the horse shared one body and one will. She could ride now as well as her brother ever had. Her skill with the sword was as yet still rudimentary, but she would work on that.

Even if her future companions noticed the changes in her face or her bearing, she doubted they would ever guess the truth. It was too preposterous to be believed. As far as the world knew, Sophie Delamanse was dead of the plague and Gerard, after a lucky escape from the disease that had killed his entire family, was on his way back belatedly to rejoin his regiment.

Her brother had boarded with a widow in a respectable lodging house near the barracks. Sophie paid a street lad a couple of sous to guide her there. The boy led her through dark alleys and dirty streets, stopping in front of a shabby tenement with a ragged sign proclaiming rooms to let within.

The widow looked sideways at Sophie when she rapped at the door, travel sore and weary from her days on the road. "So, you've come back then." She bared her gums in a attempt at a smile. "I heard you was dead, but I guess I heard wrong. You're in luck. I've got a room free if you want to take it. The gentleman who was in there hanged hisself the other week. Still, I don't 'spose you'll worry about that, having just come from the parts where there's the plague and all."

The room was in the garret, up four flights of stairs. The heat at the top of the house was stifling, the open wooden shutters did nothing to move the air, and there was barely enough room for the small bed and a dresser that were the room's sole furnishings.

Tired and longing for a rest as she was, Sophie looked at the pokey accommodation with distaste. "How much?"

The withered old crone named an exorbitant fee, nearly the whole of the recompense Sophie would receive from her duties as a musketeer.

Sophie shook her head in disbelief. "For such a small room? With barely a window?"

"I'll be charging you a mite extra coz you've come from the Camargue," the old woman said, her beady eyes fixed relentlessly on Sophie's face. "It's not everyone who'll take in those as have had the sickness. The other boarders don't like it. It's bad for business."

The old woman had a point, Sophie was forced to concede. She might find it difficult to find another place to stay. But still she hesitated. Paying so much for her board would mean draining badly needed funds away from the family estate. She was reluctant to do that, but both she and Seafoam were close to collapse and needed to rest.

At her silence, the old woman relented slightly in her greed, fearful of losing a paying customer. "Ach, seeing as you're an old friend, I'll let you have it for a bit less." She named a sum Sophie could live with. "Payment in advance though," she said, as she stuck out her skinny claw.

Sophie tipped a couple of livres into the outstretched hand. "Bring me some hot water and food." She added a couple of sous. "And have your boy take my horse to the stables."

The old woman tucked the coins away in the pocket of her apron with a feral look in her eye. Sophie doubted her poor boy would see any of the coins for himself.

When the landlady had shuffled away again, Sophie sat down on her bed, the thin straw rustling beneath her. She was in Paris. She had found herself lodgings, meager though they were. She was going to be a musketeer. No one had questioned her sex. As far as the world was concerned, she was a man. Maybe, just maybe, she would succeed in her mad scheme.

Her confidence had evaporated into heat and worry by the time the landlady returned carrying a small basin of barely lukewarm water for her to wash away the grime of travel, and a bowl of thin, watery-looking gruel.

She shut the door, pushed the dresser against it to be sure she was free from interruption, and washed as well as she could in the rapidly cooling water. How could she ever pull off her masquerade when she was so obviously a woman? Would it not be evident by the way she walked and talked, even by the way she wore her clothes? She would be exposed in front of all of Gerard's companions and shame him for ever.

The gruel was edible, but little more than that. In her hunger, she wolfed it down anyway. The hard winter had robbed her of most of her reserves of body fat. She hoped the food at the barracks would be more appetizing than her landlady's meager mush, or she would grow thinner than ever. She had to build up her strength or she would easily be discovered.

The night was warm, and the city air that crept in through the open casement window was heavy and putrid. She tossed and turned throughout the night, disturbed by the cloying heat and unfamiliar noises and smells of the city that surrounded her, dreaming of discovery and shame.

In the early hours of the morning, she was wakened by the calls of the street-sellers peddling their wares. With a groan she rose, wrapped her breasts in a thick layer of linen strips and covered them with her shirt, tucked into her leather breeches. The wrappings felt doubly uncomfortable and constricting in the thick, moist heat of the city, but she was woman enough that she had to bind her breasts tightly to hide them. She would not allow her womanhood to be discovered through such an elementary mistake.

The barracks were close by the lodging house, in the very center of the heat and noise and dirt of the city. By the time she arrived there on foot, the perspiration was dripping down her neck and soaking into her clothes.

Men in the uniform of the King's Guard hustled hither and thither, all seemingly engaged on errands of supreme importance. Sophie stood confused in the midst of the commotion, feeling lost and out of place, not knowing which way to turn.

She felt tears prick the back of her eyelids. Gerard would have known what to do and where to go.

Gerard was no longer there to help her. She was on her own. With all the resolution she could muster, she squared her shoulders and began to stride off in a random direction, hoping she looked more purposeful and in control than she felt.

She was arrested in mid step by the shout of a fellow musketeer. "Gerard? Gerard, is that really you?"

Sophie stopped dead in her tracks and instinctively turned away from the voice. A critical part of her plan had been to avoid all Gerard's old friends as much as possible, to lessen the chance of discovery. "What do you want?" She pitched her voice as low as she could, making it sound curt with impatience.

The musketeer stopped short. "Gerard?" His voice was puzzled and hurt. "Where are you off to in such a confounded hurry? Have you no time to greet your friend?"

Sophie took in his appearance out of the corner of her eye. He was taller than average, certainly far taller than she was, and broader in the shoulders than most men. Despite his bulk, he wore the flared jacket of his uniform with an unstudied grace she couldn't help but envy, though he walked with a slight limp and noticeably favored one side above the other. His hair was a rich wheaten gold that curled around his shoulders, and his thigh-high boots were gleaming with polish. She wondered which one of Gerard's friends or acquaintances he was, but short of exposing herself by asking him, she had no way of knowing.

Whoever he was, he was well worth the looking at, did she ever have the liberty to look. She crossed her arms over her chest and tapped the toe of her boot on the ground. "I'm looking for the captain. Have you seen him?"

The musketeer gestured to the group of buildings on the far side of the courtyard. "Last I saw of him, he was giving the captain of the foot soldiers an earful."

Without another word, Sophie strode off in the direction he indicated, and the musketeer fell into step beside her. "I was sorry to hear about your loss. I grieved that I could be of no help to you."

Sophie grunted. Even after all those months of solitude as she recovered her strength and taught herself how to fight, her loss rubbed raw against her spirit. She did not trust herself to speak of it.

"I knew how close you were to your sister, and how much you loved her."

Her heart swelled with an anguished pride to hear herself so spoken of and to know Gerard had confided his brotherly love to his comrade in arms. She had to clear her throat several times before she could speak. "We were twins. We had seldom been apart from each other. We were two, and now I am one. I feel as though a part of me is gone."

"I, too, mourned her death. I was more than half in love with her already from the reports you had made of her. I had hoped to be your brother by now . . ."

Lamotte. Of course, such a handsome fellow had to be Lamotte—the author of her ruin. She stopped dead and faced her enemy for the first time. "No matter," she interrupted, stopping him in his tracks. "Sophie is dead and buried, and nothing can bring her back."

Lamotte stood still, gazing at her with an earnest puzzlement. "You are not the man you used to be." His voice was tinged with a sober melancholy. "The sickness has changed you in both mind and body."

"I am the man I always was." She shrugged her shoulders and began to walk away, the memory of her solitary winter in a house of death making her shudder. Lamotte had promised her brother he would take care of her, but he had broken his vow. How she hated him for that. "I had no time for coward, and scoundrels a year ago, just as I have no time for them now. Good day."

The words had barely left her mouth when she felt a sudden prick in her belly.

The count, moving quickly despite his limp, pressed the point of his sword uncomfortably hard against the leather of her jerkin. "No man, not even you, Gerard, calls me a coward. Draw your sword."

So this was it, Sophie thought, as she moved back a step and drew her sword. Had she been cooler and more detached, she would not have provoked him so readily. In the heat of the moment, she had been overcome with her hatred of all he stood for—the death of her brother and her loss of faith in humanity. Forgetting she was now a man and her words would be construed as a deadly insult, she had given in to the temptation to taunt him.

Now they would fight. She had no illusions about her skill with the sword. She had done her best to learn on her own, but she was direly in need of an expert teacher. Unless she was lucky or he was a worse than usual swordsman, she would most likely die.

She had no fear of dying by his hand, only of dying without honor.

She focussed all her concentration on the sword in her fist. She would acquit herself well in this fight and avenge her family if she could. If she were unsuccessful, at least she would die in peace, knowing she had done her best.

Gerard, this is for you, she screamed in her heart as she made the first lunge, which he deflected with a quick flick of his wrist.

He feinted and then lunged back at her. She knew that trick. Her brother had taught it to her when they were both still children. She twisted her body to one side, and the force of his blow cleaved only the empty air.

Backward and forward they went, now attacking, now defending, the clash of their swords drawing a crowd of the curious around them. Sophie was breathing hard and her sword arm was starting to tire. Lamotte, though his limp was more pronounced than ever and his face pinched with pain, had barely broken into a sweat.

She attacked once again. He parried her thrust, bowed awkwardly to the onlookers and was upright again, his sword at the ready, before Sophie could react.

The audience guffawed with laughter. He was ridiculing her lack of skill in front of their comrades.

"Are you ready to eat your words yet, boy?"

His mocking words made Sophie redouble her effort. He was baiting her, toying with her, as a cat played with a mouse. "Never."

She attacked him with a renewed fury, concentrating all her attention in the movement of his body, seeking for hints of his next movement, those tiny clues that would give her the advantage in the attack.

One of the onlookers called out an encouragement. Lamotte unwisely turned on his heel to acknowledge the favor with a tip of his hat.

In an instant Sophie was on him, drawing blood from the fleshy upper part of his arm with a lucky hit.

He cursed at the sight of the blood staining his jacket and his levity fled on the instant. Sophie quaked in her borrowed boots at the new determination on his face. Even the rowdy onlookers fell silent, sensing the fun was now over.

Thrust after fatal thrust he aimed at her, steadily driving her back against the wall of the courtyard, until she could retreat no further.

He lunged again.

Sword raised to parry his blow, she tripped and fell sprawling on her back in the dirt. The force of the impact knocked her weapon out of her hand, out of her reach, into the mud.

He stood above her, blocking the sunlight, his sword at her throat. She stared up at him, hatred in her heart, willing him to slit open her gorge with his blade and end her struggle.

His eyes were the steely gray of ice in winter. She felt the chill of descending death. "Take back your words."

She spat in his direction, her spittle only reaching halfway up his boots before running slowly down. She stared at its slow journey, knowing it was the last thing she would ever see.

The tip of the sword slowly lifted from her throat. She dragged her eyes away from Lamotte's boot and watched him resheathe his weapon by his side.

She had thought to be with Gerard in paradise by now. He had cheated her of death.

He reached down toward her and offered her his hand, but she scrambled to her feet again, unaided. "Why will you not kill me?"

He was looking at her in puzzlement, as if he saw her and yet didn't see her. "You're not worth dirtying my blade on," he said at last. "You've forgotten everything the captain and I ever taught you about fighting. Come back and insult me again when you are worth clashing swords with."

Sophie watched as he limped away, shaking his head. His face was etched in her memory: her brother's false friend and her own worst enemy. By refusing to kill her, he had insulted her to the death. Next time they met, she would not rest until she had killed him.

She retrieved her sword from the ground, wiping it clean on her jerkin before returning it to her side. He had escaped her vengeance today, but no matter. He would not find her so unprepared another day.

A burly man with shoulders as wide as the back end of an ox detached himself from the onlookers. "Delamanse, my lad," he said, slapping her so hard on the back that Sophie nearly toppled over with the unexpected force of it. "I'm glad to see you back in my regiment, for all you are so thin and pale and as cack-handed with a sword as a girl. A regimen of hard training with your betters will have you fighting like a man again, and a dozen pints of port drunk of an evening with your fellows will put the color back in your cheeks."

He heaved a huge sigh. "Ah, I know it's a good thing to have peace in Paris, but I miss the good old days of rebellion in the streets when a man could carve up a dozen rebellious frondeurs before breakfast just to work up a hearty appetite."

D'Artagnan, the captain of the Musketeers. Sophie groaned to herself as she doffed her hat and bowed to her superior. Covered in mud and sweat and smarting from the utter humiliation of an ignominious defeat was not the way she had dreamed of meeting him.

Ricard Lamotte bowed painfully to his monarch as he took the folded paper from the desk. He glanced at the direction. Yet another missive for Madame Henrietta Anne, the Duchesse D'Orleans.

He knew the way to her apartments with his eyes closed. A brief knock at the door had the Duchesse's pretty red-haired maid opening it for him. He handed her the letter. "For your mistress."

He did not wait for a reply. He knew of old that the Duchesse D'Orleans had no particular love for her brother-in-law, King Louis XIV, and would give any messenger from him curses in place of gold coins for his efforts.

How he longed to be back on active duty on the front, any front, instead of acting as pander to the king.

He limped slowly back to his station, his side aching abominably as he moved and a trickle of blood seeping through his shirt. He hoped the edges of his wound had still held together. He had no desire to be sewn up again as if he were made of leather rather than of flesh and blood that felt every movement of the needle that pierced his side. He had been foolish to pick a fight with Gerard when he was still so lamed, but such provocation as Gerard had offered him could not be ignored.

The other guard sat morosely by the wall, a pint of porter in his hand. He tipped his jug by way of a greeting, but didn't speak.

How Ricard missed Gerard's light heart and easy tongue that had made even the coldest, wettest, longest, and most miserable night of guard duty bearable.

Gerard had returned, but he was not Gerard any longer. It was as if the body of Gerard had remained, but his soul had been replaced with that of a stranger—a stranger who bore a deep grudge against him.

He had read the hate in his old friend's eyes, and it had shaken him to his soul. The cause was a mystery to him, an inexplicable twist of fate. He could only think that Gerard's sickness had affected his reasoning, along with his strength and skill with a sword.

He shrugged his shoulders, wincing where Gerard's blade had cut deep into his flesh. Another scar to add to his rapidly growing collection. He still could not believe Gerard had deliberately wounded him.

Worse still, he believed Gerard would have killed him if he could. He had no idea why, but he intended to find out as soon as he could.

In the meantime, he would have to watch his back with care. There was none so treacherous, or so much to be feared, as a friend who had turned against you.

Three

The days passed in a haze of exhaustion for Sophie in her new role as musketeer of the King's Guard. Every day she completed her allotted guard duty and then trained to the point of collapse, and early each evening she passed out on her bed as soon as she lay her head on the prickly straw of the mattress.

Now she understood only too well why Gerard's letters had been so few and far between when he had been in Paris and she had been waiting anxiously in the provinces for some sign he was still alive and well. He had had no time to write them.

Even if he had had the time to write to her, he would have had no strength to lift the quill to the paper. She surprised herself each morning that she could still move the aching, protesting muscles of her body. She surprised herself even more that she had the will to roll off her bed and into her uniform. She surprised herself that she was even still alive, what with the punishment she was inflicting each day on her poor, mistreated body.

She barely noticed that her attic room in the lodging house was small and dark and pokey. Nearly every second she spent in it was spent sleeping. The thin gruel her landlady provided for her meager supper was left untouched as often as not. She would eat well at the officer's table at the barracks at midday, and come evening time she would rather sleep than eat.

Gradually she became inured to the hardships of her new life. The muscles in her arms became bigger and better defined, and they no longer ached unbearably after a long day's practice with sword or spear. Her legs grew accustomed to the punishment of spending hour after hour on horseback, dressed in the heavy leather riding boots that were part of her uniform.

Thanks to her love of horses and hunting, she could ride better than most of her fellows already, but her skill with the sword was well behind. Her arms were simply not strong enough to fight hard for long. After a short bout of swordplay, her right arm would begin to tire and her opponent would eventually conquer her not by dint of great skill, but simply by battering her down through brute strength.

She watched her fellows closely as they dueled with each other. None of them were as inept as she was, though some were little better. After some weeks of watching every move they made, she had to admit that of all of them, Lamotte was the most proficient with the sword. Now that he had recovered from the limp that had slowed him down, not only was he strong, but he was agile and clever.

She loved to watch her enemy fight. He was as strong as the village blacksmith back home in the Camargue and as graceful as a dancer at the same time. He could cleave a post in two with one blow from his sword in one moment and leap as high as the acrobat from the traveling fair at whom she had marveled as a child in the next. At times, he looked as light on his feet as a butterfly in flight, while at other times his legs anchored him to the ground more solidly than a hundred-year-old oak tree.

When he took off his jacket and pushed his sleeves up his arms, the bronzed muscles of his bare arms rippled in the sunshine as he parried and thrust with an ease and grace that made her heart pound in her breast and her breathing quicken. Half dressed as he was, he looked like a warrior of old, a wild and cunning berserk, whom none could stand against and live.

She wondered anew at her foolishness at picking a fight with him on the day she arrived. Had he not been hurt already, she would have suffered a far more ignominious defeat than she had dreamed possible. None of the others came close to his skill. None could match him for speed, and he could disarm an opponent who was twice as large and heavy as he was with a clever feint and twist of his blade.

She would learn from him, she decided one day, as she stood outside the fencing ring watching him demolish an entire regiment of men, one after the other. She needed to learn what he could teach her. She would never outclass her enemies in strength, so she would have to outfox them with her agility and her cunning.

She would ask Count Lamotte to help her. Putting herself in his way was risky, but she had little to lose and much to gain from him. If she was to outshine her peers, she must learn from the best—and Lamotte was indisputably the best.

Besides, she needed to learn all his tricks so she could turn them against him when next they fought. She liked the idea of learning all he could teach her until she could defeat him with his own weapons. It carried a sense of poetic justice.

As each day passed, she had grown more and more confident in her role as Gerard, less fearful her masquerade would be discovered. Even Lamotte, who had been her brother's closest companion, had not discovered she was an imposter. She was accepted by the entire regiment as Gerard. She no longer even thought about her sex much herself, except when she bound her breasts up tightly in the morning and unbound them again in the evening.

She was in no danger from Lamotte. She would learn everything she could learn from her enemy and, God willing, she would eventually use her hard-won knowledge to defeat her teacher. Then would her brother be avenged on his false friend, and his ghost would sleep easier in the grave.

Lamotte noticed immediately when Gerard started to watch him practice his swordplay once more. However early he was at the fencing ring to practice his thrusts and feints, Gerard was there before him, waiting with hungry eyes, watching his every move, just as he had when the boy had first arrived in Paris nearly two years ago.

This time, however, Lamotte did not rush in to offer his services as tutor to his old friend. Since the day Gerard had tried to kill him, the two of them had more or less studiously ignored each other.

He was biding his time, sure if he left Gerard alone, the boy would come to him in the end. He would find out sooner or later why the lad hated him with such intensity. In the meantime, he contented himself with watching his back whenever his former friend was around.

His skill with the sword had always been the lodestone that attracted Gerard. It seemed the magnet had lost none of its power. The attraction was still there, despite the hatred that festered in the lad's heart for him. He was not surprised when his old friend approached him one day after fencing practice.

Gerard looked directly at him with those blue eyes that were so clearly Gerard's and yet not Gerard's. "Teach me how to fight." A demand, not a question. How like a boy he was still, with his smooth, pink cheeks and his awkward ways. He would lay a wager Gerard still had no need for a razor to keep his chin smooth.

He grabbed his towel from where it hung on the fence and wiped the sweat off his forehead. The weather showed no signs of cooling yet, and fighting in the heat was hard work. Thank the Lord his wounds had healed well and no longer slowed him down so much. They had left his skin feeling tight and puckered down one side, but they no longer pained him except when it rained. He moved his shoulders in a circular motion, feeling the muscles stretch and pull. In time he would regain more of the flexibility he had lost. He would have to be patient. "Why should I do that?"

Gerard shrugged his shoulders and shuffled his feet in the dirt, not looking him in the eyes. "Because I need to learn, and you're the best swordsman in the barracks."

He drank deeply of the water from his flask and wiped his mouth on the back of his hand. Gerard had used exactly those words the first time he had asked to be taught, and in exactly the same tone. There was no flattery in it. It was simply as if his skill was a matter of fact. He shook his head. He could not put his finger on why he was so uneasy in Gerard's company, but the lad still troubled him.

"You do not want to teach me?" Gerard sounded more determined than distressed.

Maybe some lessons would give him the time he needed to unravel the mystery of Gerard's sudden change of attitude toward him. "Come. Put up your sword."

Gerard's mouth dropped open. "Now?"

"Is there any better time?"

Gerard gave a tremor. "I suppose not." He drew his sword and held it in front of him as if it were a charm against evil.

After a few minutes of cut and thrust, Lamotte tossed his sword up into the air and caught it in his left hand. He could not believe how Gerard's skill with the sword had so utterly disappeared over the past six months. "Have you forgotten everything I ever taught you?" he asked in puzzlement, as Gerard failed to protect himself from the most simple feint.

Gerard tripped over his feet and righted himself with a curse. "I was sick. I had the plague."

The excuses made no sense. "The plague does not affect your brain. Or your sword arm."

Gerard was sweating heavily and beginning to tire. "It left me weakened. I am no longer as strong as I was."

He grinned. "You were never going to be the strongman at the fair."

Gerard did not take offense at his teasing comment. "I need to learn how to compensate for my lack of strength. That is what I want you to teach me."

"Swordplay is not about strength. It is about speed and agility, and the ability to read the mind of your opponent so you know what thrust he will make as soon as he knows himself."

Gerard looked as intrigued as if he had never heard him say that before, though indeed he had drummed it into the boy's head time and time again when he had taught him before. "How can I do that?"

"Keep your eyes on your opponent. Never take

them off him even for a second, or"—he glanced pointedly at the still red scar on his upper arm—"you will find yourself stitching up a rather painful flesh wound or two."

Gerard blushed like a girl and look slightly shamefaced.

He felt a small measure of satisfaction at Gerard's discomfiture. The wound had hurt like the very devil, especially when the surgeon had stitched it up with his clumsy fingers. "Watch his eyes. They will give him away every time."

They would have to go back to the basics, Lamotte decided, as Gerard stumbled once again and dropped his sword on the ground. He would start from the beginning and teach Gerard once more how to fight like a musketeer.

For the next hour, he drilled Gerard unmercifully. Cut, thrust. Cut, thrust. He made Gerard practice the first simple movement over and over again until it was perfect. Then he made Gerard practice it over and over again until it was fast. Then he made Gerard practice some more until it was faster. Only when the boy had achieved pinpoint accuracy at lightning speed did he let him drop his sword on to the ground to rest.

Gerard had not uttered a word of complaint or asked to stop, though Lamotte could see he was near to passing out from exhaustion. The plague might have changed him in many ways, but it had not altered the strength of his will or his hunger to excel. "You'll soon learn how to fight again if you practice that hard."

Gerard's breath was so labored he could hardly speak. "Good."

"I hope you do not forget again so quickly."

"I will not forget a single lesson ever again."

He eyed the lad curiously. Gerard was only a handful of years younger than he was, but lately those few years had yawned like a huge, impassable gulf between them. "Why do you want to fight so badly?" Once he thought he had known, but now he was no longer sure of anything.

Gerard grabbed the flask from his hip and took a long swallow. Water dribbled over his mouth and chin as he drank. "What man doesn't?"

"So you can safely insult me again another day?"

"Of course."

Lamotte could not tell whether Gerard was serious or making a jest. "You would have killed me that day."

"Yes." There was no apology in Gerard's tone, just a simple admission of the facts.

"Why do you hate me so much?" The question had been seriously troubling him for some time. "Why did you try to kill me?"

Gerard crouched down on his heels in the dirt and ran a dirty hand over his forehead, leaving trails of grime in the sweat. "Because you are alive."

Of all things, he had not been expecting this. It made no sense. "Because I am alive?" he repeated stupidly. "What do you mean?"

"You are alive, and my bro—everyone else I have ever loved is dead."

He did not understand. Had Gerard loved his sister so much that her death had warped his mind? "Everyone you love? You sent me word your sister was sick, but that the rest of your household had been spared."

"Sophie was the first to fall sick. She brought the plague into the household." Gerard's eyes were glistening with tears and his voice sounded choked. "One by one, everyone fell sick after her. One by one, everyone died. Everyone. My mother. My father. Everyone. My twin was the last to die."

Lamotte felt his words pierce his heart. No wonder Gerard had lost his light heart and friendly spirit. "I had not known. I am sorry to hear it."

Gerard stared at the ground, his head between his knees. He spoke quickly, as if the words were burning him. "I buried them all in a pit. I tossed the bodies in one after another until the pit was full, and then I covered it over with earth." Tears were running down his face and dripping into the dirt as he spoke. "They all died. All of them. Even the person I had thought to marry."

What could he say? Words were inadequate to express his pity for his friend or his sympathy for the horrors he had suffered. "I tried to come to help you."

Gerard raised his head again, wiped his eyes on his sleeve and made a visible effort to regain control of himself. "Better men than you are afraid of the plague."

"The plague did not stop me." Lamotte crouched down beside his old friend and pulled open his shirt to reveal a jagged scar that ran from his breastbone to near his waist. The scar tissue was red and angry, the edges knitted together in a vicious welt. "That did."

Sophie felt sick to her stomach as she looked at the scar. It made the cut she had given him on his arm look like the merest scratch of a wayward bramble. His side looked as though it had been ripped open by a pack of wolves. Certainly no sword would leave such a mess. She reached out and touched the ribbed edges with a gentle fingertip. "What did that to you?"

"A pitchfork."

She wiped her dirty sleeve across her face. She

knew men and soldiers did not cry, but she had not been able to stop the tears from coming. She had kept her pain bottled up inside her for so long that she had not been able to stop it from flooding out in a torrent when she opened the lid just the smallest bit to let a stranger get a glimpse of it. "How?"

"The roads to the Camargue were blocked and the villagers would allow none through, either in or out. They feared the spread of the plague far too much. I knew how you loved your sister, and I had medicines with me that the king's physician swore were a guaranteed remedy against the plague."

Tears filled Sophie's eyes anew as she thought of her brother's death and how easily it could have been prevented, if only things had turned out differently. "You tried to bring them to me?"

"I was stopped by a mob as I approached Provence. They would not listen to my pleas to be allowed to pass through. Why was I traveling? they demanded. What was I running from? What sickness had God struck me with? They would not believe I had come from a place of no sickness. They would not believe any medicine made by men would be proof against the plague.

"They were mad with fear; I could not reason with them. I tried to ride past them, but there were too many of them. They grabbed hold of me and dragged me off my horse." He gave a wry smile. "I am lucky to be alive at all. I thought I was a dead man."

"You recovered well." Try as she might, she could not keep the distress out of her voice. Did he know how lucky he was to have lived when so many others had died?

"A priest found me and took me in to care for me. Despite his care, the wound went bad and I was sick with the fever most of the winter. Even in my moments of lucidity, I could not rise from my bed. I tried to find a messenger who would bring the medicines to your sister, but they thought I was raving or mad or worse. At any rate, none of them would risk a journey in the middle of winter to a house with the plague. By the time I was well enough to travel, word had reached me that Sophie was long since dead and you were on your way to rejoin the regiment."

Sophie crouched in the dirt still, her heart aching for what she had done, wallowing in the newfound sense of her guilt. She had misjudged Lamotte and sought to murder him, when he had risked his life to save her. He would have saved Gerard, too, if he could. He had not forsaken them in their hour of need as she had thought for so many many months.

She rose unsteadily to her feet to make what belated amends she could. "I apologize for my actions when I first saw you again. I was deeply upset. I thought you had ignored my plea for your help out of fear." She cleared her throat. The words stuck deep down in her chest until she thought she would choke on them. She had to force herself to give them voice. "I take back my words. It seems I had no cause to call you a coward."

Lamotte bowed his head briefly. "Apology accepted."

She sheathed her sword with a hand that trembled. "Thank you for the lesson." She had been so used to seeing him as the enemy that she did not know how to handle this sudden change. Her thirst for revenge had given her the strength to struggle on when even her desire for honor could not have kept her on her feet. Losing the guiding force of her life in an instant made her feel suddenly lost and alone.

She had to believe him. His body could not lie. She had seen his wound with her own eyes and touched the raw edges with her fingertips. He had taken that wound for her. For Gerard. He had nearly died of it.

She had much to think about now, more than she had ever imagined possible. She wanted to be alone in her lodgings with her thoughts.

She could feel his eyes on her as she strode away. "Come back tomorrow," he called after her.

She waved her agreement. She would be back for another lesson in the morn, though her desire to use her newfound skill against her teacher had utterly disappeared. She would learn her best so she would bring honor to Gerard's name.

Her brother had been right. Lamotte was no coward. He was an honorable man, and he deserved her respect. He had well-nigh died trying to bring her the medicine she needed. She would not seek his death any longer.

Still, she could not afford to let him get close to her. Only by holding herself aloof from her companions could she guarantee her secret would be kept. She would learn from Lamotte, but she must nonetheless avoid his friendship, as she avoided the friendship of all her fellow musketeers. She would never be his companion, as Gerard had been.

The thought pained her even as she admitted its absolute necessity. He was an honorable man, and the best fighter she had ever seen. She would have liked to become close to him, to share his hopes and fears, to become a part of his life.

She understood now why Gerard had chosen him for her husband. She sent a silent apology up to Gerard's soul that she had ever doubted him. Her twin had known her better than she had known herself, choosing for her with eyes unblinded by childish liking, choosing her a man she could both love and respect. Lamotte was more of a man than Jean-Luc ever would have been. He was a hawk, a fierce predator, to Jean-Luc's good-natured robin. Lamotte's wife, whoever she would be, would be blessed with a courageous and loyal husband.

Her life as a man gave her freedom to do as she pleased, she thought to herself as she lay awake on her narrow bed that evening, but it cut her off from the rest of the world. She could trust no one, neither man nor woman, with her secret. She had never felt so alone or so lonely before. Even her ambition to do her family honor was cold comfort for her in the dead of night, when all the world but she was asleep in the arms of those they loved.

Henrietta jumped into sudden wakefulness at the sound of the timid knock on her chamber door. She had retired for the night some time ago and was halfway into sleep by now. She turned over grumpily and pulled her bedclothes up to her chin. Maybe if she ignored the noise, whoever it was would go away.

Tap tap tap, a little louder this time.

She sat up and drew back the curtain around her bed a fraction, resigning herself to the annoying inevitability of being thoroughly awakened. "What do you want?"

Her maid opened the chamber door a crack and peeped through. "You have a visitor, Madame Princesse," she whispered.

Henrietta frowned at her maid. The girl, though not overly bright, was not usually quite so dense. "It is the middle of the night and I was asleep. I am not in the mood to receive anyone. Tell them I am not at home."

"But, Madame . . ."

"No buts." She waved her hand in the air to dismiss her maid. "Tell whoever it is to go away."

Her maid squeaked with fright. "Please, Madame," she gabbled, tripping over her words in her haste to get them out of her mouth. "Your visitor is the king."

Henrietta swore under her breath—in English. In the crowded quarters of the palace in Saint-Germain-en-Laye one never knew who might be listening.

The maid looked at her, her frightened face silently beseeching her mistress not to make her tell her king a lie. He could have her whipped to death for less.

Henrietta sighed. She liked her little maid too well to give the king any reason to punish her. "Show him in."

The maid's face lost its terrified pucker and sank into its usual look of agreeable docility as she scuttled off to do her mistress's bidding.

Henrietta patted her hair straight and tucked the bedclothes securely around her. Not for the first time she wished her husband's brother was not the king of France. It would not be politic to offend the king, howsoever much she might be tempted to.

At that moment, the door to her chamber opened with a flourish and King Louis XIV strode in, an ermine nightcap on his wigless head and a purple dressing gown loosely belted around his corpulent waist.

He gestured to his young page, who pulled back the curtains from around her bed.

She bent her head in a gesture of respect, shivering in the cold draft that tickled her shoulders. "Your Majesty."

"You may call me Louis," he said with a benevolent

smile, as if he were conferring the highest honor of the land upon her. Indeed, he probably thought he was, Henrietta thought to herself with a grimace. He had always so loved pomp and ceremony above all else that to voluntarily ask her to address him without his title was most likely a sign of greatest love.

A great love from the king, however, she could very well do without. "You do me too much honor, sire."

He raised her hand to his lips and kissed it with his wet mouth. "If the whole world came to pay homage to you, sweetest Henrietta, it could not give you more honor than you deserve."

She drew her hand away again and tucked it out of sight under the bedclothes. "I trust monsieur, my husband, is well?" Perhaps he needed a timely reminder that she was his sister-in-law—married to his younger brother.

He sat down on the side of her bed with an air of dignified complacence. "Monsieur was perfectly well when I left him last. He was quite surrounded by a pack of adoring boys. You know how much he enjoys that." He gazed at her greedily, his beady eyes shining with desire. "I know my brother is no fit husband for you, Henrietta."

She forbore to remind him that he had arranged the match himself, in full knowledge of his brother's proclivities toward those of his own sex. "I like my husband very well."

"Then you are not being unfaithful to him with one of his friends, I suppose? Not with the Marquis de Torbay, for instance, or the Comte de Guiche?"

Henrietta felt the blood rush from her head. She and the comte had been so careful in their liaison. They had thought they had kept it a secret from all around them. Someone must have spied them together and gone running to the king with the tale. "Did monsieur request that you put such a question to me?" Though trembling with fear for her lover inside, her guilt made her seem haughty. "Would it not be more fitting for monsieur to ask me himself, were he worried about the fidelity of his wife?"

The king gave an uncomfortable harrumph. "I would not like to think you give freely to the Comte what you refuse your king." His words held a wealth of warning.

How many times would she have to tell him the same thing? Would he never accept her refusal? "I refuse you nothing that is lawfully mine to give you."

"You refuse me your love, which I, your king, have many a time begged you for, though it doth humiliate me to my very soul to beg for aught."

She could never give him her love, even were it hers to give. The Comte de Guiche was embedded deep in her heart, and no blusterous words from the king could drive him out again. "I owe my love to my husband."

"Pah. You owe such a husband nothing. You refuse me your kisses, you refuse me the sight of your naked body, you refuse me the pleasure of being abed with you. Such things would cost you nothing but a little complaisance to bestow, and they would make me the happiest of men."

She shuddered at the thought of his body atop hers, his thick, slobbering lips kissing her face, neck, and breasts. She would rather die than submit to his embrace. "I cannot give you such things. I am your sister-in-law, and to be abed with you would be a mortal sin. You have no right to ask it of me."

He drew himself up in anger at her words. "I have the divine right of a king to ask of you anything I require. When you refuse me, you refuse God's messenger on earth. To refuse me is to commit not only treason against your ruler, but blasphemy against God himself."

Were he not the king of France and the ruler of much of Christendom, she would call him a deluded old fool. "I love God, and I cleave to my husband as the Church teaches me to do."

He gave an ugly laugh. "You do not ever cleave to your husband. He is far too busy cleaving to young boys to bother with you."

How true his words were, she thought to herself with an inward smile. Had it been left up to her husband to deflower her, she would be a virgin yet. Still, monsieur had been good to her and had protected her from those at court who bore her and her brother, King Charles II of England, little goodwill. She loved her husband dearly as her friend, though he would never be her husband in more than name only. "My husband is what he is. I do not judge him for it."

He edged closer to her on the bed. "I would give you wealth and honor that my brother Philippe could never match. I would dress you in silks of royal purple and shower you with sapphires and rubies."

She did not wear half the silk dresses or jewels she possessed already. Monsieur could be generous when he pleased—particularly when he had no young boy to lavish his affections and gifts on. "The greatest honor a woman may possess is a good reputation."

"I would make you my chief mistress. None would dare say a word against you."

His breath was foul and his teeth stained a dull brown from too much wine. She drew back as far as she was able. "My conscience would not be satisfied.

It would not leave me to rest peacefully, knowing I had done wrong."

He drew back again, his back straight with anger. "You are refusing me again?"

She was silent.

"Will you be my mistress?"

"No, sire. I cannot."

He glowered at her. "I will have the Comte de Guiche thrown into the Bastille at sunrise."

She decided to brazen it out. If he had proof of her liaison, no doubt the comte would already be in the Bastille, upon the rack or worse. "The Comte de Guiche is nothing to me."

He rose from his seat on the bed, his face red with bottled rage. "I am a patient man. You have a month to reconsider your foolishness. If your only answer is still to refuse your king, I swear you will live long enough to regret your obstinacy. Not even monsieur will be able to save you from my anger then."

Three weeks of lessons. Three weeks of rising before dawn to practice each movement until she could run three paces at top speed, leap in the air, and spit a tiny caterpillar off the wall with unerring accuracy and without so much as blunting the very tip of her blade on the stone.

Lamotte had worked her harder than a mule, and she risen to the challenge as well as she could. She had done her best and more for him. For hours each day, she watched each movement of his lithe body, mirroring him as best she could. She knew his body almost better than her own—she could see every scratch or scar on his arms and neck, even with her eyes closed.

Every day she trained with him to the point of exhaustion, and each night she dreamed about fighting him again. Day or night, sleeping or waking, he was with her. She lived only for his approbation and for the casual nod of his head that told her more eloquently than the floweriest of words that she had done well.

Her obsessive attention to his lessons had paid off. Her skill had improved to the point where she could hold her own against some of her companions. She would always be better with a bow or a knife, where skill was all and strength nothing, but she was no longer a disgrace with a sword. Even D'Artagnan had noticed the difference and had growled his appreciation of the fact that she no longer fought like a lily-livered girl.

How proud Gerard would be if he could see her now, Sophie thought to herself as she flicked her opponent's sword out of his hand, grinning to herself at the look of shock and surprise on his face. Gerard had always believed she could do anything if she set her mind to it. She had proven him right.

Her opponent, a likeable red-haired Tuscan called Pierre, threw up his hands in defeat. "God damn it, Gerard, but you must have been practicing like the very devil was driving you. You've beaten me fair and square."

She shot a glance out of the corner of her eye toward Lamotte as he stood in the slowly lengthening evening shadows watching her. No doubt he would have a dozen criticisms of her style for tomorrow's lesson, but she wouldn't worry about that now. She had beaten Pierre in a fair fight and it felt good.

She inspected her blade carefully for nicks. Finding none, she wiped it carefully with a soft cloth impregnated with oil, just as Lamotte had taught her to do, and put it away by her side. "Lamotte has been teaching me."

Teaching was too easy a word for it. He had been drilling her unmercifully, but with such success that she had disarmed one of her fellows for the very first time. In her delight at winning, she momentarily forgave him every harsh word he had ever aimed her way.

Pierre wiped the grime off his blade on his shirt, and shoved his sword back into its scabbard with an easy motion. "Ah, so that's your secret. He's the very devil when it comes to fighting. Maybe I should get a few tips myself before I cross swords with you again."

His good humor was infectious. Sophie let down her habitual guard enough to smile. "Lady Luck favored me today, that was all."

Pierre flung his jacket over his shoulder. "Lady Luck and a lot of practice. I'm for a drink of something a mite stronger than the feeble ale you get around here. You interested?"

Sophie hesitated, wavering between desire for company and the ever present need for distance and caution. She glanced at Lamotte again, hoping he would call her to him now that her bout was over, but his back was turned away from her. She sighed with disappointment.

"Come on, Delamanse. All work and no play makes Jack a dull boy. You've been working like the very devil. You must need a drink for sure."

She could go back to her tiny room and eat watery gruel for supper in her stifling attic room in safety, or she could accept Pierre's offer of uncomplicated company. Pierre was as new to the musketeers as she and posed little danger to her masquerade. He had never known Gerard.

She gave a quick sideways glance. Lamotte had disappeared into the shadows at the far edge of the courtyard. There was little point in staying in the hopes of prolonging her lesson with him. She did not want to impose too much on his good nature. He had been giving up all his free time to her lately to tutor her.

She felt as though she could never be sick of his company, but she did not want him to tire of her. His friendship, so casually offered and so gratefully received, had made her feel less lonely. He made her feel as though she belonged as part of his world, and that she need never be alone again.

Her craving for company decided for her. "Lead on." She could not rely on Lamotte to always be there for her. She had to make a place for herself in the world she had chosen. A drink in the tavern with Pierre was an uncomplicated start. She only hoped she would not regret it.

The tavern was full to the bursting point with soldiers of all descriptions. Sophie recognized a few of them from her regiment, but most of them were strangers to her.

Pierre elbowed his way to the front, fending off the complaints of those he jostled with a quick grin and a few easy words, and ordered them some stew and a pint of porter apiece.

They sat down on a pair of stools at a rough-hewn table in a dark corner, away from the worst of the crowd.

Lamotte, she noted, appeared not long after they did. She avoided catching his eye, and to her mingled relief and disappointment he did not join them, but made his way instead to a quiet group in the far corner.

He unsettled her and made her feel more on her guard than anyone else in the regiment, though she enjoyed his company more than anyone else's as well. She did not want him to think he was her only friend. Besides, she was tired tonight and Pierre's unthinking comradeship was far easier for her to deal with.

She ate her thick meaty stew with relish, but dared only to sip at her drink. She had never touched anything stronger than small beer before. In her situation, and with Lamotte and others who knew her brother all around her, drinking was too dangerous. She needed all her wits about her.

Pierre was under no such restraint. Before he taken more than three mouthfuls of stew, he had finished his pint and was calling loudly for another. The drink made him merrier than ever, until Sophie was laughing harder than she had done in a long while. She had not shed her cares for the simple enjoyment of food and laughter for longer than she could remember.

She could feel Lamotte's gaze on her, and could not resist sneaking the odd glance back at him. He did not seem to share her enjoyment of the evening. He ate his stew slowly and with a black look on his face. The ale he drank only deepened his frown. She wondered what ailed him that he was so morose on such a pleasant evening.

She was wiping out the last of her stew with a thick chunk of bread when a harried-looking serving maid, her hands full of brimming pewter mugs, finally answered Pierre's call for more ale. She plonked one of the mugs down in front of him, and he swiped it up immediately. "To your health, darling," he said with a flourish, raising his mug in her direction.

The fellows at a nearby table were less polite. One of them, a big, burly, oafish fellow with hands the size of trenchers, put his arm around the serving maid's waist as she passed by and drew her on to his lap.

Sophie looked up from her plate at the woman's squeal of protest. The maid was holding her brimming pints of porter high above her head as she tried to wriggle out of the oaf's grasp. With her hands occupied, she was powerless to escape.

The landlord passed by, plates of food in each hand. He made no attempt to rescue her. "Don't spill 'em girl, or I'll dock the price of 'em out of your wages."

The oaf roared with ribald laughter at the girl's cries for help, and grabbed at her breasts with his huge, meaty hands. Sophie was close enough to see tears of pain and terror come to the girl's eyes as she struggled in vain to break free.

Without stopping for breath, Sophie vaulted off her stool and drew her dagger out of its scabbard. A few quick steps, and she was at his side. Just touching the tip of her sword against the oaf's neck, she growled into his ear, "Drop the girl."

He looked around in drunken surprise. "You talking to me?"

Sophie pressed her knife a little harder against his neck, so that a trickle of ruby-red blood ran down into the collar of his shirt. She had no patience for bullies who preyed on those weaker than themselves. "Drop the girl."

He roared in fury as the pain hit his fuddled brain. He let go of the serving maid, who quickly scuttled away to safety, and lumbered drunkenly to his feet. "I'll take you apart with my bare hands for nicking me, you poxy little son of a whore," he bellowed.

He was taller than a mountain and just as solid-looking, Sophie thought with a faint stirring of dismay, as she swapped her wicked little dagger for her equally sharp sword. She stood her ground, sword in hand, defying him to wreak his revenge on her. Mountain of a man that he was, she was far more nimble on her feet than he could ever be, and the porter he'd drunk had slowed him down even further.

With a rumbling bellow of outrage that reverberated in the rafters, he drew his sword and aimed a tremendous blow in her general direction—luckily for her with more enthusiasm than finesse. She barely needed to twist sideways a fraction and the blow landed harmlessly on a nearby stool, shattering it to pieces.

The scabrous landlord materialized out of nowhere, wringing his hands at the sight of such damage to his precious property. "My chair," he wailed, in tones of heartfelt anguish. "Gentlemen, gentlemen, put up your swords."

She ignored his cries, as he had ignored the cries of the serving maid. He deserved to have all his chairs broken for the meanness of his mercenary soul.

All her attention was concentrated on the fracas she had started. She had no desire to kill or maim the oaf, only to teach him a lesson to not mess with maids who didn't welcome his attentions. With a quick twist of her wrist, she cut through the lacings that tied up his breeches. She heard Pierre behind her convulse with laughter as the oaf's breeches fell to his knees.

The draught of cold air around his nether parts sobered the oaf. With an inarticulate grunt of fury, he gathered a fistful of breeches in one hand and came after her again, vicious determination squinting crookedly out of his bloodshot eyes.

She could see out of the corner of her eye that Lamotte was watching her once more. She could not resist showing him how well she had learned her lessons. Pivoting on her heel, she leaped on to the table behind the oaf, hooked the tip of her sword in the back of his leather jerkin and ripped it cleanly in two.

The two halves of the jerkin fell over the oaf's shoulders and down his arms, tangling in his sword and inhibiting his movement. Still he came after her, blundering through the crowd with his breeches in one fist and his sword in the other, intent on vengeance, striking this way and that at whatever got in his way.

His drinking companions had roared with laughter along with the rest at the oaf's mishap with his breeches, but their mood turned ugly when they saw how useless all his strength was against Sophie's speed. They misliked seeing one of their own mocked by a musketeer in the service of the King.

One by one they clambered to their feet, swords in hand, advancing against Sophie, trampling over anyone who got in their way.

In a few short moments, the entire tavern was in a complete uproar. Stools were being flung and tables overturned. Each man was fighting against everyone else, for no other reason but the love of a brawl. Sophie was in the thick of it, hoping Lamotte was still watching her as she called on every lesson he had ever taught her to keep herself from harm.

She would have done better to keep her attention focused on the rolling waves of the fight in front of her rather than trying to spy Lamotte's reaction to her agility. One wrong move, and she found herself trapped, her back against the wall, the oaf and his friends having cut off her escape routes.

She wasted no time in cursing her foolishness. There would be time and enough for recriminations when she was safe out of trouble. Her mind focused on all the tricks she had been taught, she fought her attackers fiercely, calling on every dram of strength and courage she possessed. Her agility was little use to her in such a tight corner.

Despite her best efforts, they were crowding in on her. Much closer, and she would not be able to lift her sword arm to fend them off. She searched desperately for a friendly face among the crowd. Pierre was trading blows with a fellow in the corner, too occupied to come to her aid. Lamotte was standing idly in the far side, raising his sword only when necessary to ward off any stray blows that came in his direction.

She caught his eye in a frantic plea for him to come and assist her. He raised an eyebrow in her direction, crossed his arms over his chest, and made no move to help her.

Damn him to hell and back again, she thought to herself, as she parried another blow. The force of it sent shock waves up her arm and she nearly dropped her sword. Her wrist would ache for a sennight. *He can see I'm struggling. Why won't he come to my aid?*

She dodged another blow. Damn it, she hadn't meant to start a full-scale war, just teach a villain some manners.

Just as her attackers were closing in on her for the kill, from out of nowhere a tall, blond musketeer appeared beside her, his sword ringing with ferocity as he carved his way into the middle of the fray. "Into the kitchen," he hissed into Sophie's ear. "We can get out through the back door and into the alley that way."

Sophie flashed her rescuer a smile of relief and thanks. She could not understand why Lamotte had left her to her fate so callously. She had been in for a beating to end all beatings to be sure, if she had even survived. She had thought he had begun to like her and to enjoy her company while he was teaching her. Thank God and all his angels that some of the musketeers knew the meaning of chivalry and would come to the aid of their beleaguered comrades.

Back to back she and her rescuer battled along the wall, swords clanging as they went. Her companion battled valiantly and seemingly without fear. He did not even try to dodge many of the blows that were aimed at him. He took them square on his sword and struck back again with a vengeance. With a flurry of vicious blows that sent their opponents reeling, they popped through the nearest door, a narrow opening recessed into the wall, and slammed it shut behind them.

"Damn. Wrong door," the blond musketeer said, as they found themselves in a storage room, with neither door nor window except for the tiny opening they had just popped through.

Sophie swore vigorously as she wiped the sweat out of her eyes. "We're trapped in here."

Kegs of ale were stacked up to the ceiling, and huge hams and bunches of onions and other vegetables hung from the rafters. A wiry, dark-haired soldier, dressed as they were in the uniform of a musketeer, crouched in the corner with his back to them, stuffing onions in his boots. He looked up as they burst in, dismay and then shock registering on his smudged and grubby face.

The blond musketeer grabbed the thief by his hair and yanked him to his feet. He clinked and clanked as he stumbled to his feet and a bottle of pilfered wine fell out of his shirt to smash on the stone flags of the floor. A red stain that looked uncomfortably like blood began to spread out through the gaps where the stones were joined.

The blond musketeer kicked the shards into a corner. "Drop your booty, thief, and help us fight our way out. Three of us together stand more of a chance than two."

The thief groaned as he began to pull the onions out of his boots. "Do I have to? I'd really much rather stay here."

"Coward," Sophie hissed at him from over her shoulder, her sword clashing fast and furious as she held the door against all comers. "You shame the uniform you wear."

The thief took a bottle of wine out of his shirt and gazed lovingly at it. "I can fight as well as you when I'm in the mood, but I have just scored a couple of bottles of truly fine wine and my heart aches to have to leave them behind."

The blond musketeer laughed as he prodded the thief with the tip of his sword. "Drop them, you little gutter rat. They'll only weigh you down."

The thief put the bottle carefully down in the corner and drew his sword. "For liberty and justice and three square meals a day," he muttered. "Let's get out of here."

Standing shoulder to shoulder, the three of them forced their way out of the storeroom and along the wall to the next door—into the noise and heat of the kitchen.

"Get out of here, you brawling sons of whores," the landlady screeched at them as they edged their way in, swords flying. "Get out of my tavern and take your quarrels elsewhere."

Sophie ducked the moldy onion thrown at her head. It hit one of her attackers with a dull thud, splattering rotten flesh over his cheek.

He shook his raised fist at the red-faced landlady and shouted a string of obscenities at her.

The irate landlady gave one last screech of protest and fled through a side door, shooting the bolts into place behind her as she went.

The maidservant was no such coward. Besides, she had an insult to avenge, and the kitchen was her own territory. Seizing a sizzling hot pan from the fire, she swung it around her head and laid into Sophie's attackers with a vengeance. "Take that," she screamed, as she swatted the oaf on his overgrown backside with the fiery pan. "And that. And that." Every word was punctuated with another blow to his breeches.

The oaf squealed like a pig being slaughtered and dropped his sword. He danced around from one foot to the other, holding his smoking backside in his hands and yowling with anguish.

Emboldened by her success, the maidservant clocked another of the combatants with a vicious blow to the back of his head. There was a dull thud as the pan hit his thick skull, and then a clatter and crash of broken crockery as he fell to the floor, knocked out stone cold.

Seeing their comrades felled by such a virago, the rest of the attackers beat a hasty retreat back out into the tumult of the tavern.

The maidservant dropped her pan and stood, arms akimbo, gazing at them with fierce exultation as they decamped in defeat. "Get out with ye, you scurvy sons of dogs," she screeched at their backs. "Don't be coming in here again, or ye'll get more of the same."

Sophie bowed to the maidservant. "You have a fierce arm on you, miss, and a fierce weapon to boot. You have our thanks for rescuing our sorry skins."

"Thanks be to you, sir," she said with a grin. "I didna like being pawed over by that beast, but I couldna clock him with the mugs or I wouldna have eaten for a week. He'll think twice afore messing with me again now."

The blond musketeer guffawed with laughter. "You served that lecherous bastard right enough. You'd do well in uniform. You're the sort of comrade I'd like to have beside me in battle."

The maidservant laid the pan back on the fire. "You'd best scarper off yourself, sirs. The master will have sent a runner for the guards by now, and there'll be trouble if you're caught brawling here. He'll have you taken up for breaking his chairs."

Without wasting another second, Sophie raced for the door, with the blond musketeer and the thief both close on her heels. It seemed as though all three of them had their own good reasons for not wanting to be caught by the guard.

The alley out back was covered in stinking refuse. Sophie started to pick her way over delicately, unwilling to get her boots covered in such filth. She had only one pair.

A bugle blast and the sound of horses hooves on the cobbled stone decided her that dirty boots were the least of her problems. She stood stock-still, not knowing which way to turn to avoid capture and the punishment always dealt out to brawlers.

The thief wasted no time in looking about him. With a muttered curse, he took off running. "Come on," he called softly back at the two others. "This way."

With surprising agility, he scrambled up to the top of the stone wall on the other side of the alley. "Up here," he called, as he dropped down the other side.

Sophie and the blond musketeer followed as best they could, clambering up the wall and dropping down the other side.

They were only just in time. As they leaped down,

a couple of mounted guards turned into the alley. The foremost guard gave a shout as he saw them escape over the wall. "After them!"

Sophie and the blond musketeer both turned to look at the thief at the same time. He gave an exaggerated sigh. "Follow me if you want to get out of here in one piece. But you've got to keep up with me. If you slow me down, I'll ditch you both without a second thought."

Coward, Sophie thought to herself.

"Dirty little gutter rat," muttered the blond musketeer, aiming a filthy look at the thief.

Still, he was their best chance and they knew it, so they both followed him. For the next half hour, he led them a merry dance over rooftops and walls, into courtyards, under archways, and through dirty back alleys. Sophie's side hurt with running and her feet were rubbed raw on the harsh leather of her boots. The blond musketeer beside her was panting heavily.

At last the thief stopped, and they doubled over, their hands on their knees, to regain their breath. "I think we've thrown them off the scent."

The sound of a bugle close by made them groan. The chase was not yet over.

Sophie thought of her blistered heels with near panic. She wasn't sure she could run another step. "Or maybe not."

The thief shrugged his shoulders. "We should get inside if we can. That horn is only for show. They won't find us now if we can get off the street."

The surroundings were completely unfamiliar to Sophie. All she knew of Paris was her lodging house and the street that ran to the barracks. She was utterly lost. "Where are we?"

The street the thief named was of no help to her.

The blond musketeer, however, brightened up at the name. "My lodgings are only a quarter mile away. They're big enough for all three of us to hide out there until the hue and cry dies away."

Much as she misliked this suggestion, Sophie had no choice but to accept. She had no desire to be dragged in front of the tribunal to be punished for brawling in the streets. As instigator of the ruckus, she would be sure to be punished most harshly of all. If the captain was in a foul mood that day, she could even be deprived of her commission and sent home in disgrace.

She had joined the musketeers to bring honor to Gerard's name, not drag it through the gutters. Her blistered heels complaining at every step, she followed the others through the darkening streets, staying in the shadows as much as possible and keeping a wary eye out for any guards who might still be on the prowl.

The blond musketeer lodged in a fine house not three streets away from her own. Sophie started to relax a little now that she was in familiar territory and not lost in the dark in some back alley in an unidentifiable part of Paris.

Like a trio of thieves, they crept in the front door as quietly as possible and dashed up the stairs to the blond musketeer's apartments on the second floor.

The blond musketeer sank into a comfortable chair with a sigh of relief and motioned his visitors to do likewise. "God in heaven, but my feet are killing me in those damned boots," he said, unlacing his boots and tossing them into a corner. He wiggled his toes with relief. His feet, Sophie noticed, were surprisingly small and dainty for such a tall man.

She resisted the temptation to do likewise. "Gerard Delamanse, at your service, sirs," she said, as she sank into a chair in her turn. "And I hope I don't have to run like that again for a while."

The blond musketeer gave her a lazy salute from the depths of his chair. "William Ruthgard at yours."

The thief pulled a bottle of wine out from under his shirt with a flourish. He grabbed a couple of glasses off the sideboard and poured a generous measure into each, before tilting the bottle to his own lips, taking a long drink and wiping his mouth clean again with the back of his hand. "Since we are in a formal mood, let me introduce myself to you both," he said, and aimed a mocking bow in their general direction. "I am JeanPaul Metin, at your service. To your health, gentlemen."

Sophie glugged a mouthful of the rich, warm wine. It trickled down her dry throat like manna from heaven. "You carried this all the way in your shirt without breaking it?"

The thief tilted the bottle to his lips again, smacking his lips with satisfaction. "It slowed me down some, but it was worth it. The very best Rhenish wine doesn't come my way every day."

The blond musketeer swirled the wine around his mouth and then shook his head. "Not the very best, but a damned good bottle, anyway. How did you manage to swipe it when I wasn't looking?"

The thief laughed as he flexed his fingers. "Years of practice and a good eye."

She was drinking stolen wine, Sophie thought with an uncomfortable feeling in the pit of her belly. The landlord had been duly punished for his callousness by having his tavern destroyed in a brawl. Drinking his wine without paying for it was adding insult to injury. Still, she was very thirsty, and the wine was too good to waste. She would pay him for it on the morrow, she decided, as she drank another mouthful.

A few more mouthfuls and Sophie started to feel light-headed and bone weary to boot. She closed her eyes briefly for a moment, and then shook herself awake again with a start. She did not dare fall asleep in company. She must concentrate on staying awake. Her eyes focused on the blond musketeer's face. Something was awry. She couldn't put her finger on exactly what it was.

The blond musketeer grew uncomfortable under her scrutiny. "What are you staring at?" His voice was brusque and less than friendly.

Sophie had finally worked out what had been bothering her. "Your moustache is coming loose," she said, without thinking of what she was saying. "You need to glue it on again."

The blond musketeer's face turned bright red. He rose half upright in his chair and laid his hand on the hilt of his sword. "Just what are you implying?"

The thief laughed. "She's right, you know. You need better glue that doesn't lose its grip when you sweat. Personally I find false moustaches are seldom worth the effort. They're damnably itchy, and it's so hard to get them looking natural. It's easier to pretend you shave religiously every night and morning."

The blond musketeer froze, half in and half out of his chair, looking completely nonplussed.

Sophie barely heard past his first few words before she leaped up in horror in her turn. "She? You called me 'she'?"

The thief put his hands in the air, palms out, in a gesture of conciliation. "Just a guess. Based on the simple observation that your breast wrappings have come a little loose, and you don't see many men on the streets with a chest like yours."

Sophie glanced down at her chest. Sure, her wrappings had come a little loose in their wild scramble across the rooftops and over walls, but not unduly so. The faint jiggle of her breasts could hardly have been noticeable, especially not in the dark. How had this mere stranger guessed her secret so easily?

And why was the blond musketeer wearing a false moustache?

Sophie and the blond musketeer looked at each other, and then at the thief, in burgeoning understanding.

Sophie was the first to speak. "You're a woman," she said looking at the blond musketeer. "That's why you're wearing a false mustache." She turned next to the thief. "And so are you."

Four

The thief drained the bottle dry and put it down by her side with a look of regret on her face. "Guilty as charged. Do you have another bottle of wine, or shall I have to make do with ale for the rest of the night?"

The blond musketeer looked utterly bemused. She was staring straight at Sophie, not seeming able to accept what was in front of her. "That's why you attacked that lout in the tavern, isn't it? Because you're a woman, too?"

Sophie was still reeling from the shock of finding two musketeers with the same secret that had weighed her down for so many weeks. She had companions now, two of them. She had someone to talk to, to share her life with, someone who would understand, and who would never give her secrets away. She was not alone any more. She wanted to shout out loud with the joy of it. "I don't like bullies who pick on people who can't fight back," she said. "He needed to be taught a lesson."

"I wondered at the time what had possessed you to fight him. No man would have gone to the serving girl's aid." The blonde musketeer's voice was laced with bitterness. "Whatever pretty words they may whisper in your ear, men are all alike in their selfish, stupid, pigheaded ways. They all believe women are there only to be used, not protected."

"I owe you my thanks for coming to fight by my side. I thought I was done for."

"I couldn't let you fight that battle on your own. It was a battle all women should fight against the men who abuse and oppress their sex."

A snort of muffled laughter came from the other side of the room, where the thief had given up waiting for an answer to her request for more wine and was rifling through the sideboard in a search for something else to drink. "Pah. All women indeed. Don't feed me any of that codswallop or I'll puke."

The blond musketeer growled. "Trust a dirty little gutter rat not to know the meaning of morality or respectability or human decency. You may as well stay a man and be done with it. You act just like men do."

The thief turned around to glare back at her. "Street rats can't afford morals. You can take your morality and shove it up your arse for all I care."

Sophie spoke up quickly, trying to distract their attention away from their quarrel. She wanted them to be sisters and work together, not to snarl and spit at each other like fighting cocks. "How did you guess our sex?"

The thief was still not mollified. She looked pointedly at the blond musketeer as she spoke. "A life on the street teaches to look beyond how people seem on the outside. If you don't learn that lesson quickly, you're dead."

Surely she couldn't have seen through them on the instant. No one else had so much as suspected her disguise for weeks. "When did you realize we were women?"

"As soon as you burst into the storeroom and rudely

disturbed my booty gathering," the thief said, her back turned to them again. "You could have knocked me down with a feather when I saw the pair of you evidently with the same idea as I had—to become a musketeer. I thought I was the only woman daft enough to try it, not to mention smart enough to carry it off."

Sophie knew just what that felt like. She could hardly conceive there were three of them in the same boat. She had to wonder if there were any more of them hidden away in different regiments—women passing themselves off as men, just like the three of them.

"It's the only reason I stuck with you both," the thief continued, her head deep in a cupboard. "If you'd been men, I would've ditched you three times over and left you to be taken up in irons by the guard without a qualm. As it was, I figured you two could do with a helping hand.

"Ah ha, success." She turned around again, a fresh bottle of wine in her hand. "Come, gentlemen, shall we make our introductions again?" she said, as she poured them all another generous measure. "Let me start. May I introduce myself not as JeanPaul Metin but as Miriame Dardagny, born and raised in the back alleys of Paris, lately a pickpocket, recently turned musketeer in the hopes of making my fortune with rather less risk to my neck."

The blond musketeer stretched out her legs in front of her. "Courtney Ruthgard at your service. I have a cousin named William of around my age." She wrinkled her nose. "He is a sweet-natured simpleton who grows tulips in Holland and hasn't a martial bone in his body—he is one of the few men in the world who is worth the food he eats. I borrowed his name to become a musketeer and avenge the wrong one of them did to me and my family. God willing, he will sleep with the worms before too much longer and I shall sleep easy in my bed again."

"Sophie Delamanse. My twin brother, Gerard, was a musketeer before he died of the plague—the plague that I brought into the house. I loved him dearly and would have given my life for his, but I was the cause of his death. I decided to take his place and win in his name the honor that should have been his."

The three of them sat in silence for a while, drinking their wine and looking at each other in bemusement. Sophie did not know what to say to the other two. She had trained herself for so long to act and think like a man that she did not know how to be a woman again.

Finally she dared to do what she had been longing to do for hours. She reached under her shirt and pulled free the wrappings that bound her chest, sighing with pleasure as her breasts swung free. "Ah, that feels so good. I never dreamed how uncomfortable men's clothes could be until I had to wear them myself."

At her cue, Courtney pulled off the tattered remains of her moustache, tossed her hat aside and ran her hands through the strawberry blond hair that fell straight to her shoulders. "I detest wearing hats, but I look impossibly feminine without mine." Her usually somber face relaxed into a grin. "I think I'll forgo the moustache in future, though. I would hate to have it fall off in my dinner. How shockingly disreputable that would be."

Miriame perched comfortably on the arm of a chair. "Breeches are far more practical than dresses when you live on the street. I don't know that I've ever worn a dress in my life—certainly not that I can remember."

All three of them were silent with their own

thoughts. The silence was broken only by the sound of them breathing, the faint ticking of the grandfather clock in the corner, and the night noises that filtered their way up from the street.

Sophie lay back in her chair and stared at the ceiling. This discovery had changed everything. "So what now?"

Miriame rested her boots on the low table in front of her. "We have a drink, we rest our feet, and then Sophie and I make our way home again once the guards have given up the chase."

"That is not what I meant."

Miriame looked genuinely confused. "What do you mean?"

"Well, we can hardly go on pretending we don't know each other's deep, dark secret, can we? So what do we do about it?"

Courtney nodded. "I see what you mean."

Miriame raised her glass. "You keep my secret close and I'll keep yours to my dying day. Either of you betray me by so much as an incautious word, and I throw the pair of you to the wolves. Deal?"

"And that's all?"

"What more do you want?"

Sophie shook her head at Miriame's obtuseness. "We could make each other's lives far easier. Alone as we are now, we risk attracting unwanted attention from those who may want to befriend us. If we succeed in keeping our fellows at a safe distance, we may garner suspicion because of our solitary ways. Alone, we are vulnerable. Together, we can form a barrier against the rest of the world our enemies will not be able to break."

Miriame raised her glass in a cynical salute. "All for one and one for all and all that stuff? How quaint."

Sophie glared at her. "I'm serious."

Miriame looked suspiciously at the wine in the bottom of her glass. "Why? What do you get out of this?"

Sophie thought of the lonely nights she had spent in her attic room, longing for companionship. She would not let this chance slip out of her hands without a fight. "How long can you be a musketeer and yet not be one?" she asked. "How long can you survive surrounded by people you cannot afford to trust or confide in?"

Miriame crossed her arms across her chest in a defensive gesture. "All my life, so far."

Sophie could not imagine such solitude. She had always had Gerard to love her and listen to her. She hated to feel so alone. "That is no way to live. It is existence, not life. Are you not sick of it? Don't you ever long to have a friend to talk to?"

"How long will it take before your fellows notice you never go swimming with them?" Courtney chimed in. "Or that you never strip down to wash off after a hard day's fighting? Won't they start to think you strange? Of course, most men wash infrequently enough that they may not notice."

Miriame was not impressed. "Each to his own. If I don't bother them, they won't bother me."

Sophie shook her head. "You may spit and curse along with the rest of them, but you'll never be able to piss in the corner of the courtyard like they do. Sooner or later, one way or another, they'll find you out."

Courtney screwed up her face in disgust. "Men are such pigs."

Miriame was silent for a while, her forehead furrowed in thought. "So what do you suggest we do about it?"

"We band together. Not just for one night, but for all time."

"We eat and drink together."

"We keep each other's secrets."

"We go on duty together."

"We look after each other's interests."

"Brothers in arms."

Miriame lifted her nearly empty glass. "Fellow musketeers, sisters in arms, we have a deal."

Courtney filled their glasses to the brim one more time.

Miriame drained her newly filled glass and lifted it to the ceiling with a whoop. "Pour me another one then, sisters. I feel a celebration coming on."

Sophie tilted the warm rich wine down her throat. She had two new companions, and life was good. All the three of them needed now was an adventure that tested their mettle and their fighting spirit and proved their worth to the world.

The Comte de Guiche raised himself up on his elbow at the sound of the rustling at the door. "Henrietta," he whispered urgently into the ear of the woman sleeping soundly beside him. "Wake up."

She half woke up and pulled him toward her for a kiss, her hand moving to touch him in between his legs. "Darling," she murmured, her voice husky with sleep, "you're insatiable, and I love you for it."

He could see the glow of a lighted candle through the curtains around their bed. They had dismissed all their servants the previous eve so they could be alone together. Whoever held the candle was here to spy on them and discover their loves. Whoever it was bore them no goodwill.

He hugged her tightly to him. "Henrietta," he whispered again, the knowledge of mortal danger clutching at his heart. "We have been betrayed."

In that same instant she was wide awake. She sat bolt upright in the bed and clutched his arm with a bruising grip. "How?"

He stroked her hair with his free hand—her beautiful dark brown curls he loved to bury his face in, breathing deeply of the perfume of her soul. The how was not important at a time like this. "Just remember that I love you forever. You are my one true soul mate, and I will love you until the waves stop crashing on the sand and the sun ceases to rise in the morning sky."

The voice of the king cut through his avowal. "How quaint, Monsieur le Comte. I see you have the soul of a poet."

Henrietta groaned softly and buried her face in her hands. "I'm sorry, my love," she whispered in the Comte de Guiche's ear. "I have ruined you."

The king pulled back the curtains around the bed. "My dear sister-in-law," he said, and gave a grimace that tried to pass as a smile. "I see you were not altogether honest with me, or else you have been cruelly toying with the comte's heart. The comte swears he loves you until the end of the world, but I vividly recollect you telling me a few short weeks ago that you cleaved to your husband and the Comte de Guiche meant nothing to you."

Henrietta looked at him with abject misery and guilt writ large over her face, but said nothing.

"Monsieur le Comte, I am most displeased with you," the king continued. "I had heard an idle rumor you were cuckolding my brother by foutering his wife, but I had discounted it as a vile slander. What courtier, I thought to myself, would sink that low?"

The comte looked the king straight in the eye. "I love Madame Henrietta better than her husband ever could."

"The charges laid against you, treasonous intercourse with the king's brother's wife, were so serious I thought it politic to investigate the rumor myself. Unfortunately"—and King Louis gave a loud sigh of satisfaction, quite at odds with his words—"I have proven them true instead. "What will I do with you now, Monsiuer le Comte?"

Henrietta felt the king's beady eyes on her as he spoke.

"A ruinous fine for corrupting my sister-in-law? An oubliette in the Bastille for the rest of your natural days? Or a torturous death for treason?"

Henrietta squeezed the comte's hand under the bedclothes. How much she regretted now falling in love with him. Had she not loved him, he would have been safe from the malice of the king.

The king gave an unpleasant smile, looking from one to the other with a gaze of malignant satisfaction. "Enjoy the rest of your night," he said, as he let the curtain fall. "It will be the last night you ever spend together."

As soon as the door closed behind him, Henrietta sprang out of bed. "You must leave at once," she said to the comte, thrusting his clothes into his hands. "He will take some minutes to rouse the guards and send them to arrest you. You must be on your horse by then and on your way out of Paris. Once you are out of his sight, hidden away in the provinces, he will forget about you."

"You must come with me," the comte said, pulling on his breeches. "I will not leave you behind."

Henrietta shook her head. "I cannot run from here. King Louis will take it as an insult to the royal family of France from the royal family of England. In his anger, he might even declare war on my brother, King Charles II of England. I cannot be the cause of war between England and France."

He stopped in the middle of putting on his boots. "The king will punish you if you do not come with me."

"He cannot harm me. My husband will protect me from the king's anger."

He shook his head. "Monsieur is weak. I do not like to leave you here at the mercy of the king."

She helped him on with his riding jacket. "You are wasting precious minutes. Even now the guards may be on their way to arrest you. If ever you loved me, be off with you right away. I would die if you were caught."

He grabbed his hat in one hand and his riding crop in the other. "I leave my heart behind with you."

She wiped away a tear. "You take my heart with you wherever you go. Now be on your way. I would never forgive myself if you came to harm through loving me."

Still he hesitated. "Call me if you have need of me, and I will come to your side, though a thousand kings stood in my way."

She crushed him to her in one last desperate embrace before pushing him out the door. "Fare thee well, my love. Forgive me."

Sophie's head felt as though it was about to split in two the next morning as she staggered off to the barracks with her two new companions. Courtney looked as seedy as she felt: her face was pale and tinged with green, and big purple hollows ringed her eyes. Sophie was glad she could not see her own face. She was quite sure it would be bad enough to scare crows and make pregnant women miscarry from fright. She was not sure how she managed even to stay upright.

Miriame was disgustingly chirpy, despite having swallowed three times what either Sophie or Courtney had managed. She had no sympathy for either of them. "You can't even hold your liquor like a woman, let alone like a man or a soldier," was her disparaging comment as Sophie turned aside for the second time to be violently ill by the side of the road.

Sophie could only groan in response as she rinsed her mouth with water from her flask and spat it out again. If anything, her stomach felt worse than her head. Her head only hurt—and as a soldier she was used to dealing with pain. With every step she took, her stomach felt as though she were on board a tiny boat in the middle of a raging storm. All she wanted to do was lie down and die to stop the sick feeling in her stomach from completely overwhelming her.

She got no sympathy from Lamotte, either, when she staggered on to the grounds for her lesson, late for the first time ever.

He was singularly unimpressed with her condition. "A good soldier never drinks so much in the eve that he cannot fight in the morn," he said, his voice dry, as she stumbled into the courtyard, pain shooting through her head with every beat of her heart and her stomach still heaving. His brows were knitted together in a look of disgust.

She did not even try to justify herself in his eyes. She had no will left to do so. Thank the Lord he thought she was a man, and didn't know her true sex. Drunkenness in a man was tolerable—barely—as long he did not make a habit of it or cause trouble when he was in his cups. Drunkenness in a woman, though, she thought to herself with a giggle that made her stomach heave again, was another matter entirely. Lamotte would no doubt be disgusted unto death were he to know. It was the best reason yet for him never to find out she was not Gerard.

She was having a hard time keeping up the charade this morning. She could not even concentrate on her lesson with more than the outermost edges of her mind. She was in no state to leap or thrust to meet Lamotte's blade. The most she could manage was to stand in the dust, parrying the blows he aimed at her as best she could. Even then, her arm felt like it was made of lead and she winced with shooting pains in her head at the harsh metallic ringing made by their clashing blades.

After a few minutes of coaxing her to greater effort, he threw his sword down on the ground with disgust. "Be off with you," he growled. "You are wasting my time and your own."

Sophie sheathed her sword gladly and sank down on her heels, willing herself not to vomit up the bile in her throat in front of him. She had already given him more than enough of a disgust for her. She felt so sick that she wished she could die, if only death would take away her pain and nausea. She looked up at Lamotte's clear countenance with envy in her heart. "You were not drinking last night, then?"

He gave a wry smile that twisted up the corners of his mouth but did not reach his eyes. "You spoiled my evening. After your brawling in the tavern last night, no one was able to drink anymore."

"Drinking is bad for you anyway," she said moralistically, forgetting for the moment what had put her into the sorry state she was in now.

"Yes, drinking to excess," he said pointedly, "tends to make one a little slow the next day."

She felt herself blush. He was right. She ought to take her own words to heart.

He had not been drinking last night and had not the excuse that he was too tipsy to fight alongside her. So why had he not come to her aid? She had a vivid recollection of Lamotte standing by, watching her struggle and refusing to lift a finger to rescue her. "I know you saw me beg for your aid yester night. Why did you not help me?"

"Musketeers do not waste their skill brawling in taverns." His eyes were cold and gray. She shivered as he looked straight through her. "No musketeer should be brainless enough to start a brawl he is not prepared to see through to the end. By himself. I will not always be around to see you out of every foolish scrape you get yourself into. Even when I am around, I may not choose to aid you. You may as well learn that lesson sooner rather than later, in a place where your foolishness will mean only a beating and not your death."

She rested her head in her hands, keeping it as still as she could to stop the pounding in her brain. "You would see a woman abused, then, and not go to her aid?"

He made a dismissive noise. "She was no innocent maid, but a sluttish serving girl in a tavern. Why should you rush to her side?"

Sophie felt her gorge rise up in her throat. How easily he had labeled the woman as unworthy of his protection. Were not musketeers supposed to protect the weak and prevent injustice wherever they found it, regardless of whether the victim was a Queen or a lowly serving maid in a tavern? "She was a woman and so worthy of our protection."

"She worked in a tavern. What else could she expect but to be treated that way?"

She was growing angry now. "Women have to eat, just the same as men. Or would you rather she starved on the streets? Would you help her then, or would you consider her equally unworthy of your protection? Is your honor so meager and uncharitable that you protect only wealthy virgins?"

He shrugged his shoulders. "There are other ways to earn a crust than spreading your legs for every soldier in the barracks. Still, she would have come to no lasting harm in his hands. Henri is a brutal bastard, but he would've paid her well enough. She would have had nothing to complain about."

She was almost too angry to speak, and far too angry to hold her tongue. "You think a handful of pennies would make amends for being abused in such a way? You are a fool with no feeling. Have you no imagination to put yourself in that poor woman's place for a moment and to feel what she might feel?"

He picked his sword up off the ground and weighed it in his hand with a threatening air. "I do not care for being called a fool."

Sophie's temper was still too riled for caution. "If you are not a fool, then you must be a vile, whoremongering bastard. Take your pick."

She saw a blur of motion and the tip of his sword was suddenly at her breast. "That was not a wise thing to say."

She felt too ill to defend herself. She did not even

attempt to rise or even reach for her sword. "Not wise, maybe," she readily admitted. "Honest, but not wise."

The tip of his sword pressed sharply against her breastbone. "Those are fighting words."

For the first time, Sophie was glad of the wrappings around her chest. The thick cloth cushioned her from the point of his sword, preventing his blade from breaking her skin. "Go away," she said wearily, lifting her aching head from her hands.

Why did men always take offense at the slightest insult and want to cross swords over it? She could not have so much as a simple disagreement with a man without him wanting to slit her throat for it. Men needed to learn to save their energies for battles that were worth fighting. She was running out of patience with the lot of them.

"I'll fight you tomorrow, if you insist. I am too sick to fight this morning."

He did not move his sword. "musketeers do not always have the luxury of choosing when to fight."

She looked at him with disdain. "Attack me now if you insist, though it would be the work of a braver and more honorable man to wait until I could defend myself."

He looked at her with growing disbelief. "Are you calling me a coward? Again?"

"If the hat fits . . ." she muttered under her breath.

His face grew tight with rage. "Damn you, I am no coward," he said in a voice of scarcely controlled fury. "I will whip you tomorrow until you beg for mercy. But to last you until then, I think you deserve a taste of your own medicine." With a quick flick of his sword, he ripped the front of Sophie's shirt in two.

His blade had caught some of her bindings. With a feeling of horror, Sophie watched the linen rags she kept wrapped around her chest start to unravel. If they came undone any further, her breasts—and her secret—would be exposed for all the world to see. All she had achieved would be wasted in the work of a moment. She would be utterly ruined.

With a strength born of desperation, she sprang to her feet, clutching the two pieces of her shirt together in one hand and her sword in the other. "Damn you, damn you, damn you," she shouted, driving him off with a sudden fury that caught him completely by surprise.

The effort of standing up so suddenly and moving so quickly was too much for her badly hung over body to cope with. Her stomach protested violently at the movement, her eyes grew misty, and her head began to swim. After fewer than half a dozen steps, she collapsed to the ground, retching violently into the dust.

He ran to her side, his anger dissolving into concern as she made no move to get up again. "Gerard?"

She lay motionless on the ground, exhausted. She could not move. Her only thought was to get away from the barracks somehow and hide in her tiny room until she was better. She would never touch a drop of wine again. She closed her eyes to block out the pain. "Go away," she whispered.

He grunted with annoyance as he crouched in the dirt beside her. "Gerard, you are more trouble than you are worth. You insult me and then refuse to fight. Then when I goad you just a little, you attack me as if all the furies in hell had taken possession of you. You deserve for me to leave you here for crows to peck out your eyes."

She could not wish for anything more. "Leave me alone. I do not need your help. I will wait until Jean-Paul comes looking for me. He will help me."

He ignored her complaints. With a fluid motion, he picked her up in his arms as if she were a baby. "Where do you lodge?"

She struggled briefly, but the effort only caused her head to swim with pain until she was too dizzy to think. "Put me down," she croaked, when her head had stopped pounding enough for her to speak.

He wrinkled his nose at the mess she was in, but he did not drop her. "Where do you lodge?" he repeated.

It seems he would rescue her whether she would or no. "With the Widow Poussin in the Rue de Fosset."

His hands were gentle as he cradled her head to stop it from jolting around with every step he took, and his arms were strong and held her safe.

She shifted a little in his grasp to make herself more comfortable, resigned to being carried home like a child. Once she was safe inside her lodgings, she would barricade herself in her bed and sleep the pain and nausea away. Her secret would be safe there.

Lamotte picked his friend up with a less than gentle touch, only just resisting the temptation to fling him over his shoulders like a sack of potatoes. The only thing stopping him was the fear that the boy would puke all the way down the back of his jerkin and over his favorite leather breeches and well-shined boots.

Did the boy have a death wish that he insulted him so at every turn without rhyme nor reason to it? Twice now the boy had called him a coward and lived unscathed to tell the tale. No other man could boast of that.

The lad in his arms was more fragile than he looked. He must have been starved by the plague, for he weighed scarcely more than a feather. His legs were slim and his arms positively puny, but his hips were wider than most men's would be. For all his lightness, the boy had a surprisingly broad, well-muscled chest.

He looked a little more closely at his burden and felt his whole world turn over. It was no young man he was carrying, he would wager his life on that. He would swear on the Bible he held a woman in his arms, and no man at all.

He shifted his burden a little, feeling the round softness of her hips under his hands. No man could have such curves there.

A woman dressed as a musketeer, masquerading as his friend.

Gerard had a twin sister, Sophie. She had supposedly died in the plague that had swept over the south of France, destroying half the human souls there in the path of its relentless fury. Out of his whole family, Gerard had been the sole survivor.

He looked down at the girl he was carrying in his arms, so like his friend in every feature. He had no doubt about it. Gerard's twin sister, Sophie, had not died. The woman in his arms had to be Sophie, the woman to whom he was betrothed.

How unlike she was to her portrait! In her picture she had seemed all sweetness and light, all softness and welcoming love. How far removed her appearance was from reality. She was as beautiful as he had imagined, if not more so, despite the purple rings of exhaustion under her eyes and the green tinge of sickness to her face. Her look of sweetness had been replaced by a hardness he had never seen before in woman's face. Either the portrait had lied from the beginning, or in becoming a soldier, she had become less of a woman.

However much of her sweet softness she had lost, he was still betrothed to her, and he would not break his word. This brawling, fighting woman who had the temerity to call him a coward must needs be his wife.

Her eyes were shut, puckered against the light. No sign of a whisker marred the softness of her skin. He marveled that he had never noticed it before. Few of his fellows were such dandies that they shaved every day, but even they could never rival this young woman's complexion. He touched her chin gently with the tip of his finger. Only a woman or a child could possibly have such smooth, soft cheeks.

He stumbled over an uneven patch on the cobblestones and she gave a groan. He held her tighter to his body to protect her against the roughness of her ride. He was carrying a woman disguised as a man, and wearing the uniform of a soldier. He had never even imagined such a thing before.

A woman. No wonder she had rushed to the aid of the serving wench in the tavern. She had seen her own self in the figure of that poor bedraggled maidservant and had rushed to her defense.

Fool that he was, he had not gone to her aid but had let her battle it out on her own against the drunken mob intent on her blood. He shivered with the realization of the danger she had been in—that he had allowed her to face without him by her side. She was only a woman, and fighting against half a dozen men twice her size. She could have been killed as he stood by.

She relaxed in his arms, nuzzling her cheek against his rough linen shirt.

No wonder her face had gone as white as milk when he had torn her shirt. He'd intended it only as a lesson for the lad to hold his tongue when he was in no fit state to fight. Better he learn that lesson in a hurry from one who wished him no harm, or he would not live long.

He'd caught a glimpse of some strange undergarment the lad was wearing, and then his pupil had surprised him by leaping to his feet with more agility than he would have thought possible, given his sorry state.

From the moment his friend had returned from the Camargue, he had been Gerard and yet not Gerard. Those blue eyes that were so like Gerard's had looked right through him without a shred of recognition or warmth. He had recognized the face of his friend, but that familiar face had hidden the soul of a stranger.

No wonder he had been so confused, wondering how his friend could be the same on the outside but different in every other way from the man he had once known. The explanation had been so obvious he had never seen it hiding under his nose all the time. Gerard had never returned.

Instead God had sent him Gerard's sister, so like her brother in face and feature. He would marry her as he had promised and look after her as well as he could. He owed his friend that much. Foolish, impulsive, beautiful girl that she was, she would need a lot of protection.

He gathered her closer to him, thankful for her safety. He would never let her be in such danger again. Now he knew who she was, he would protect her with every last drop of blood in his body.

He could not take her back to her lodgings as he had first intended and leave her there to the scant cheer of her landlady. He knew the Widow Poussin from old. She was a grasping, cheerless old woman, concerned only with feeding her avarice and adding to the pile of coins she had stacked up under the mattress of her bed.

His own lodgings were close by. He could take her there and keep an eye on her until she was better again. Once she was well, he would find out both the reason for her masquerade and the fate of his friend.

Soldier that he was, he felt his eyes fill with tears as he though of his friend. He had little hope Gerard had survived. If he were alive, his sister would not be alone in Paris, living an unnatural life as a common soldier.

He could not imagine the desperation she must have felt to have driven her to such extremes. Once again he cursed his own foolishness that had so nearly gotten him killed by a peasant with a pitchfork. He had made the ultimate error then in underestimating his enemy. He vowed he would never do so again.

She opened her eyes as he carried her over the threshold. "Where are we?"

"At my lodgings."

She groaned, sounding as if she were about to breathe her last. "I thought you were going to take me back to the Rue de Fosset."

He climbed the last of the stairs and pushed open the door to his apartment on the second floor. "The devil take me if I was going to carry you that far, you great lump of lard," he said, as he put her down gently on an ottoman. In truth, she was such a lightweight he had barely noticed carrying her. "This is quite far enough."

She looked like she was going to protest. "Besides, you reek of stale wine," he added. "It almost made me sick to the stomach to carry you."

She looked at her stained shirt in embarrassment. "Lend me a shirt to go home in, will you?" she said with forced cheer. "I'll bring it back to you on the morrow."

He shook his head. "No shirt of mine is going on your back until you've had a bath."

The look on her face was almost comical in its dismay. If he hadn't already known she was a woman, he would have guessed at it simply by her horror of taking a bath in his company. "N-no bath," she said. "I shall catch cold."

He could not resist teasing her. After all, he still owed her for that annoying scratch on his arm. How humiliating, to have been wounded by a mere girl! "Don't worry, I'll have the water well heated."

"I'm perfectly clean," she said. "I wouldn't want to bother your landlady for hot water when it isn't necessary. All I need is a clean shirt and I'll smell as fresh as a daisy."

He looked tellingly at her soiled breeches and stained jacket. Her entire outfit looked as if she had been carousing in it all night. "You will?"

She looked down at her battered clothes and sighed. "I had a rough night last night. I'll bathe in my own lodgings."

He sighed. What kind of a virago was this strange fiancée of his? "More brawling?"

She held out her hands. They were cut and torn and covered in weeping blisters. "No more brawling. I never fight without good reason. I was escaping the effects of the first one. I never knew I could climb a stone wall in less time than it takes you to snap your fingers."

He took her hands in his and stroked them, probing gently to see how deep the sores went.

She winced at the touch of his fingers.

"They look bad. They need to be tended to."

"They are little enough." She gave a wry smile. "My feet are worse."

Despite her protests, he unlaced one of her boots and pulled it down her thigh and over her ankle. It made his guts churn to see how the stocking on her foot was covered in crusted blood. "Have you been walking in them all morning?"

She nodded.

Was his pretty Amazon slow-witted as well as quick-tempered? "Did you not have the sense to tend to them last night?"

"I did not make it home last night," she admitted, her face going pink around the edges. "I was drinking with two of my fellows deep into the night, until I fell asleep on the floor with my boots on. I had no time to change my stockings and no clean linen to change into."

A pang of fury shot through his heart that Sophie, the girl to whom he should be married by now, had spent the night with a couple of his own comrades. "Who did you spend the night with?" he growled, barely able to disguise his anger.

She put her nose into the air and gave him a haughty stare. "That is no concern of yours."

She was wrong. It was definitely a concern of his.

He had promised Gerard he would take care of his sister if anything were to happen to him. He had thought Sophie's death had absolved him of his promise. Now that he knew better, nothing on earth would keep him from her side. He would even marry her as he had promised, beautiful, brawling Amazon that she was. He owed his dead friend that much. "A simple question deserves a simple answer."

The haughty look had not left her face. "Is there a law against sleeping on your comrade's floor?"

He glared at her, wishing he could shake some sense into her pretty head. "Don't be absurd."

"Then why do you care?"

What kind of a foolish question was that? She knew full well he was her betrothed husband, even if she didn't yet realize that he knew it, too. "You should not be sleeping on the floors of strange men."

"They are not strange. They are musketeers, the same as you and I."

He shook his head at her answer. He still could not get over the fact that she had successfully disguised herself among the regiment for so long. How could he have missed the signs that were so obvious now that he knew the truth? How could he have missed the feminine tilt of her chin or the haughty way she had of looking down at him, as if he were a maggot under her heel? How had he so easily managed to dismiss her sudden incompetence with a sword, when his efforts with Gerard the year before had turned the lad into a passably good swordsman? Suddenly, she made sense to him, where before he had seen only confusion and contradiction.

She was a woman. There was no point in arguing with her any longer. If she was like every other woman he knew, she would talk the head off a donkey before he would ever convince her he had a right to care for her.

He stuck his head out of the door and shouted for the landlady. She appeared in a bustle of warmth, smelling like the good roast beef she turned out daily for his evening meal. "I need a tub and some hot water up here right away. A comrade of mine has been in the wars and needs attending to."

She smiled at him. "Certainly, Monsieur le Comte. Would you be wanting anything else?"

"Some bandages, too, if you would be so kind."

"Right away, Monsieur le Comte." She bustled away again with a busy air.

Sophie was glaring at him with a look that would freeze the ocean over, her arms crossed over her chest. "I will not get into that bath."

He would not argue. He would demand. "Yes, you will. You're filthy."

Her dagger was in her hand, threatening him with its shining blade. "I will not get into that bath. You cannot make me."

Did she think she would frighten him with that little pinprick of a knife? He sat down opposite her and looked her straight in the eyes. How could he tell her kindly that he knew her secret? "Believe me, I know why you do not want to bathe."

Sophie looked back at him with defiance writ large over her face. "I doubt that very much," she muttered, so low he barely caught the words. "I will catch my death of cold," she said aloud.

He could not imagine her catching her death of anything, unless it was at the point of an enemy's sword. "You're a good deal stronger than that, if I'm not mistaken."

She dropped the dagger in her lap, gave an artificial cough, and looked up at him with a face full of misery. "The plague weakened me."

He would have laughed at her had he not known how unpleasant one's very first hangover felt. "Did it also turn you from a man into a woman?"

All the blood rushed from her face and her whole body was trembling. Even her voice shook with shock and disbelief when she spoke again. "What did you call me?"

He felt sorry for her distress. She had guarded her

secret so well he hardly had the heart to tell her her disguise had been penetrated. "I called you what you are."

She picked up her dagger again and held it in a wavering hand. "I will kill you for that insult."

He did not move. He doubted she could see straight to kill anything that morning. She was probably still seeing two of him. "Come, Sophie. The time for playacting has past. I know what you are. I know who you are."

All the fight went out of her suddenly and she collapsed on to the ottoman as if she had lost all the strength in her legs. "What did you call me?"

"You are Sophie, aren't you? Not Gerard, but his twin sister?"

"You are mistaken. I am Gerard." Her voice was flat and lacked all conviction.

He looked at her in silence. Her lip wobbled as she tried to face him down.

After a moment, she hung her head and looked away.

He spoke with utter certainty. "You are not Gerard."

She nodded, her face blank with desolation. "I am not Gerard."

"You are Sophie?"

"I am." Her voice was dead and cold.

"What happened to Gerard?"

Her eyes filled with tears. "He died of the plague."

Lamotte bowed his head in grief to have his suspicions so baldly confirmed. "I guessed as much."

He took her hand in his and held it in silence for some minutes as together they mourned for the death of the brother and friend they both had loved. The touch of her hand was comforting in his grief. Gerard had passed on to a better world, but he had left a part of him behind on earth. He would cherish and protect Gerard's sister as best he could.

After some moments, she wiped her eyes on her shirtsleeve and made a visible effort to control her grief. "How did you find me out?"

The real question was how had he taken so long to find her out? "You have been bothering me for weeks. You were Gerard, and yet not Gerard. I watched you and took note of everything you did, but I could not work out why you had changed so much. Then when I picked you up in my arms this morning, it all became clear. I knew then you were no man. I knew you were a woman."

She raised her head again and looked at him with a spark of her usual fire. "What are you going to do about it?"

He had been thinking about that since the moment he realized who she was. "I will marry you, as I promised Gerard I would, and send you to safety in Burgundy as we had agreed. My mother was looking forward to meeting my new wife. She will take good care of you. She has run the household by herself for many years, and will no doubt appreciate some help now that she is growing older."

Sophie shuddered. "I became a musketeer so I would not have to marry a stranger and be sent off to exile in Burgundy. I will not marry you now."

He shrugged his shoulders. She was not being reasonable. What other kind of marriage could she expect? With no father to arrange matters for her, and after her time spent as a musketeer, what other marriage could she possibly make? She was lucky he was contracted to her and his sense of honor obliged him to marry her. She would find no other husband else. "What else can you do?"

"I can be a musketeer, as I am now."

How unreasonable and impractical women could be sometimes. "But you are a woman. You cannot survive the rigors of the barracks."

She looked at him in silence for a moment. "I already knew how to ride before I came to Paris," she said at last. "In the last few weeks I have learned how to fight. I have worked every day until I collapsed on my bed with exhaustion. I fought off a dozen louts bent on mischief last night, and escaped the guard sent to arrest the brawlers. I wounded you in a fair fight and faced death with my eyes open. Exactly what rigors can I not survive?"

He could not understand why she wanted to accept such hardship when an easier option was open to her. "You are a woman. You should be allowed to spend your time raising children and running a household, as other women do. You should not have learned to fight."

"You taught me how."

He could not argue with that. He was already regretting everything he had taught her. "You are a woman, not a soldier."

The look on her face would be enough to make a seasoned warrior quail. "I will kill you before I let you disclose my secret."

He believed her capable of killing him—had she not tried to once already?—but he would not fight a woman.

"My comrades believe me to be Gerard. They will laugh at your claim. I will deny I am a woman. I will fight you over the insult."

She seemed to forget he could easily prove his claim. She had shown him how the prior evening. All it took was the sharp point of a sword to rip apart the lacings of a man's breeches and he would not need to say word. "You want to be a musketeer that much?"

She nodded. "I brought the plague into the household that killed Gerard and all my family. I owe him the honor he would have received as a musketeer. I loved my brother, my twin, more than I loved anyone else in the world. I will not let you rob him of that honor I will win in his name."

He thought of how fondly Gerard had spoken of her. Her love had been returned in good measure. "Gerard loved you, too."

Surprisingly, her eyes filled with tears at his words. He would have thought her heart was hardened beyond her sex. He was glad to see she was capable of some softer, more feminine emotions. "I know he did," she whispered.

A knock at the door heralded the arrival of the tub and plenty of pitchers filled with steaming hot water.

He saw the yearning in Sophie's eyes as she looked at the water being poured into the tub. "Bath time," he said.

She glared at him again, but held her tongue until the landlady had left the room once more. "You know I cannot bathe with you here," she said, not taking her eyes off the water as she spoke. "It would not be seemly."

For such an Amazon, she was surprisingly prudish. "Are we not soldiers together? Comrades in arms?"

"Very amusing."

At least she had some shreds of modesty left in her. He had been starting to wonder whether she was male in all but the shape of her body. "I'll find you some clean linen and leave you alone while you wash," he said. "You smell too bad to have in the house else."

Once left alone with the steaming tub of water, Sophie could not get her clothes off fast enough. How long had it been since she had immersed herself in water and gotten really clean? She could not rightly remember.

All through the winter she had washed in cold water, not wanting to waste the firewood she gathered so painstakingly on luxuries like keeping clean. She had spent all her energy on keeping herself warm and fed.

Her lodgings in Paris offered her no such luxury, either. She had had to make do with a pitcher of lukewarm water grudgingly delivered to her each evening by her ill-tempered landlady. She would never have dreamed of asking for an entire tub full of hot water. She would not have gotten it, she was quite sure. Her landlady would have swooned with the mere shock of being asked.

With an exhalation of pure delight, she tossed off the last of her filthy linen, pushed it into a pile with her foot, and stepped into the deliciously warm water.

The blisters on her feet stung, as did the cuts on her hands, but she hardly cared.

Lamotte's landlady had even brought soap—wonderful soap that smelled of heady purple lavender. She ran the precious cake all over her body, rubbing it into a rich, foamy lather over her legs, her arms, her belly, her breasts. There was even a long-handled scrubbing brush for her back. She lathered the soap on to the brush and brushed her back vigorously, feeling every particle of dirt and grime dissolve away.

She sank down into the tub to wet her hair and lather it up with soap. She'd cut her hair short before she had left the Camargue. It barely skimmed the top of her shoulders now, whereas before it had hung in a heavy plait nearly to her waist. The soap ran into her eyes as she lathered her hair, making them water.

Finally, when she had scrubbed every inch of skin until it was as pure and white as the soul of a saint in heaven, she lay back in the tub, relaxing in the cooling water. Ah, it felt so good to be clean again.

Looking down at her nakedness in the tub, she could see how much her body had changed over the last year. She had never been plump, but her body was hardened into leanness and a new firmness. She ran her hands over her arms, marveling at the new bulges of muscle she found there—the bulges she had acquired herself through hard work. Her belly was flatter than ever, with barely an ounce of fat covering her ribs, and her thighs were lean and muscular. Her body was like that of a boy, she thought with a grimace.

All except for her breasts. They, at least, made her look like a woman. Indeed, they were her only saving grace. Almost too big for her slight frame, even her winter of hardship had caused them to lose only a fraction of their fullness.

She took them in her hands, feeling the reassuring weight of them with a sense of joy. She knew it would be more convenient for her not to have breasts at all, to be as flat-chested as a young girl. Binding her breasts each morning was a chore she could well do without. Still, as she looked at the pair of them, gloriously round and full, she could not regret a single ounce. They alone reminded her she was a woman.

She dunked herself once more in the water, reluctantly pulled herself out of the tub, and wrapped herself in the soft yellow towel she found waiting for her.

She eyed her pile of filthy clothes with distaste.

Now that she was clean, she felt like burning the lot of them. Lamotte had been right. They stank.

Her head still hurt, but not as badly now, and her stomach had settled somewhat. The bath had put her in a far more agreeable frame of mind all over.

Lamotte had left some linen out for her—a pair of cotton drawers that tied together at the waist, a white linen shirt, and some white stockings. There was also a pair of soft leather breeches, the finest quality, but decidedly too generous for her small frame. She had nothing to bind her chest with except the dirty old wrappings she had been using before. She could not use those. She would have to let her breasts swing free.

She felt uncomfortably vulnerable, half dressed as she was in borrowed linen and too-big breeches. Still, she was at least decent again. She felt much more able to deal with Lamotte on his own ground.

She yawned. Somehow or another, she had to convince him not to reveal her secret. She had no future as a woman. If she were to leave the regiment, her brother would be undeservedly forgotten.

Besides, she was a musketeer now, and a good one. She had no desire to return to the confines of a woman's life, all sewing and scouring and making gooseberry preserves. How much more glorious it was to protect the king from his enemies! How much more worthwhile she could be as a man than ever her life would be as a woman.

No, whatever he threatened, her mind was made up. She was Gerard now, and she would not give up her new identity until her death.

Five

Lamotte returned to find her sitting on the ottoman, laboriously combing the tangles out of her hair with a comb carved in intricate swirls of bone. Dressed in his oversized clothes, she looked surprisingly fragile and vulnerable. "Feeling better?" he asked.

She nodded. "Smelling better, too."

He set down the jar he was carrying on a low table by the ottoman. The apothecary in the next street over had a failsafe recipe for blisters and cuts of all kinds. He'd spent the time while Sophie was in the bath replenishing his stocks. He sat down on the ottoman beside her. She smelled of soap and mint, a huge improvement over sweat and dirt, stale ale and vomit. He breathed deeply of her scent. "Give me your hands."

Her hands were large for a woman's, strong, capable hands, though badly battered. He took a gob of ointment from the jar and smoothed it over one raw palm. She bit her lip at the sting of it, but she did not utter a sound of protest. He had to admire her courage. He knew firsthand how much the stuff hurt.

"Climbing stone walls, huh?" he said with a grin, trying to distract her from the pain as he began to work the oily unguent into both her palms with a gentle, circular motion. "Not what I would have expected from an ambitious young musketeer."

"We didn't want to be caught by the guards." Sophie was biting her lip with her white teeth, trying not to cry out with pain, he'd wager. "I have the honor of my family name to uphold."

He worked the ointment gently around a vicious blister. She was a woman. Her hands should not have to look like this. "Not for much longer. Soon you will have the honor of my family name to uphold."

He could feel her arms stiffen. "We have already discussed that. I told you I would not marry you. I will be a musketeer."

He looked at her straight in the eye. He would not let her win this battle. It was best she were to know it from the beginning and not waste her efforts fighting the inevitable. "I made a vow to your brother I would take care of you if aught should happen to him. I will not let you make me break that oath. Marry you I will, if I have to tie your hands behind your back, gag you, and drag you to the altar kicking and scratching."

Her face was deadly serious. "You forget I am a soldier now. You would not live long as my husband were you to force me like that."

What had happened to Gerard's sister to warp her in this fashion that she would threaten to murder him for the crime of wedding her? "I doubt you would find my murder worth your while. Husband-killers are tortured and burned at the stake."

Sophie gave an evil smile. "Never fear, I would not burn. I am too careful for that. Many brutal husbands have accidentally died of eating bad mushrooms, and their wives have gone unpunished."

He did not like the thought of watching his back

for the rest of his mortal life, but he could see no other alternative. He rubbed some ointment into the back of her hand with a touch that had lost some of its gentleness. Much as he misliked the idea, he had to marry her.

He had made a solemn vow to Gerard, the man he had loved as a brother. Sophie was his responsibility now before God. Only when she was his wedded wife would he have the right of a husband, before man and his laws, to protect her as he was bound to.

"Still, I will agree to marry you."

He raised his head, temporarily ceasing his ministrations. He was suspicious of this about-face. Barely a moment ago, she was threatening to poison him did he ever wed her. "You will?"

"On one condition."

"What is it?" Knowing her as he did already, he wasn't sure that he wanted to know.

"I will continue to live and dress as a man, in my own lodgings, living my own life. I will continue to be a musketeer. You will not disclose to anyone else by word or deed that I am a woman. You will not interfere in my life, as I will not interfere in yours. We will be as strangers to one another. If you agree to this, then I will marry you and allow you to fulfil your promise."

He could not help but be amused at her audacity. She could not possibly be serious or think he would consider such outrageous demands. He was marrying her to protect her. He could not protect her if she was estranged from him so utterly. Still, at least she was willing to open negotiations. That was a good sign. "That was at least three conditions."

She did not smile back at him. "Do you accept?"

He spread his hands open, palms out, with exasperation. Was she so blinded by her stubbornness that she could not see his point of view? "I cannot marry another musketeer."

"Then I refuse to wed you." She pulled her hands from his and stood up, wincing as her injured feet touched the ground. "Thank you for the bath. I will be on my way again."

She was either deadly serious or she was the best negotiator he had ever come across. She would really leave if he did not agree to her absurd demands. "Stop for a moment," he said, pushing her down on the ottoman again. He needed to buy himself some time to convince her he would not take no for an answer. "I have not attended to your feet yet. They will suppurate if you do not let them heal."

"My feet are fine."

"Nonsense. I can see that they pain you. You can barely walk on them." He knelt down on the floor in front of her and pulled one stocking off her leg. By God, but she had a beautiful leg—trim and lean and long, with soft, curving calves. He felt a stirring in his loins at the sight of it. Maybe marriage to the little termagant would not be so bad as he thought, as long as he could chain her to his bed and keep her there. Especially if the rest of her body was as tempting as her naked leg.

He let his eyes travel up her body, slowly, almost luxuriously. Her thighs in the breeches he had lent her were shapeless, but her waist was tiny and her belly as flat as a girl's. Not so her chest, though. His eyes nearly popped out of his head in amazement as he saw her large breasts, barely covered by the thin linen of his shirt. He itched to touch them, to take them in his hands and knead them gently between his fingers. He ached to touch the dusky pink of her nipples, to take them into his mouth and suckle on them until she arched her back and cried out with pleasure. How had she managed to hide them so successfully, and for so long?

She caught the direction of his gaze and brought her arms over her chest to cover herself again. The tips of his ears burning at being caught staring at her breasts like some callow schoolboy, he bent his attention to her feet.

Her feet were worse than he had thought, covered in bulging blisters, running sores, and half-healed scabs. "You could not have done this all last night," he said, as he smoothed the ointment into a huge blister the size of his thumbnail.

She shrugged. "Not all of it."

He rubbed ointment into each of her toes, one after the other. He would rather be smoothing sweet, scented oil on her stomach and her beautiful white breasts than treating her badly wounded feet. Her nipples would pucker under his touch and she would make soft, sweet mewing sounds like a newborn kitten as he caressed her.

He shook his head to dispel the sweet image that bewitched his brain. Time enough to think about the pleasures of her body and the pleasures he could give her with his touch when she was his wife. "What about the rest?"

"Gerard's boots rub my feet."

Once she was his wife, he would see to it she would never have to wear borrowed boots again. "You must buy some new boots of softer leather and some thicker stockings. Your feet are rubbed raw."

"One pair of boots was enough for Gerard. One pair of boots will have to do me, as well."

Her feet had to feel like she was walking on broken

glass. He did not know how she could have kept upright for the last few weeks, let alone learn to wheel and leap as she had. Once again he was struck by the force of determination that had fueled her in her life as a musketeer. His job of convincing her to marry him might well be harder than he had first thought. "Marry me, and I will buy you a new pair."

Sophie wiggled her toes appreciatively and broke into a grin. "That's got to be the best offer I've received yet."

"Better still, I will buy you soft velvet slippers embroidered with silk, and you'll never get another blister in your life." No other woman he knew would wear harsh leather boots when she could have silken slippers in their place. Why should his errant fiancée be any different?

"I would rather have a pair of boots. Musketeers cannot fight in slippers."

He smoothed the ointment into her callused sole, trying to be gentle with every patch of blistered and broken skin. He would not bear down on her with the full force of his mind and body and force her to marry him. She would only resent him. He needed to convince her that no other course of action was possible for him to keep his word to her brother. "I am honor bound to marry you."

She shrugged uneasily. "Your honor is not my concern."

The first foot done, he rolled the stocking up to above her knee and tied it with a ribbon. Her thighs were white and soft, though leaner than most. He let his fingers linger on her thigh for a moment before turning his attention to her other foot. The insistence of his desire for her disturbed him. He was still getting used to viewing her as a woman and not just a soldier. "You are determined to stay a musketeer."

"I am."

"You do not want to live a life of ease, a life of luxury and warmth, silk dresses and fine wines, in my castle in Burgundy?" He touched a raw patch and she gave an involuntary wince. He still didn't understand a woman who would not choose ease over labor. "As my wife, you need never have another blister in your life."

"I will not lead a life of selfish idleness and sloth, without meaning or purpose. I would rather die."

He knew how she felt. He felt exactly the same way himself, but he had never known women could feel that way as well as men. "You would rather live a life of hardship and privation as a soldier, prepared work hard all day and night too if necessary, to go cold and hungry when there is no food or fire to be had, prepared even to sacrifice your life if need be?"

"I would rather be a humble honeybee and serve my colony as best I could than be the most beautiful butterfly ever seen, draped in luxury, and be of no use for anything."

"What would you do if I turned you in to D'Artagnan?" He would not betray her so calmly—her courage deserved better than that. He wanted to know, though, just what she would do. "He would turn you out without a second thought."

"I would kill you, or die trying." Her voice was matter-of-fact, as if death was a minor detail.

He heaved a huge sigh as he rolled the second stocking up her leg and tied it with a ribbon around her white thigh. He could read determination in her eyes, but he was just as determined. He would compromise for now, but it was only a strategic retreat so he could prove the ultimate victor in the battle between them for dominance.

He had few other options unless he were to force her, which he was loath to do. He would not set her against him so badly right from the start. There would be time enough for bringing her round to his way of thinking once they were safely wedded. Heaven knew he would need to if he were ever to have a quiet house. No household could safely contain two soldiers without them eventually coming to blows. "Then I do not see that I have a choice. I will marry my musketeer. But I have a few conditions of my own."

She looked at him suspiciously. Such as?"

He tried to frame a compromise he could live with and that would allow her to bend graciously into wedlock without too much of a blow to her pride. She was like a skittish wildcat he had to tame into eating out of his hand. Moving too fast or demanding too much of her would scare her away, and she would be doubly hard to come close to again.

He cleared his throat. "In public you will be a musketeer, and I will not give rise to any suspicion by word or deed that you are a woman and my wife. In private, you will be my wife, in both word and deed. You will live with me in my lodgings, and you will be faithful and true to me in every way."

She shook her head and the ghost of a smile flitted across her face. "I cannot be your wife in deed. What would D'Artagnan do with me if he discovered I was not only a woman, but I was breeding to boot?"

She saw his intent exactly. Did she once have a babe in her belly, she would surely lose interest in fighting and become a proper wife and mother. Motherhood would tame her to his hand faster and more surely than anything else ever could. "I would have you faithful to me, Sophie, and not seek to break your contract later on for lack of consummation. This must needs be a real marriage."

Her brows drew together in a frown. "I am a musketeer and a woman of my word. I will not betray your trust in me, but I cannot be your wife in every way. I will not wed you if you insist on that condition."

He needed her close to him if he were to succeed in winning her over. "You will live with me in my lodgings?"

She nodded. "Yes, I will do that, if I must, but as your comrade, not as your wife."

He would have to seduce her into his arms. If he put his mind to it, he would wager she would not resist him for ever. She was only a woman, after all, without the self-control or iron determination of a man. Sooner or later she would weaken, and he would be there to catch her when she fell. "Then I will not insist you share my bed, though I must insist I have the right to try to change your mind."

"I will not change my mind."

He grinned. He would enjoy trying to seduce his lovely wife and tame her to his hand. She would present a worthy challenge to him, but he was sure to win in the end. "I am willing to take a gamble on that."

"Then I agree."

He made a quick calculation in his head. "We will have the banns read at church on Sunday for the first time, and then we shall be as good as wed."

She made a move to get up again. "I will see you on Sunday, then."

He could not let her go as easily as that. She might yet run from him. He would make sure of her while he could and not take the risk that she would back away from the bargain he had forced upon her. "I will send a boy around for your belongings. As of today, you are living with me."

Sophie's mouth fell open in horror. "Live with you? We are not yet man and wife."

"I am not sure I trust you yet, my beloved wife-to-be," he confessed. It would not hurt her to know he distrusted her as much as she distrusted him. "I have no guarantee you will not slip my traces and be off to Lyons or to Reims, to pop up as a soldier there. I have you here now, and I intend to keep an eye on you as best I can. Besides, if I have you sleeping here with me, I can be sure you are not sleeping on the floor of one of your other comrades."

"I cannot share apartments with you while we are as yet unwed. I am a woman, you are a man. It is . . . it is unthinkable."

"You have slept in a drunken stupor on the floor of another musketeer's bedchamber," he reminded her. He did not like thinking on that himself. Sure, it must have been innocent enough, or her fellows would surely have let out the secret of her sex by now, but he still did not like it. If they ever discovered her sex, they would think her a loose woman, and treat her accordingly. She was no light skirt to be so abused. She was a gentlewoman and his wife-to-be.

He would have to impress upon her the risks she ran and make sure she did not ever run them again. He would not like to have to run through a dozen of his fellow musketeers for mistreating his wife. "Is that not equally unthinkable?"

She made a noise of protest. "That was different. It was only one night, and it was quite harmless."

Harmless? He hardly thought so. Whether or not

she was willing to admit it, she had run a huge risk. She was only lucky she had not been caught. "We have been promised to each other for some months. The contract between my uncle and your father is signed. In the eyes of God, we are as good as wed already."

"The contracts may have been signed a thousand times, but I have plighted no troth to you. I have promised nothing."

That was easy to remedy. He stood up straight, his arms by his side. "Sophie Delamanse, I do hereby plight my troth to you. From this day forth you shall be as my wife to me. Unto you will I cleave and all others forsake. I shall marry you and none but you, so help me God."

Sophie groaned. This was not how she had envisioned her betrothal day, dressed in ill-fitting breeches and suffering from a head that threatened to split in two with every movement she made. What choice did she have? The comte was determined to fulfil his promise, and come what may she would stay a musketeer for her brother's sake. This way, at least they would both get what they each demanded.

She stood up on her stockinged feet. It did not seem right to perform such a solemn vow while lolling at her ease on a sofa. "Comte Ricard de Lamotte," she said, trying not to wince at the pain in her feet, "I do hereby plight my troth to you. From this day forth you shall be as my husband to me. Unto you will I cleave and all others forsake. I shall marry you and none but you, so help me God."

The comte had a look of triumph on his face. Sophie was too worn out to care. He had won this battle only because she was too tired and sick to fight anymore. "My head hurts and my feet hurt. I want a drink of water and I need to sleep." She did not even care if she sounded like a querulous child. All she wanted now was oblivion.

He pushed open the door to another chamber with a huge canopied bed in the middle. Picking her up as he would lift a child, he carted her over and placed her gently on the coverlet. "I'll bring the water for you in a moment. Then you can sleep for as long as you like."

The sheets were crisp and white and smelled of lavender, just like the soap she had used in her bath. She tossed her oversized breeches on the floor and crept between the sheets, thankful to close her eyes at last and block out the light that made her head pound harder. Baths, clean sheets, the smell of lavender. Maybe her marriage would be tolerable after all.

A glass of water in his hand, Lamotte looked at her as she lay tucked up in the bed, her damp hair fanned out over the pillow. Asleep, she looked soft and sweet-tempered—far more like a woman—than she did when she was awake and spitting at him with her teeth bared and her claws unsheathed.

It would be so easy to throw off his clothes and climb into bed beside her to hold her naked body against his own. She would be too sleepy to protest. He would be able to hold her in his arms all night. His hands could rove freely on her luscious breasts, her hips, her legs, and that soft sweet cleft between her thighs. He could make her his wife in more than name only and she would not be able to say him nay.

He felt his manhood rise at the thought of entering her tantalizing body until he was embedded inside her to the very hilt. He would prepare her well with kisses and touches until she was as eager for it as he was. Her channel would be wet and warm and welcoming and he would thrust into her body, losing himself in her as he had dreamed of doing when he had first seen her portrait.

He knew he was only dreaming. He would never do that. She was sick and tired, and he would never force himself on her. She would never forgive him. He would never forgive himself.

He squatted down and put the water on the floor beside her. No doubt she would wake in a while with a desperate thirst. He hoped her headache was a salutary lesson not to drink to excess in the future. Drinking had ruined more good soldiers than he cared to think on. He would not have the same vice ruin his wife.

There was little point going back to the barracks now. Training would be over for the day, and he was not on duty until the morrow. Besides, he wanted to be there when Sophie woke again. He intended to see her properly bedded down in his apartments before he took his eyes off her. She belonged to him now, and he was determined to take good care of her.

A boy was soon dispatched to the Rue de Fosset to bring back her belongings. She had little enough—a small cloth bag filled with clean linen and an ornate dagger. He recognized it as having belonged to Gerard.

She was still sleeping peacefully when he opened the door quietly and put her bag at the foot of her bed. With a grunt of satisfaction, he sat down at his desk and began to polish his weaponry. The simple tasks of a soldier should help him keep his mind off the soft white body of the woman sleeping in the next chamber, in his bed.

He was giving Gerard's old dagger, now Sophie's, a final polish when he heard a strangled cry come from the chamber where she lay asleep. He dashed next door to find her sitting bolt upright in the bed, her eyes wide open and staring blankly at some horror that only she could see. "Water, give me water," she moaned, not seeming to see him.

He grabbed the water glass from the floor and held it to her lips. She drank it down greedily, not caring when it dribbled over her chin and onto her shirt. The glass drained, she lay back on her pillows and was immediately deep in slumber again.

He stayed for a while, stroking her forehead gently with the palm of his hand, making sure her nightmare did not return to disturb her sleep once more. She was so brave and strong that it was easy to forget how much she had suffered and how much grief she must still carry around in her heart. The horrors she had faced as her family died around her would have been enough to break the spirit of most men he knew. And she was only a woman. A remarkable woman, but a woman nonetheless.

The shadows were lengthening into night when Sophie woke again, the remembrance of a nightmare weighing heavily on her mind. In her dream she had had the plague and none would help her. She cried out for water, and an angel of mercy had poured water into her desperate mouth and chased her demons away. She could not fathom why, but the angel of mercy had worn the face of Lamotte.

Her headache was only a dull throbbing now, she was ravenously hungry, and a tantalizing smell of roast meat was wafting through the room. She had not eaten all day and her stomach growled at the thought of being fed at last. Stopping only to pull on her breeches, she padded out of the silent bedchamber in search of food to satisfy her suddenly desperate hunger.

Lamotte was sitting in the last of the evening sun, reading a leather-bound book. He raised his head when she came padding through the door. "I thought you would sleep all night."

She hoped he was not reading poetry. She despised poetry. "I'm famished. What have you for me to eat?"

He gestured toward the table. "I was about to start by myself. Now that you are awake, would you care to join me?"

She had no time to waste on words. Roast beef, roast chicken, dishes of vegetables, and, glory of glories, even a couple of fresh peaches. She had not seen such a feast in months—not since before the plague had struck her family. Her mouth watered until she thought she would drown in saliva.

She could not resist the sight of the peaches. Grabbing the nearest one, she bit into it with relish, licking her lips as the juice tried to escape and run down her chin. She could not bear to let a single precious drop escape her. "I have died and gone to heaven," she said, through her mouthful.

"If you came to Burgundy, you could eat your fill of peaches every day," he said as he helped himself to a plateful of roast beef and delicious-looking dressings. "We have an orchard of them there. When I was a boy, I used to gorge myself on them until I was sick."

The last succulent mouthful of peach turned to ashes in her mouth at his words. Silently she laid the knobbled pit on her plate.

He looked guilt-stricken at her actions. "I did not mean to spoil your simple pleasure."

She shrugged. "It is of no matter." She loaded her plate and ate mechanically, barely tasting her meal. She would not let herself be seduced by the richness of the beef gravy, she vowed, or by the delicate flavor of the chicken wings he served to her. She would not let the devil tempt her with luxury so he could imprison her in his castle in Burgundy. She would be strong and steadfast against him.

He offered her a glass of wine, but she shook her head with a feeling shudder. "Water, if you please." She had had her fill of wine for now. She would not care if she never saw another glass in her life again.

The meal was scarcely over when Sophie began to yawn once more. Her craving for food satisfied, she wanted only to sleep again. "Seeing as you have demanded I live here with you, where shall I sleep?"

"There's only one bed."

She rolled her shoulders with a grimace, feeling the ache in them from sleeping on the floor of Courtney's lodgings the night before. "It's mine." She would not sleep on the floor tonight for all the gold in Christendom. She would rather walk in her stockinged feet over the rough cobbled streets to her own apartments and sleep in her own narrow cot than bear the hardness of the floor of her aching muscles for another night.

He shrugged. "As you wish. I shall not ask you to share it with me until we are wed."

She tossed her napkin down on the table and rose to her feet. She would not fall for his seductions. She would not even notice the muscles in his arms, or the way his hair fell in waves down to his collar. She would not long for the touch of his hand on hers, or for the caress of his lips against her neck. She wanted nothing of him but to be left alone.

She would be strong and steadfast against him and live the life she wanted to live. She would make him regret it if he were to presume on his role as her husband and try to talk her into what she was determined against. "Not even then, Monsieur le Comte, if you know what is good for you."

Ricard Lamotte watched her stride toward his bedchamber, a feeling of regret tugging at his loins. She was a desirable woman, for all her fighting ways. He very much wanted to plunge into her body and lose himself in the soft sweetness of her milky thighs and breasts, to use her as a woman should be used by a man. He had sworn to wed her. There would be no shame in trying to seduce her into his arms even before the marriage ceremony.

He thought of her remark about poisoned mushrooms and shuddered. The wench had a mean streak. Were he to disturb her rest with such demands, he would not put it past her to knife him as he slept. He would not be crawling into bed with her until he was duly invited.

He would work on getting that invitation. He took his marriage vows seriously and would be true to her once they were wed. He had no desire to live a life of married celibacy for the rest of his days, or at least until his beautiful, desirable, hotheaded, sharp-tongued wife managed to get herself killed.

Sophie strode into the barracks the next morning, feeling halfway human again. Her stomach was blessedly quiet, her head no longer ached, and the dressings Lamotte had rubbed into her feet were working miracles. She could walk almost without pain.

Pierre greeted her with a slap on the back so hard and unexpected it nearly made her go sprawling. "You brawling bastard," he said, with a note of admiration in his voice. "You have more courage than sense to take on such a big bastard." He chuckled with delighted glee. "I will never forget the look of surprise on his face when he lost his breeches."

Sophie looked at him in surprise. Lamotte had been so aggravated by her behavior she had not considered her other comrades might look at it in a different light. Evidently some of her comrades enjoyed a brawl for no other reason than the love of it.

She could not understand it herself. Fighting for a good cause was just and glorious, but she did not comprehend how men could enjoy fighting for the sake of it.

"Damned good swordsmanship this morning," another musketeer grunted at her as she shoveled food into her mouth after a hard morning's training.

She choked on her mouthful. His face was vaguely familiar, but she'd never so much as spoken a word to him in her weeks in the barracks. She'd been at pains to keep herself to herself, and none of them had bothered her in her self-imposed solitude before.

"Almost as good as the other night when you showed that big bastard what we musketeers are made of," said another.

"May you live to fight many more battles," called a third.

Yet another lifted his mug of ale into the air for a toast. "Long live the king's musketeers, the cream of the crop."

"Death to the king's enemies," shouted another, to loud cheers.

Courtney, seated by her side, nudged her with a sharp elbow, lifted her mug of ale in a salute, and grinned at her. "Welcome to the club of brainless brawling bastards, Gerard, my man," she said softly into Sophie's ear.

So elated was Sophie by her newfound sense of

acceptance into the group she almost didn't mind when the captain of the musketeers set her to scrubbing the barracks on her knees with a bucket and mop all afternoon. "That ought to cool your hot head down for a bit," he muttered at her, as she scrubbed away. "Doing the work of a woman for a day will teach you a lesson not to go picking fights just for the fun of it."

She grinned at him, her mood quite undeflated. "Yes, sir."

"Why, oh why, do I have to look after a regiment of foolish young boys?" she heard D'Artagnan grumble as he stomped away over the wooden boards she had just scrubbed. "Young fools who think they're invincible. Why, in my day, I had a healthy respect for my enemies, those damned frondeurs. Musketeers these days wouldn't stand a chance against them. Ah, they don't make rebellions like they used to anymore . . ."

Sophie stared out the window in Courtney's apartments at the gray sky and the drizzling rain. She had been made to scrub floors all afternoon and had had no chance to get the three of them alone together all day. Her news was burning up inside her.

Now that the chance had come, she felt her courage fail her. There was no easy way to tell her comrades what she had to tell them. She would have to be blunt and hope they would forgive her. "I am to be married tomorrow to the Comte de Lamotte."

Courtney dropped her glass in astonishment and stared stupidly at the thousand shards scattered on the floor, winking up at her in the light from the wax candles. Her face was white and strained as if she had just seen a ghost. "You are to be what?"

Miriame drained her glass dry and put it down on the table with a hand that trembled slightly. "If you have given away my sex to the comte, you are a dead woman."

Sophie shook her head. Paris in the rain was the most drear and dismal place in the world. Gone was its gaiety and song. All that was left was the cold and the wet and the mud. Everywhere you looked there was mud and filth and more mud.

"Your secret is safe with me. I was affianced to him before I became a musketeer, and he will not release me from the bargain. I have agreed to wed him on condition that he keeps my secret. He has agreed to my terms and is content to be my husband in name only."

Courtney's eyes went from astonishment to excitement in a flash. "Oh, I love weddings," she said dreamily. "What kind of a dress will you wear to the church on the morrow? What color have you chosen? What flowers will you carry? Something blue to match your eyes?" Then she suddenly seemed to come to herself again. "The only thing wrong with a wedding is that there has to be a groom involved," she added with her usual bitterness.

Sophie was puzzled by Courtney's reaction. Did she not see how her news would affect them all? Dresses were the last thing on her mind. "I had not thought of what I would wear. I have no dresses in Paris. I left them all in my father's house in the Camargue. I shall have to get married in my breeches or not at all."

Miriame shrieked with laughter at the thought.

"You would scandalize the priests to within an inch of their lives."

Sophie shrugged. "I wore breeches at home and Father Capin did not mind. He only lectured me occasionally about the proper place of a woman, but he ate the ducks I shot for him nevertheless."

Miriame laughed even harder. "You do not know the priests in Paris," she said, as soon as she could get the words out between her gales of mirth. "They are a different breed from those in the country. I doubt they could be bought with a brace of freshly killed ducks. They would demand a fat haunch of venison at the least."

"So I will pay them whatever it takes for them for their eyes to convince their consciences that I am wearing a perfectly proper and suitable dress."

Miriame poured herself another glass of wine. "I will have to come and watch this wedding. It will be better than a play. The priests will excommunicate you as an unnatural man-woman, not marry you."

Sophie dropped her hands into her lap in despair. She had not thought of what she would wear. Miriame was right. She could hardly get married in her breeches, and yet how was she to obtain a dress without giving away her secret a thousand times? She would have to call the wedding off again. Lamotte would simply have to understand she could not go through with it.

"I have plenty of dresses you can wear," Courtney offered. She scurried to the corner of her chamber, where a large wardrobe stood half hidden by a heavy velvet curtain. Opening it with a flourish, she riffled through the brightly colored silks hanging inside. "I loved them so much I could not bring myself to part with them all when I came to Paris to be a soldier. It is lucky I did so. You could not possibly be so disrespectful to God and the Church as to get married in breeches. Just imagine what your parents would think if they knew."

She held up a dress of sparkling emerald green with lace dripping from the sleeves, lovingly stroking the silk with her glance. "Try this one on. It is still quite fashionable and would suit your complexion very well. Besides, the lace is real Brussels lace. That never goes out of style."

Sophie sent up a quick prayer of thanks to the Lord for her friends. They had saved her twice now. She owed them a debt she would not forget in a hurry.

She kicked off her boots and breeches and unwound the bindings from her breasts. She hadn't worn a dress in so long she had forgotten what it felt like to have the feeling of luscious, smooth silk slip over her body.

She was shorter than Courtney, and several inches of silk pooled at her feet. "It's a bit too long," she said doubtfully. "I would ruin the hem in the mud." Wealthy though they had been, her father had not approved of dressing her too fine. He had spent his savings on fitting out Gerard as a musketeer and on improving their estate and had dressed her and her mother in wool and cottons. Silk gowns were reserved for special celebrations, and even then they were plain gowns, without a speck of lace or ribbon to be seen. She had never had a dress half so fine before as the one Courtney was so casually offering her.

"I can shorten it for you in an hour," Courtney offered. "musketeer that I am, I haven't forgotten how to sew."

"And a little tight in the bodice."

Courtney inspected the seams. "That can't be

helped. There's no spare fabric to let out for you. Besides, it makes you look every inch a woman."

Miriame's eyes were round and wide at the sight of such finery. She touched the green silk with reverential fingertips. "I've never worn a dress this beautiful in my life."

Courtney went back to the wardrobe and picked out another dress, this one a deep crimson with gold trimmings around the neck and sleeves. "This would suit your dark hair," she said, and she tossed it at Miriame. "Try it on."

Miriame struggled into it with a few muttered curses. "I feel all trussed up like a goose ready for the oven," she complained, as she turned this way and that in front of the looking glass.

Sophie could only stare in amazement at her friend. The crimson dress turned her from a striking-looking young man into a woman of quite exotic dark beauty. "You look beautiful."

Courtney had chosen a yellow dress for herself. "This was used to be my favorite," she said, as she deftly did up the buttons that ran the length of her back. "I wore it on the happiest day of my life." She wiped a tear from her eye. "Before I realized what heartless bastards men are."

Sophie felt like a goose among swans, a plain brown homespun mouse next to a couple of exotic creatures from another world, but the magnificent silk of her dress and the presence of her friends gave her some comfort. "Come to the church with me tomorrow," she pleaded. "Be my attendants so I will not be quite alone."

"Oh, to feel like a woman again," Courtney said, picking up her skirts and doing a little dance in her stocking feet. "I am so sick of pretending to be a man.

I despise filthy men and their even filthier clothes. Soldiers have to wear the most uninspiring clothes in creation. If I could wear my favorite dress into battle, I'm sure I would fight the harder for it. The man who muddied this dress would die a thousand deaths."

Miriame craned her neck over her shoulder to look at the back of the dress. "If this is what feeling like a woman feels like, I'd rather stay a soldier, thanks very much. It's much more practical." All the same, she didn't move away from the glass.

"Forget that you're soldiers for the morrow," Sophie begged, "and come to my wedding. I shall need some friendly faces to get me through. Lamotte would not like me to have an escort of musketeers, but he could not quibble over an escort of women. Besides, nobody will recognize you in a silk dress."

Courtney's face creased in indecision. "As a woman, I knew more than a few people in Paris. I would not like to be recognized by anyone. Besides, I have business that ought to take me out of Paris tomorrow."

"I suppose I can be a woman for one day," Miriame said, smoothing the silk over her hips with covetous hands. "It might be the only chance I ever get to wear a dress worth this much."

"We shall be three women, not three soldiers. None of our comrades will know us."

"Ah, damn it," Courtney said, and she banged her hand on the wardrobe door with the finality of decision. "I shall be there for you. Every woman deserves a proper wedding day."

Lamotte stood at the door of the church, waiting for his bride. He felt little other than a decided impatience to get it all over and done with. His honor demanded he marry the wench. He was sure he could like her well enough, did she but douse a little of her martial spirit. He certainly lusted after her body as a man should lust after his wife. He had no doubt but that once she had accepted him as her lord and master, they would eventually find a measure of sexual satisfaction with each other. He might never find true love and happiness in her arms, but he must needs be content with what he had and forbear from pining for what he could never realize.

A hackney coach stopped a little way down the lane and three female figures alighted, stepping carefully through the mud of the street in their high pattens. He glanced at them briefly before turning his head away again. *Where the devil was Sophie? Did she think to keep him waiting all day?*

"Monsieur le Comte?"

He turned his head back again with a snap.

His mouth fell open in shock to see Sophie, with her soft brown hair in ringlets about her face and looking like a dream in a dress of a rich green, holding out her hand to him. "You are rather lacking in gallantry, Monsieur le Comte, to ignore us so pointedly."

He blinked his eyes to make sure that he was not seeing visions. "I did not know it was you. You look . . . different."

"I am the same Sophie Delamanse I always was—only in a dress."

He could not get over how feminine and fragile she looked—how unlike a soldier. He had an overpowering urge to take her in his arms and hold her close, to protect her from the world outside. "It suits you."

She gestured first to one and then to the other of the women accompanying her. "My friends, Mademoiselle Ruthgard and Mademoiselle Dardagny. They have come to see me wed."

One of them dropped into a graceful curtsey and the other nodded her head awkwardly at the introduction.

He bowed perfunctorily to them both, but his eyes were captivated by Sophie. His wife-to-be was beautiful, truly beautiful. He had not thought a dress could make so much difference. In her gown of emerald green, her blue eyes shining, she was the woman he had dreamed of marrying. She was the Sophie he had always imagined her to be.

He held out his arm to her, still in a daze. "I cannot imagine anything I would rather do than marry you."

He nodded to the priest, who stood waiting on the steps at the door of the church. "Here is my bride."

The priest cleared his throat and started to read. Lamotte stood facing his soon-to-be wife, her cold hands clasped in his own. He waited impatiently for the priest to reach the crucial part of the ceremony. He didn't trust Sophie not to run off before the words that could tie them together as man and wife were finally spoken.

Finally the priest asked the question he had been waiting to hear.

"I do." He spoke the words loud and clear, surprised to find he meant them with all his heart. He wanted to proclaim his marriage to the whole world. Sophie was his wife now and he was glad of it.

"I do." Her voice was soft and clear, but her eyes were troubled. He smiled at her to put her at ease but she did not smile back.

He bent his head in the symbolic kiss that would seal their union. Her breath was sweet and fresh and smelled faintly of mint. He wished he were not on the steps of the church and could kiss her thoroughly instead of merely pecking her chastely on her closed lips.

She gave no outward reaction to his kiss, but there was a telltale flush on her cheeks when he lifted his head again. Maybe his wife was not as immune to him as she made herself out to be.

She was his wife, and he had promised to seduce her into his bed. He was looking forward to this night, their wedding night. He would tempt her palate with sweet dainties and her body with sweet caresses until she melted into his arms. If kind words and gentle kisses could woo her, she would be his wife in earnest by the morrow.

Sophie stood outside the king's apartments, her legs apart and her arms crossed over her chest. Her emerald green wedding dress was safely packed away in Courtney's wardrobe with all the others, as if it had never taken part in such a momentous occasion. She was back to boots and breeches as if she had never left off wearing them.

This was hardly the way she had envisioned spending her wedding night when she was a young girl, still dreaming of her neighbor Jean-Luc's brown curls and steady hand with the bow. Then she had dreamed of her new husband's kisses and caresses and longed for him to make her a real woman.

Lamotte had not been pleased when she had cut short the repast he had arranged for her in their apartments. She herself had been sorry to leave the candied fruits and spiced jellies he had brought in for her, but duty called. She was a musketeer, and the king must be guarded even on her wedding night.

Guard duty was a good reason to escape the apartments she shared with Lamotte. He was too big and overpowering and he made her feel uneasy. Now that they were married, he made her more uncomfortable than ever. She could not have borne spending her wedding night in an uneasy silence, eating a splendid wedding feast with a heavy spirit and tiptoeing around the big hulk of a man who was now her husband in the eyes of man and yet would never be her husband in the eyes of God.

The angles of his face had sat in shadow while the bronzed muscles of his arms had gleamed in the dim candlelight. He looked like a Viking of old as he sat cross-legged in front of the dainties on the low table, inviting her to partake of their wedding feast—a strong and proud warrior who owed his allegiance to nobody.

She would rather guard the king a thousand times over than be subjected to the temptation she had sworn to avoid.

Miriame lounged at her feet, a hip flask in her hand. "I dunno why we have to guard the king anyway," she grumbled, tipping the hip flask upside down and watching the last drop drip onto the dusty floor. "Who are we supposed to guard him from anyway? Discarded mistresses with poison in their eyes? He'd have enough of them for sure. Rumor is he's slept with every damned scullery maid in the palace, not to mention most of the Queen's ladies as well."

Sophie shrugged her shoulders. "His enemies, whoever they might be."

"Why should he have enemies? Everyone loves him. He's the king. The sun rises and sets in his glorious majesty." She spat on the ground beside her and ground the spittle into the dust with her heel. "That's what I think about kings."

The door in front of them creaked open a little way and Sophie glared down at her friend. "Be quiet, you fool, if you want to keep your head joined onto your neck," she hissed. "Someone's coming."

A little page boy poked his head around the door. "The king wants to see one of you," he squeaked.

Miriame stayed where she was. "Tell the king he can go piss in the wind for—"

Sophie kicked her—hard. "Tell the king I am coming right away," she said, hurriedly, to cover up Miriame's insolence as best she could. "In fact, I'll come along with you and tell him myself."

She heaved a sigh of relief as the door shut behind them. Miriame had a hearty disrespect for authority and no sense of self-preservation. Sometimes it felt dangerous to be her friend.

The king was seated in a tall-backed chair at a desk with his back to her, his quill pen scratching away as he wrote busily on the paper in front of him.

She swept a low bow at his back, ending up on one knee. "Gerard Delamanse at your service, sire."

He ignored her.

She waited on one knee for some minutes as the King scratched away, hoping she would not overbalance with a thud but not liking to get to her feet again without his permission. Finally he laid his pen down on the desk, sprinkled sand over the paper to dry the ink, then shook it off again.

With a hand that seemed to shake slightly, he folded the paper in two, dropped a blob of red wax on it from a candle on the desk to seal it, and pressed the imprint of his ring into the seal.

He turned around and handed the letter to Sophie without a word.

She took it as she knelt, and waited for further instructions.

The king ran his hand through his hair. He looked older than she had imagined, Sophie thought to herself. He was hardly a young man anymore. His complexion was almost gray in its paleness, and his forehead was creased with a frown. "The duties of a king are not always pleasant," he said, addressing Sophie with an abstracted air, "but they are duties nonetheless. One cannot shirk what one must do simply because the doing of it revolts the soul."

He fell silent again.

Sophie felt some response seemed to be called for. "No, sire."

The king gave himself a shake. "I do not like what I have to do, but I must do it regardless. Musketeer, you must arrest me a traitor and take the criminal to the Bastille. The *lettre-de-cachet* I have given you is for the Governor of the Bastille. Give both the letter and the prisoner into his hands and his hands only. Take your fellow guard with you for safety in the streets. Whatever you do, you must guard the prisoner well—kill the traitor if you must, but do not allow an escape. Take care none else may know of this."

She was to be entrusted with an important and secret mission for the king. Her heart leaped with excitement. What a perfect chance had landed in her lap to win honor for the name of her brother. She would destroy his enemies down to the very last one. She would not fail the trust her monarch had placed in her. "Yes, sire."

He turned to his page boy. "Go with the musketeer and show him where the traitor resides." He looked down at her with a cold eye. "Do not make a noise. The Comte de Guiche has already fled beyond my reach. I will not allow another bird to escape the noose I have prepared. If the prisoner escapes, your life will pay the forfeit."

She was happy to serve him with her life. "Yes, sire."

Without another word, he waved her away.

Sophie roused a reluctant Miriame with the toe of her boot and the two of them followed the page boy through the maze of winding corridors. Sophie's heart pounded in her breast. She was about to arrest a dangerous traitor to the crown and must guard him with her life. Maybe he would put up a struggle and she would have to subdue him by force. She was not afraid. With God and the king of France on her side, she would be sure to conquer him.

The page boy stopped outside a carved wooden door. "She sleeps in there."

Sophie stopped dead. "She?" She was prepared to give her life in the service of the king, fighting his enemies in a desperate battle to the death. She had not been prepared for the traitor to be a woman.

The page boy nodded.

"Who is it?"

The page boy turned his head to make sure there was nobody hiding in the shadows who might hear him. "Madame Henrietta, the sister of the English King."

Suddenly she thought she understood the reason for her mission. She could hardly bear to be the means of punishing a woman for her loyalty to those she rightly loved. *What would a woman not do for the love of a brother,* Sophie thought to herself with a heavy heart as she reached out to knock on the door. *Even treason.*

The page boy stayed her hand. "Shush," he whispered. "I have a key." He unlocked the door, pushed it open, and melted back into the shadows.

Sophie tucked the letter into the inside of her jacket and the two of them shuffled their feet at the door, unsure of what to do next.

"I hope the king pays us a good bonus for doing his dirty work for him," Miriame grumbled in a low whisper. "I don't like arresting sleeping women for nothing."

"Do you think of nothing but your own profit?" Sophie hissed back at her. "The woman is a traitor and must be dealt with." With a heart full of determination, mixed in equal amounts with trepidation, she squared her shoulders and marched in.

The first chamber was empty. Sophie gave a cursory glance over the rich furnishings and made for the connecting door on the other side.

A young woman with disheveled curls peeping out from under her nightcap was sitting in the bed, a shawl around her shoulders. She looked at the naked sword in Sophie's hand. "You have come to murder me?" she asked in a voice that did not waver at all.

Sophie shook her head. She had to admire the traitor's courage in the face of death. "I have orders from the king to take you to the Bastille."

The other woman sighed. "It is the same thing. Please, will you allow me to get dressed before you take me away?"

Sophie examined the room with a careful eye. There was no obvious exit other than the door by which she had just entered. "I shall wait in the antechamber for you while you dress. Go quickly."

The young woman gave a wan smile. "I will not try your patience for longer than I must."

Miriame was wandering around the outer chamber, picking up the dainty objects that littered the room, examining them closely, and putting them down again. "Damn me if I couldn't make a fortune flogging off this lot to old Malvoisin," she muttered under her breath. "And all of it just sitting here waiting to be nicked. It'd be enough to tempt a saint to thievery."

Sophie glared at her. "Just remember that you are a musketeer now, not a thief."

"'Once a thief, always a thief,' is my motto," Miriame said with a grin. "Lucky for your sense of honor I value my skin too highly to steal from the royal family."

Sophie barely had time to get impatient when the young woman appeared again, richly attired in velvets and jewels. "You are going to the Bastille, not to a royal pageant," she could not help exclaiming. "Have you nothing more fitting to wear? You will ruin your beautiful clothes."

The young woman fingered the string of rubies around her neck. "I am a princess of England and a duchesse of France. My brother is the king of England and my husband is the only brother of the king of France. What care I for ruining a paltry velvet? I shall go to my death with my head held high."

A covered carriage was waiting for them in the street below. Sophie could not help but admire the straightness of her back and the calmness of her demeanor as they clattered over the dark streets toward the cold, forbidding dungeons of the Bastille. Her prisoner was a brave woman and not afraid to die for what she had done. Whatever treason she had committed, she was reaping her just deserts with honor and bravery.

The governor of the Bastille was none too pleased to be awakened at such an hour. He stumbled into view, a sputtering wax candle clutched in his hand and his tasseled nightcap hanging drunkenly over one eye. "What do you want?" he grumbled through the iron grille.

Sophie stood to attention. "I have orders from the king to deliver a prisoner to you."

The governor grunted with displeasure. "You didn't need to have the sentry wake me up for that, you damn fool," he said as he turned away again. "Toss him to the guards and be done with him."

"You misunderstood me. I have orders directly from the king himself that I am to deliver this prisoner to no one but you. Here is the letter that will explain more." She reached into her jacket for the letter, but it was not there. Had she put it elsewhere? She fumbled in the other side of her jacket, to no avail. Surely she had not dropped it in the coach? The king would be highly displeased with her carelessness, after he had enjoined her to strictest secrecy as well.

Miriame stepped forward, gave a deep bow, and handed the letter through the grille. "From the king himself."

Sophie looked daggers at her comrade. Miriame had given her the fright of her life. Her light-fingered companion must have picked her pocket so neatly she had not noticed her loss before.

"Just practicing," Miriame murmured in Sophie's ear as she straightened up out of her bow. "So as not to lose my touch."

At least the letter was not lost, Sophie thought, as

she elbowed Miriame sharply in the ribs for her mischief.

The governor opened the letter and read it by the dim light of the candle. "Where's the prisoner?" he demanded, once he had reached the end.

Sophie stepped back and urged the prisoner forward with one hand in the small of her back.

Henrietta looked up at the strong walls of the Bastille and shuddered as if she could already feel the cold air of the dungeon on her face. Without further urging, she stepped daintily to the grille in her high-heeled shoes. "Here I am." Her voice was strong and clear. She was too proud to show her fear.

The governor's face grew pale at the sight of the prisoner. He drew up a big bunch of keys from his waist and unlocked the grille with fumbling fingers as he ushered her inside. He turned to face her again, his hand on the gate. "You have arrested madame the Duchesse D'Orleans on the order of the king? Are you sure this is not a mistake?"

Sophie watched as the prisoner stepped forward into the shadow of the Bastille. The governor bowed nervously to her as she passed, the keys in his belt clanking with every move her made, but she went by him with her nose in the air.

The iron grille clanged shut behind her with an ominous bang.

Sophie watched her go with a feeling of foreboding, which she tried to squelch. She was there to serve the king, not to question his orders, and his orders had been very clear. The woman was a traitor who deserved her fate. "Quite sure. The king does not make mistakes."

* * *

Henrietta sat on cold stone bench in her prison cell. The thick velvet of her dress shielded her from the chill of the night air, but still she shivered. King Louis would not forgive her for helping the Comte de Guiche to escape. She had read the fury in his eyes when his guards had come back empty-handed, and had trembled. She had known then her punishment would not be long in coming.

Still, she had not expected him to move so quickly or so viciously. Few returned from the Bastille, and those who did were broken in body and spirit. Imprisonment in the Bastille was a death sentence. The King had doomed her to a long, slow, torturous demise.

She wiped a renegade tear from her eye. For the first time since she had crossed him, she realized in full how badly she had underestimated her opponent, the king. Thwarted of his intended prey now the comte had fled to safety, he had struck at her instead.

She would not feel sorry for herself. She had known she risked her life in helping her lover, and she had done so gladly. She loved him more than she loved her own life or even the hope of her own salvation. She would not want to keep living if de Guiche had been harmed on her account.

It was too late to ask her brother for help. He had plenty of troubles of his own in his island kingdom. She would not ask him to sacrifice his peace of mind for her and declare war against France to save her.

Besides, she was not sure he would answer her call for aid. His brotherly love did not run so deep as his love for his country, or even his love of frivolity and idleness. She loved her brother dearly—better, perhaps, than he deserved. She would rather die in peace and quiet than risk testing the depth of Charles's love for her and finding it wanting.

She fingered the necklace around her neck. She might still manage to break free from her jailer if he were to prove sufficiently greedy. She had put on her jewels not to salvage her pride—a prisoner of the king could not afford such luxuries as pride—but to pay for the help she might need in escaping from her prison.

Any of the rings on her fingers or the necklaces she kept hidden under the velvet of her dress might buy her freedom. She relied on no man to come and rescue her from the hole she had dug for herself. She was not without resources of her own to save her own skin. She would explore them all before she gave her soul up to despair.

Six

Sophie threw her sword down on the ground in disgust and glared at her opponent. She wanted to stamp her feet and shout at him, but she doubted it would do her cause any good. She counted up to ten to master her anger before she spoke. "What do you think you're doing?"

Lamotte put up his own sword, looking relieved at the cessation of hostilities. "Teaching you to fight, as I promised."

Teaching me to fight? Teaching me to dance is more like it! He is big enough to break me in two with his bare hands if he feels like it. Why, then, will he not fight with me?

"Have I suddenly turned into fragile porcelain overnight and you're scared I will break if you touch me? Does becoming your wife somehow make me less of a soldier? You're not even trying to batter through my defense."

He passed his hand over his eyes, his face suddenly weary. "You know I cannot fight you."

What nonsense was he talking now? "How can I learn if you do not teach me?"

He leaned on his sword. "I cannot fight a woman, especially not the woman to whom I have pledged my troth," he said, soft and low so none would overhear him. "To fight my own wife? It goes against everything that I have ever believed in."

She spat on the dust at her feet. "I suppose you think that women are soft creatures, to be cosseted in silks and velvets in high towers far from the world?" She kept her voice soft, but she knew he could not help but hear her exasperation. She wanted him to hear it. She wanted him to know how absurd she thought he was acting.

He shrugged his shoulders, plainly agreeing with her assessment but not wanting to admit it. "I cannot fight a woman."

She picked up her sword again. She must break him out of his foolishness if she was to continue her education as a soldier. Did he not see her life might one day depend on how well he had taught her? She prodded him in his leather jerkin with the point of her sword. "What if a woman insists on fighting you? What then?"

He did not rise to her bait. "I do not think it likely. Women should not fight."

She smiled to herself. She would make him admit his error before she had done. She would force him to fight her. "This one does." She prodded a little harder until he gave a slight wince as the tip of her sword came uncomfortably close to his navel. "Would you strike back at me, or would you stand still and let me carve you into little pieces?"

He stood in the middle of the courtyard, his legs apart and his arms crossed in front of him. "I doubt you would go that far, wife."

She looked around her in panic at his words. Thank the Lord there was no one close enough to hear him call her wife for all the world to know. "Maybe not," she said, and she flicked her sword to give him a light scratch on his cheek. "Just spoil your beauty a bit, maybe."

He stood where he was, but his fists clenched at his side and his green-brown eyes grew dark with rage as a tiny trickle of blood dribbled down his cheek. "That was not a wise thing to do, wife."

"Why not?" she asked, her voice all mock innocence. "You won't fight me, so what have I to fear from you?" She flicked her sword again to cut his other cheek and flashed him a mischievous grin. "That was just to even you up a little. You shall have matching scars now—one on each side. They will remind you each time you look in a mirror what a woman can do to do if you will not fight back."

His knuckles were white, he clenched them so hard. "Sophie, my sweet, you are playing with fire."

"Fire?" She snorted in derision. "Pah. There is nothing fiery about you. You are as full of sober melancholy and phlegm as the saddest friar in the abbey." She moved the point of her sword rather lower and prodded him gently below the waist. If this did not rouse him to rage, then nothing would. "I wonder if you even have as much manhood as a friar, sworn to celibacy, does."

With an inarticulate roar of fury at this last insult, Lamotte grabbed his sword out of its scabbard and forced her blade away from his groin. "I warn you, wife, I will not stand much more of this."

Sophie grinned to herself as she felt the strength of his blade connect with hers and the force of the impact travel up her arm in waves. Success! She had angered him into fighting her. "So stop me then, if you can."

She thrust in the general direction of his breeches and he parried quickly this time. Around the courtyard they went, back and forth, from one side to the other, now advancing and now retreating, blades flashing in the sunlight and clashing at every step.

Lamotte was still holding back, she could tell. He was not giving it his all. He would only defend himself against her attacks. He would not make a positive move against her. She would not be satisfied with that.

To test her theory, she deliberately made a lunge that left her side open to attack, but he failed to press his advantage.

Damn him. She would not let him get away with this. She needed him to forget she was a woman, to see instead that she was a fighter intent on doing him an injury. Could he not see his misplaced sense of honor was putting him in danger?

She redoubled her efforts, desperate to get through his defenses and prove to him she was in earnest. She watched him like a hawk watches the rabbit marked out for its prey. Her eyes did not leave his, reading in them the movements he would make as soon as he knew himself what they would be.

He would not attack her. She would use her knowledge of his weakness against him. With a flurry of thrusts that left her vulnerable to counterattack, she moved against him with renewed vigor. She was never dare such a dangerous move with anyone else, but his foolish sense of honor meant she ran no risk.

He would not attack her, not even to defend himself. With a last, frantic lunge, she broke through and scored him in the pit of the belly with the tip of her sword.

He looked up at her, surprise and disappointment written all over his face. "You cut me." He sounded as if he could not quite believe it.

She had not meant to cut him quite so hard, just to prove to him she could. Guilt made her defensive.

"What else did you expect? We were fighting and you would not defend yourself."

He put his hand over his stomach, and when he drew it away again, blood was dripping off his fingers. He looked at the blood with a puzzled eye. "I did not think a woman would do this to me."

Sophie gazed at the blood in horror. She had meant only to provoke him into forgetting she was a woman and fighting her soldier to soldier. She had meant to wound only his pride, not to seriously hurt him. She tossed away her sword and fell to her knees in front of him to see how badly he was hurt.

Blood was seeping from under his tunic. She wanted to be sick at the sight of it. "Lie down," she commanded him in a shaky voice. "You are hurt. You need to be attended to."

With unaccustomed obedience, he stretched out on his back in the dirt, his face unusually white. "I don't know that I trust you to treat the wound you caused in the first place," he grumbled. "You are a vicious woman. You'll be the death of me yet."

With fumbling fingers, she pulled open his jerkin and unbuttoned the white linen shirt he wore underneath. She cut through the lacing of his breeches with her dagger and pulled the fabric back to expose the wound she had made. The shirt was ruined with blood anyway, so she tore a strip off the hem and dabbed away the blood that seeped out of the cut.

The cut was long but not deep, and the bleeding had nearly stopped already. She felt her stomach settle as she realized she had done him no lasting damage. "It could be worse," she said as she started to bind him up with more strips torn off his shirt.

She liked the look of him without his shirt, she decided as she bandaged him up. His chest was a deep golden brown with well-defined muscles. Her fingers itched to run her hands over his chest, over his hard, flat stomach, and into the curls of golden hair that peeked through the opening of his breeches.

She stopped herself just in time. She couldn't do that. They had agreed he was her husband in name only. She had no right to touch him. Besides, it would be asking for trouble to let him see her curiosity about his body. "You won't die of it."

He looked aggrieved at her lack of sympathy. "I might."

Her composure had returned now she was satisfied she had not hurt him. "No man worth his salt would die of such a pathetic little scratch. I doubt it will even leave a scar."

"Sacre bleu! Is that all the sympathy I get? If you had caught me an inch or two lower down, I wouldn't be a man at all anymore."

She gave a snort of laughter which she hastily muffled in the sleeve of her jacket. No wonder his face was white. No man could face the fear of being unmanned with any equanimity. She leaned over and patted him gently on his groin. "Don't worry, monsieur. Your manhood is still intact, as far as I can tell."

He gave a grunt of annoyance. "Men do not cut other men below the navel in case the favor is returned one day."

She leaned over him to secure the bandages. "In case you hadn't noticed, I'm not a man."

He gave a pointed glance at her chest, just inches from the tip of his nose. "How could I possibly forget?"

She sat back on her heels again to remove her chest to a safer distance, where he could not ogle it so obviously. "Besides, I did not mean to hurt you badly, just to shake you up a little."

"Kiss it to make it better, then, and I will be happy."

She glared at him. What pathetic kind of plea was that? "Soldiers do not kiss other soldiers to make their booboos better."

He screwed up his face in disappointment. "But wives kiss their husbands better when the poor men have been wounded in battle with fierce, bloodthirsty Amazons."

She took a quick look around. No one was in the courtyard. She leaned down and, under pretence of adjusting his dressings, planted a light kiss on his scratched belly. Then, before she succumbed to the temptation to kiss him again, she knotted the lacings of his breeches together as best she could and pulled his jerkin shut. "There now. I thank you for the compliment you paid me in calling me an Amazon, and I have paid in full for wounding you. Are you satisfied?"

He put his hands under his head and looked at her with a measure of triumph in his eyes. "You were worried you had hurt me and you kissed me to make it better again. I knew you still had some semblance of a true woman about you."

His idea of true womanhood was so narrow and unenlightened that she wanted to shake him. Could she not be a woman and a soldier both at once? "I was concerned I had disabled my mentor, that is all. Who but you can teach me all I need to know?" She swatted him lightly on the shoulder as she squatted next to him on the dusty ground. "Get up, you lazy lump. I've done bandaging you now. Besides, it was only a scratch and we have work to do."

He didn't move. "Kiss me again first."

He was teasing her and she didn't know what to do with him. "Why should I do that?" she temporized, not moving any closer to him, but not moving away either.

"Because you hurt me."

He didn't exactly look very hurt, lying on his back at his ease in the sunshine with a satisfied grin on his face. "I've already kissed you once to make your stomach better. That excuse won't wash with me."

He gave a mock frown. "Because you're my wife, then."

She frowned in earnest at his words. "In name only. Don't forget that."

"Then how about because you have the most beautiful blue eyes in the world and I love to look at them until I feel I could drown in their cool depths?"

"How poetic. Unfortunately, I have no feeling for poetry. You should save your fine words for the tavern girls—they have more use for them than I do."

Despite her mocking dismissal, she couldn't help feeling disturbed by his words. Jean-Luc had never mentioned her eyes. He had complimented her on the sharpness of her vision and on her accuracy with a bow, but she doubted he even knew her eyes were blue. She had no remembrance of what color Jean Luc's eyes had been, if indeed she had ever known. She had been too intent on admiring the daring way he rode his horse to worry over much about his eyes. It felt strange to be appreciated for something so ephemeral and impractical as the color of her eyes.

He took her hand in his, holding her fingers lightly in his own. "You have beautiful eyes. Just like your brother's, only even more blue."

She looked at him suspiciously, but his voice was all sincerity. His eyes were beautiful, too. They were a deep green with flecks of tawny gold and surrounded by a band of darker tawny gold around the edge. Truly beautiful eyes, like the green of the marshes glinting in the sunlight in her home in the Camargue. "You have green eyes just like a cat."

He laughed delightedly, showing his white teeth. "Then we are well matched, you and I. I have the eyes of a cat, and you have a wildcat's sharp claws."

"Female cats are the most vicious killers," she reminded him, as she rose to her feet and stretched out his hand to help him up. "You should remember that in future before you ask them for a kiss."

He held on to her hand as he leaped lightly to his feet, showing not a sign of discomfort from the scratch on his stomach. "You have given me graphic proof of that twice. I shall not dare forget again, or I will be a dead man."

She raised her sword in front of her. "So you will forget I am a woman and fight me properly this afternoon?"

"I could never forget that you are a woman, but I will endeavor to fight you as if you were a man." He rubbed his arm where she had wounded him the first time and patted his belly a little gingerly. With a slight grimace he bent over and picked his sword up from the ground. "Indeed, I dare not do otherwise."

She attacked him before he finished speaking. He defended himself vigorously this time, testing her defenses whenever she left him an opening to do so.

Within a minute he had disarmed her with a flick of his wrist that jarred every bone in her arm. Dispite her discomfort, she smiled to herself in triumph as she bent down to pick up her sword from the dust. She had won that battle. He would see her as a danger and treat her as a soldier now. She had seen to that.

After half an hour's swordplay, she put up her sword and held her side for a moment to catch her breath again. "That's better," she said, as soon as she could speak again. "I did not like being treated as a child."

A movement from the shadows caught her eye and she turned her head to look. A figure dressed in a dark cloak and hat was signaling with furtive desperation in her direction. She sighed. She was enjoying her lesson immensely, but she was a musketeer and sworn to help those in need. "Excuse me a moment. It seems I have some business to attend to."

Lamotte followed the direction of her glance to where the dark figure waited in the shadows. "With him?"

She nodded. "It seems so."

He glowered at her. "What business do you have with other men, wife?"

She ignored his last whispered word. "I'll be back soon enough." She strode over to the shadowy figure in the corner of the yard.

Lamotte followed her, a couple of paces behind.

"You want me?"

The man blanched at her direct approach. He pulled his hat further down on his head and wrapped his cloak over all his face but his eyes. "I would speak with you only, not with your fellow."

She looked at Lamotte, a question in her eyes, but he shook his head. "Where you go, so do I," he said softly. "Even vicious wildcats need someone at their back."

She turned back to the stranger. "I will vouch for his trustworthiness. Whatever you say to me, you may say to him as well. Go on."

The stranger looked sideways at Lamotte, as if trying to make up his mind. After a moment's reflection, he shrugged his shoulders. "I suppose I have no choice, if you will insist."

Lamotte looked even more unhappy than the stranger at the situation. "I do insist."

The stranger ignored him, turning his attention back to Sophie. "Were you on guard duty last night?" His voice was soft, as if he wanted no one to overhear him.

Sophie could see nothing of his face. She misliked talking to a stranger wrapped up like a ghoul in the light of day, as if he had something to hide. "I was."

He jerked his head in the direction of the street. "Then come with me, if you would."

She stood her ground. "Where to? And why?"

He pulled urgently at her sleeve. "Come, I am in haste. I care not where we go so long as it is somewhere we can talk privately."

She swiveled her head around, but there were few others in sight, and they were all going about their own business and showing no interest in their talk. "Why not here?"

He looked around the yard with desperation. "There are too many people here who might see us together. Please, let's go. Anywhere in private where no one can see us. I swear I will not hurt you. You may search me if you please. I am unarmed. Besides," he said, gesturing toward Lamotte, "you have your own private guard dog to look out for you."

He didn't look as though he could hurt a fly, but Sophie nevertheless followed him out of the yard with some reluctance. She was glad to have Lamotte at her back. She was no dealer in secrets and shadows, but the stranger seemed so desperate for her help she did not like to refuse him.

Once in the street outside, he looked around him

as if unsure where to go next. "Have you somewhere nearby we can talk? My apartments are some way away, and I do not want to be seen walking the streets with you."

Sophie tossed the possibilities over in her mind. The apartments she shared with Lamotte were her only choice, though she misliked taking him there. Inside those four walls, she lived life as a woman, not as a soldier. She wanted no dark stranger to guess her secret.

There was nowhere else. She set off toward their apartments at a cracking pace, Lamotte close at her heels and the mysterious stranger half running beside them to keep up.

As soon as they hustled in the door, the stranger collapsed on a well-cushioned chair and rubbed his ankles with a pained expression on his face. "You walk faster than a horse can gallop," he said ruefully. "My feet are all a-blister."

She wanted to point out his feet would be in better shape if his shoes were not so absurdly high-heeled. Instead, she bit her tongue and flung herself down on a sofa. "Well?"

Lamotte plonked himself down beside her, his legs stretched out in front of him and his arms crossed defensively over his chest.

The stranger held his hand to his heaving sides. "You arrested a woman last night?"

The king had counseled her to keep it silent, but Sophie would not lie, either. "I cannot tell you that."

"So you did arrest her." What she could see of his face grew gray. "Poor, poor Henrietta."

Lamotte stirred uneasily beside her. "Who is this Henrietta you speak of?"

The man pushed his hat back on his head and let his cape fall. "She is my wife."

Sophie gave a gasp of shock as she saw his face, so like that of his brother, King Louis XIV of France. "Monsieur le Duc, Philippe of Orleans?" How could she have been in the presence of royalty and not known of it till now?

The stranger nodded gravely. "Yes, I am the duc."

She fell to one knee and bowed her head. Offending royalty by failing to give them due honor was the quickest way of finding your head suddenly separated from your shoulders. "Forgive me for my earlier rudeness. I did not know who you were."

Beside her, Lamotte doffed his hat with little sign of his earlier antagonism. "At your service, Monsieur le Duc."

Philippe of Orleans waved her up again. "You were not meant to know me. I will be luckier than I deserve if no one else recognized me, either. Now, will you tell me what has happened to my wife?"

Sophie shuddered. Monsieur did not look happy to hear of his wife's arrest, despite the gossip of the streets that claimed they could barely tolerate the sight of one another. "I arrested her and delivered her over to the governor of the Bastille last night."

Philippe of Orleans gave her a haughty stare. "On whose authority?" he asked in a cold voice.

He looked every inch as formidable as his brother. She shuddered. When royalty squabbled among themselves, the common people suffered for it. "The king himself gave me the orders. He wrote the paper I delivered to the governor in his own hand."

"On what accusation?"

She hardly dared say the word. "She was under accusation of treason."

Philippe of Orleans crushed his hat in his hands and swore like a fishmonger. "My royal brother the king, God rot his soul, is a hypocritical, whoremongering bastard."

Sophie's shock must have shown on her face. For any man to say that about his brother was unthinkable. For the duc, it was treason.

The duc shrugged his shoulders. "I forget you are a simple soldier. You need to have been a courtier to understand the intrigues that take place in every corridor and corner of the royal palace. Suffice to say my royal brother, for all his sanctimonious piety in public, has a letch for my wife. He's been obsessed about her for years, but unfortunately for him, he revolts her.

"I don't like women much in general," he continued, and gave an elegant shudder, "but I like Henrietta very well. She is my best friend and she has the most elegant taste in gowns you can imagine. I borrow hers whenever I am sick of my own. I only wish I could borrow her slippers, too, but she has such delicate feet I cannot squash my toes into her footwear."

Sophie looked at the man in front of her with a new eye. Did he really dress in women's clothes as she hid herself in those of a man? She had not imagined such a thing before. Why would any man desire to be a woman when the least of men had so much more freedom than the greatest of women ever could possess?

Lamotte was shifting nervously on his seat beside her. She wondered what was bothering him now.

"You don't look as shocked as most people when I tell them that," Philippe of Orleans said and he patted her knee in a friendly gesture. "That's a good start."

She shrugged. He confused her, but did not shock her. Little did he know she kept her own secret from the world. "Each to his own, and the devil take the hindmost."

Philippe raised his eyebrows. "I sympathize with your motto, but Henrietta is my wife and I must protect her. The king denies all knowledge of her disappearance. He swears she must have run off with her lover, the Comte de Guiche, but I cannot believe it. It would be most unlike her." He wrinkled his nose with annoyance. "I was most put out with Henrietta for seducing the comte, you know. I had an eye on him myself, but he preferred my wife to me, the silly boy."

Sophie grinned in spite of herself. Philippe of Orleans had all the infectious charm of a boy who had never grown up, and never would. "How unfortunate for you."

He patted her knee again, and let his hand rest there as if by accident. "I thought you would understand, my dear boy. I saw right away you had a generous soul."

Lamotte scowled at him and looked pointedly at the hand resting on Sophie's knee.

Philippe of Orleans looked up into Lamotte's scowl. "Ah, your watchdog is displeased with me," he murmured, as he moved his hand away again. "I had better behave myself.

"As I was saying, I love Henrietta dearly and I most heartily detest my royal brother. I must rescue my dear wife, but I cannot do it alone. I need your help."

Sophie hesitated. Did he know what he was asking of her? "I have sworn fealty to your brother, the king."

Philippe of Orleans did not look impressed with her doubts. "You would rather let an innocent woman suffer and not go to her rescue? What human vow is worth the sacrifice of your honor?"

What could a single musketeer do anyway? "She has been taken to prison. What would have me do? Storm the Bastille single-handedly and get her out again?"

Philippe of Orleans fluttered his hands in the air with distress. "Nothing as dramatic as that, my dear boy."

Lamotte scowled harder than ever. "The Bastille is a fortress. No one has ever escaped from there. Would the king not release her on your asking?"

Philippe of Orleans raised a scented handkerchief to his nose and rubbed the tip of it daintily. "My dear brother cares little for my displeasure—indeed, he would rather have me displeased than not, I fear. Duc though I am, I am powerless. Luckily, Henrietta has friends more powerful than I am. I need you to go to England and tell them of her plight."

Lamotte snorted with derision. "Wouldn't you rather we stormed the Bastille?"

Sophie raised her eyebrows and waited for the duc to explain.

"Go to her brother, King Charles, and beg his help to rescue her. He does not know of her current situation. Indeed, only a handful of people could even guess the truth. The rest will only too readily believe the lies of the King that she has fled with her lover. If King Charles has any notion of honor and decency left in him, he will save his sister."

Sophie felt torn between sympathy for the duc and pity for his wife on the one hand, and her loyalty to the king on the other. She did not know what to do.

If she were to believe the duc, then the king must have lied to her. The duchesse was guilty of nothing more than refusing the King a boon he should not even ask of her, and she herself had been complicit in punishing an innocent woman.

She could not comprehend a king who told untruths. The king of France was the fount from which all honor flowed. If he proved corrupt, her life, which she had dedicated to the pursuit of honor, had little meaning.

And yet why would the duc lie to her? What motive could he have but to protect the life of his wife? She did not know.

She rose to her feet and paced backward and forward across the room, her indecision tearing at her. "I cannot give you an answer now. I will have to think over what you have said."

Philippe of Orleans rose to his feet in his turn. "Do not take over long to decide," he said, as he paused in the doorway. "The Bastille is not a gentle or forgiving place for those poor unfortunates incarcerated within its walls. Those stones eat away at a man until there is nothing left but an empty, soulless shell."

Once they were alone together, Sophie turned to Lamotte in distress. He was more experienced that she. She needed to hear what he had to say, to hear his advice on her dilemma. "Can what monsieur says be true? Can the king have lied to me?"

Lamotte shrugged. "It is no secret in the court that the king harbors an unnatural affection for his sister-in-law and that she does not welcome or return this affection."

Of all things Philippe of Orleans had claimed, Sophie had found this one the hardest to accept. That a king could try to pervert the bonds of a family in such a fashion beggared belief. "You know of this for certain?"

He shrugged one shoulder as he lay back on the sofa. "It would be hard to ignore. I have carried many a letter from the king to Madame la Duchesse and gotten naught but a door slammed shut in my face for the trouble."

She ceased her pacing and fixed his eyes with a steady gaze. "So monsieur speaks true."

He nibbled on his bottom lip. "I do not altogether trust monsieur."

Surely both of them could not be lying—or could the truth lie in a third direction? "Why not?"

He screwed up his face in distaste. "He openly confessed to us both that he dresses in women's clothes. What manner of man would so shamelessly flaunt his perversions?"

If the duc was perverted for dressing in women's clothes, then so was she for dressing in breeches like a man. How could the one be condemned and not the other? She did not consider either a perversion. "A man who was not ashamed of the way God made him?" she suggested, her voice tart.

"The devil more like it," he muttered under his breath.

"Be it god or devil who gave the duc a liking for women's gowns is no matter. Have you no other reason to distrust Monsiuer le Duc?"

He shrugged. "I do not like the man. Did you not see the way he pawed at you, thinking you were a smooth-faced young boy? He has an unnatural liking for young men."

Sophie scratched her head. Were men always this illogical and unreasonable? "So you have no reason to distrust him other than that he dresses in women's clothes and prefers boys to women?"

"Is that not enough to distrust a man?"

"No, it is not. A man should be judged on his words and deeds, not on the clothes he wears. You tell me the duc speaks truly of the king's love for his wife, and truth is that the king has had her arrested and sent to the Bastille. Why then should I not trust the duc? Why should I not go to England?"

"It is a long, hard journey to an unfriendly land where the winters are harsh, the women ugly, the food unappetizing, and the wine positively evil."

She raised her eyebrows at his flimsy excuses. "I am a soldier. I cannot expect to live a life of ease while I fulfil my duty. Besides," she added with a smile, "I care not if the women are ugly so long as the men are brave and fair to look upon."

"The crossing will be rough this time of the year."

"I am not afeared of the water. God will keep me safe, if that is his will."

"You have sworn your allegiance to the king of France, as have I. One cannot lightly toss such an oath aside."

There was the rub. She had sworn her allegiance to the king. Should she serve him as she had sworn to, with due obedience, or should she break her troth to him for the sake of truth or pity? Which way lay her duty? Which way lay honor? "You would not come with me, then, were I to go?"

"We are musketeers in the service of the king, not in the service of his brother, the Duc of Orleans. Neither are we in the business of rescuing from prison those whom the king has deemed traitors to France. I would counsel you to remain in Paris."

She did not altogether agree with his arguments. "If I ignored your counsel? What then?"

"You are my wife. I would chase after you and drag you back to Paris by your ears, if I must."

***

"The king ordered the prisoner to be kept in darkness and isolation," Miriame said idly, as she lounged on a pile of gold velvet cushions on the rich red Persian rug on the floor of Courtney's chamber. "No candles. No tapers. No lights of any kind. No letters. No parcels. No messages to be delivered. No visitors except for the king himself. Plain black bread and a small jar of water to be stuffed through the grating on her door only every second day. Even her guards are forbidden to speak to her on pain on suffering the same fate."

Courtney lay back on the sofa and buffed her nails with a piece of soft cloth. "You're making up stories. How would you know that?"

"I read the letter the king wrote to the governor of the Bastille."

Courtney was not impressed. "When did you do that?"

"In the coach. There was enough moon to make out the letters, though the king does write in a remarkably ill hand."

Sophie, perched in the window seat with her knees drawn up to her chin, stared at her in amazement. "But it was sealed with the King's seal. Don't tell me you picked the seal as successfully as you picked my pocket."

Miriame took a blade out of her pocket and threw it in the air. It somersaulted half a dozen times on its journey, light from the candles glinting off the highly polished, wickedly sharp blade before the hilt dropped back into her hand as easily as if it belonged there. She tucked it back it into her pocket with a grin. "Nothing a sharp knife could not slit through without leaving a mark."

Sophie shook to think of the danger she had unwittingly been exposed to. Was there no end to Miriame's foolish risk taking? "What if the governor had noticed?"

"He was roused from sleep in the middle of the night. The night was dark enough, despite the moon. I took a gamble he would be too drunk from his carousing the previous night, too confused from the orders he was being given, or simply too sleepy to notice."

"What if he had noticed? Then what would you have done?"

"What's to worry about? He didn't see aught amiss."

Courtney had finished her fingernails and had moved on to her toenails. "That is not the point. The point is what shall we do about this request of monsieur's? Should we rush to the rescue of the fair Henrietta, or stay quietly at home by the fireside and let her rot?"

Miriame tossed her knife in the air again. "Will he pay us for our trouble?"

Sophie dismissed the question with a wave of her hand. The issue was one of honor and faith and obedience, not of gold livres. "Money is not important."

Miriame threw a cushion at her. "Not to you, maybe. To me it is."

Once a gutter rat, always a gutter rat, Sophie thought to herself as she caught the cushion in midair and hugged it to her knees. *Miriame has the mind of a street hawker, greedy for profit, and always will have.* "Yes, he will. One thousand gold pistoles to pay for our journey, with as much again when we return."

Miriame whistled between her teeth. "Then I say we go, and go in style."

Sophie's loyalties were torn. She wanted to do the

honorable thing, but which way lay honor? Lamotte had counseled her to stay out of mistrust of the duc and fear she might come to harm on the way. Miriame counseled her to go and earn a few gold pieces.

Neither of them understood her confusion. She did not know what to do. "The king has accused her of treason. Surely he would not imprison her so without good reason?"

Miriame laughed. "Do not be so naive. Not everyone who is accused is guilty. I know half a dozen people hanged for crimes they didn't commit. Of course," she added after a pause, "they were guilty of plenty of other things. Just not the things they were hanged for."

Courtney finished her last toenail and tossed the cloth aside. "My faith is with monsieur in this matter. I believe she is innocent of treason and the king has jailed her for not succumbing to his advances. I can see nothing here but the maliciousness of men who prey on those weaker than themselves. I say we rescue her."

Sophie still wavered. "And our vows of loyalty to the king? What of them?"

Miriame gave a great belly laugh. "I'd break a vow to God himself for a thousand gold pistoles. Breaking a vow to the king of France is no great matter."

"Justice ranks higher with me than obedience," Courtney said in a measured tone. "I will break a vow to any man, be him the king himself, a thousand times over before I will go against my conscience and do a woman an injustice when it is in my power to right her wrong."

Sophie felt the sun on her back as she sat in the window. From that day forth, her conscience could not remain perfectly clear. She had to make a choice between doing her duty and obeying her conscience.

Courtney was right, though. She had no choice at all.

She jumped down from the window seat and stretched her legs. They would be stiff and sore from hard riding soon enough. "To England, then? Tonight?"

Miriame pumped one fist in the air with a shout of joy. "A thousand pistoles among us? I am in Heaven."

Courtney looked sadly at her newly buffed fingernails. Few things were harder on fingernails than riding in all weathers. Their new shine would be lost in the first day's travel. "To England."

Miriame looked at Sophie with a calculating air. "Your new husband will not mind your sudden yen for English air? Most wedded men would surely take it amiss were their wife to disappear on the sudden."

Sophie sniffed. "The count has threatened to drag me back to Paris if I should go. He is on guard duty tonight, so we shall have to leave before he returns home. I shall endeavor to put him off the scent, but if I am not successful, we shall have to fight our way through him."

Courtney gave a delighted laugh. "I have been spoiling for a good fight for some days now. I will look forward to seeing him try."

Lamotte paced up and down outside the king's chambers. He had an uneasy feeling he could not shake. Sophie had said nothing more about going to England since he had threatened to drag her home again by the ears did she leave without his permission, but he did not trust her silence.

He stumbled over an uneven patch of flooring and righted himself again with a curse. Damn the guard duty that kept him occupied that night. If Gerard saw a soul in need of help, he could not be prevented from going to their aid, whether they deserved to be rescued or no. Sophie was far too like her brother for comfort.

He propped his elbows up on the casement window in the corridor and looked up at the night sky. The moon was full and bright, and the stars made a tapestry of light against the dark wall of the sky. The only patch of cloud lay far off on the horizon. All in all, it was a perfect night for riding, and it made the uneasy feeling in the pit of his stomach grow.

He wished only for dawn to arrive so he could leave his post. His discomfort grew greater by the moment. Sophie needed him, he felt sure of it.

He had slipped into a restless doze, napping on his feet as soldiers do, when a messenger arrived, panting and covered in sweat as if he had run fifty miles on foot.

Lamotte leaped to his feet, fully awake on the instant. Through the casement he could see the sky starting to lighten with the first rays of the sun peeping over the horizon. He heaved a sigh of relief. His duty was nigh done.

The runner put his hand on his heaving side. "An urgent message for the king," he panted, between great gasps of breath.

Lamotte, spear in his right hand, knocked on the door of the chamber. The king's boy stared wide-eyed at the messenger and gestured for him to enter at once. Lamotte made to come in with him as a guard should do, but the boy stood in his path to stop him from entering.

"The king is expecting him," the boy stammered,

as Lamotte fixed him with a steely glare. "He trusts him without a guard."

Lamotte did not like to leave his king so exposed, but he had no choice. With a snap of his heels, he remained in the corridor while the door to the king's chamber shut in his face.

It opened again a few moments later and the boy beckoned him inside.

Lamotte stood to attention by the side of his king. The messenger was nowhere to be seen.

The King motioned to his boy to pour him a glass of wine from the decanter on the table. He took the full glass and drank it down before speaking, his forehead creased with worry. "You know of one Gerard Delamanse? A musketeer in your regiment?"

Lamotte felt his heart pound in his breast with fear for his wife. What had she done to come to the king's attention in this way? Such a question from the king, accompanied by such a frown, did not auger well for his wife's continued well-being. "Yes, sire."

"It seems this Gerard has been prevailed upon by my brother, the Duc of Orleans, to undertake a mission for him. A mission that will take him all the way to England."

He felt his blood run cold. How could the king's spies have found out so quickly about monsieur's request? Had monsiuer himself betrayed her? He caressed his dagger with itchy fingers. If monsieur had betrayed Sophie, then, king's brother or no, he would have his revenge. "To England?"

The King glared at him with bloodshot eyes. "Do you doubt my word on the matter?"

He bowed his head in apology. He would not be able to help Sophie if he antagonized the king himself. "No, sire."

"It seems my brother, the royal duc, has a mind to create mischief between the king of France and his brother, the king of England. He has suborned the loyalty of one of my own musketeers to do it for him. I am mightily vexed with him."

Lamotte shivered. He would not like to be in monsieur's place now, for all that he was the king's own brother. "Yes, sire."

"I feared my foolish brother would make such a move as this. I am thankful I have some faithful servants still, who will tell me when such treasons are being plotted against my majesty."

Lamotte shifted from one foot to the other, an uncomfortable prickling in his spine. The king must have had monsieur spied on. Poor, guileless Sophie did not stand a chance against the vast legion of royal spies and informers the king could command.

The king threw his empty glass into the grate with a violent flick of his wrist. It shattered on the hearth with such force that slivers of glass went flying in all directions. "This Gerard Delamanse is either a traitor or a fool to be so taken in by my brother," he said, with vicious urgency. "I want him found—and stopped—before he gets to England. You will leave instantly on this mission."

Lamotte bowed his head. With all his heart, he would do his best to stop his wife from destroying herself on this foolish mission. "Yes, sire. What shall I do with the lad when I find him?"

Placated by the eagerness of his agreement, the king waved him away. "Kill him if you will, I care not," he said. "Just do not let him get to England to carry out my brother's mischief, or you will both suffer the fate the king of France has reserved for traitors and fools."

The king of France's spies were highly efficient, Lamotte had to admit as he returned to his empty apartments just as the sun was rising. They had known he had been deserted by his new wife long before he had. Sophie was indeed gone.

A cryptic message lay on the bed she should be sleeping in. "My conscience would not let me stay." She had signed it Gerard.

There was no doubt in his mind she was off to England. Even had the king not informed him of it, he would have known by her note.

After waking all night on guard, he was dead on his feet with exhaustion. He pulled off his boots and lay down on the bed in his clothes to snatch a few hours sleep before he began the chase after his errant wife.

Miriame reined in her horse and looked longingly at the roadside tavern that sent out a welcoming glow and a promise of food and rest in front of them. "We have a thousand pistoles to spend on our journey. Let's make a dent in them here, with a hot meal, a fine bottle of wine, and a soft featherbed."

Sophie was reluctant to stop, but their horses were flagging after a hard ride through the night and their riders weren't much better. "Should we not go a few miles further before we rest?" she asked, her voice lacking all conviction.

Courtney slipped off her horse and rubbed her backside with a rueful look. "A few miles further on there will be no warm inn and we'll be sleeping under a tree with empty stomachs and sour tempers. Besides, my bones ache. I need a few hours sleep so I can look forward to that fight you've been promising me."

Sophie did a few fast calculations in her head. They had made good time through the night. With a full moon and no cloud cover, there was light enough to travel quickly. Three musketeers traveling together had been more than enough to frighten off any brigands that might be lurking along the wayside. Roadside robbers would wait for easier game and richer pickings to pass them by.

She hoped the note she had left for Lamotte would throw him off the scent. With any luck he would think her conscience had smote her for living with him in such an irregular fashion, as his wife and yet not his wife. She hoped he would think she had departed to find lodgings elsewhere and would waste precious days looking for her in Paris. By the time he realized she had tricked him, she hoped to be halfway to England.

She had no fear of any other pursuit. None knew of their quest save for Philippe of Orleans, and he would keep his own counsel for fear of harming his wife. Her haste was for Henrietta, languishing in the Bastille, without thought or hope of rescue. The Princesse Henrietta was safe enough for the moment, though, and Sophie was as dog tired as her companions.

She vaulted off the back of her horse and threw the reins to a sleepy-looking postboy who was standing by the door rubbing his eyes. "Give him a good brushing and a generous measure of corn. Your best corn, too. None of last year's moldy crop, or, by God, I'll have your guts for garters, see if I don't."

Never had it felt so good to Sophie before to be off the back of a horse. Saddles, she thought with a grimace, were not well designed for riding long distances without a break.

After swallowing a hasty meal and washing it down

with a tankard of small beer apiece, the three of them flopped down on the huge bed in the only spare chamber the innkeeper could let them have.

"A short nap only," Sophie cautioned the others, as they pulled off their boots, tossed them in the corner with their swords and hats, and closed their eyes with a look of relief. "We should be on our way again before noon."

The two on either side of her were asleep in seconds, but Sophie could not rest. She could not shake off the sense someone was following her. She tossed and turned uneasily for an hour or more, desperate for rest but scared to fall asleep with such a feeling of dread hanging over her.

Finally, the comforting noises from the kitchen below and the stables outside, so different from the clatter and bang of Paris and so like the noises that reminded her of her home in the Camargue, lulled her off to sleep.

Lamotte turned his head at the sound of hoofbeats coming up behind him and dug his spurs into his horse's side to urge him on a little faster. Two riders were closing in on him, one on either side of him by the sound of it. He shook the reins, and his weary mare tried gallantly to pick up her pace for a few moments before subsiding again into a slow canter. She had no extra speed left to give him.

He put his hand on the hilt of his sword, ready for trouble if it came looking for him. Damn the pair of them. He was not afraid of taking them on alone, both of them together, but they would slow him up. If he were to catch Sophie before she slipped away out of reach, speed was essential.

The first horseman drew alongside him on one side, closely followed by the second on the other. He surreptitiously spurred his horse on again, but she could not respond. He was trapped.

He turned his head from one side to the other to see who they were. Their appearance gave few clues as to their character or purpose. He saw only that they were dark figures on plain brown horses, wrapped in brown cloaks and with plain brown boots on their feet. Their cloaks looked rough and ready and their hats were without adornment. They looked as if they had made some effort to blend into their surroundings and not be noticed. Highwaymen, most likely, keeping watch by the side of the road, and seeing a lone rider as fair game for robbery.

Strangely enough, they made no move to stop him, but rode in silence by his side for some minutes. Finally his curiosity got the better of him. "What do you want from me, gentlemen?"

The rider on his left doffed his hat. "You are Count Lamotte?" His voice was thick and guttural, his accent proving him to come from one of the rougher quarters of Paris, where a loaf of coarse rye bread was worth more than a man's life.

He misliked these strangers knowing his name, but he had nothing to hide. "I am."

"You seek one Gerard Delamanse, a traitor on his way to England?"

He misliked even more that they knew his business. "What if I do?" His voice was more curt than politeness called for.

The rider on his right gave an ugly laugh. "There's no cause for you to fear us," he said, his voice cold with cultured menace. "We don't want aught from you. We're here to assist you. We've been sent to dispatch the boy for you once you find him."

They were worse than brigands. They were hired killers, put on a horse and sent to murder his wife. He would not share his road or his mission with the pair of them. "Then you may go your own way again. I need no help."

"The king begs to differ," said the cold-voiced stranger on his right. "He repented that he had sent a musketeer to catch his fellow and thought you might not have the stomach to do the deed yourself. He sent the pair of us after you, to make sure, as it were, there was no trouble with his orders."

The man's words sent shivers down Lamotte's spine. "The king wanted the boy stopped, not murdered."

"You won't have to soil your pretty white hands, my fine gentleman," the rough-voiced man sneered. "You find him, and leave the rest to us."

He could take on the pair of them here and now, he thought, but it might not be the wisest move. If they were to overcome him with a knave's trick, Sophie would be left defenseless, not even knowing of her danger until she lay dead with their knives in her belly.

He would draw them into the open and warn Sophie of the new danger she faced. A couple of brigands should be no match for a pair of musketeers when the time came. If by some chance one of them escaped his vengeance, Sophie would at least be able to flee in greater safety, knowing the face of her enemy.

On he rode in silence, saving his horse's breath as much as he could. He may well need her speed before the day was done.

Every step he took drew him and his unwelcome companions closer to Sophie. His one consolation for the knowledge that he was putting her in danger was his determination to just as quickly snatch her out of it again.

The hired killers would be forced to taste of their own medicine before either of them so much as laid a finger on his wife.

Seven

Sophie was in the midst of a troubling dream when the clatter of hooves in the courtyard outside woke her. She sat bolt upright with a start. Miriame gave a sleepy grumble at being disturbed and Courtney tossed and turned over without waking.

Travelers like themselves, Sophie thought to herself, and nothing to worry about. Still, the sun was bright overhead and it was time for them to be leaving. Her conscience told her she had chosen the path of honor, but she still wanted to get well away from Paris and the king she had betrayed as soon as she could.

The casement window was open, letting in a welcome breeze of autumn air redolent with the rich scent of ripening apples. She lay down again, just for a moment, and breathed deeply of the fresh, country air. Ah, how good it felt to be out of the noise and stench of Paris. She had not realized how much she missed the country until she was back among the comforting familiarity of wide, open spaces, the greenness of the land around her, the lowing of cattle at pasture, and the song of the birds at dawn and dusk.

Despite her resolve to be on her way again, she was on the point of drifting back to sleep again when through the open window she heard a guttural voice rap on the door and cry out. "Open up in the name of the king."

Travelers with a purpose, she presumed. She would have to enjoy the autumn air from the back of her horse once more. She would lay a wager the king had found out about their mission and was not pleased. Whether they were looking for her or no, she was not about to stay in her chamber to be caught like a rat in a trap.

She nudged the other two awake with her elbows. "Wake up," she hissed at them. "I suspect we may have visitors."

There was a start from Courtney and another sleepy grumble from Miriame. At the sound of the second knock on the tavern door, they were both as wide awake as a watching hawk.

Sophie stood at the window as she pulled on her boots. She knew one of the horses there. It belonged to her husband. Had he betrayed her mission to the king and been sent after her to bring her back again? She did not want to think him guilty of such base treachery. "Three of them, I'd say," she whispered. "One of them must be Lamotte. The other two I don't know."

Courtney cursed under her breath as she thrust her arms into her jacket. "Three of us against three of them would be a fair enough match, if one of them was not the count and the best swordsman in Christendom. We could hold them off well enough from in here, but we will never break free of our chamber. The bastards can hole us up in here until we starve."

Miriame poked her nose out of the casement in time to catch a glimpse of one of them. She paled. "I mislike the company your husband keeps," she said to Sophie.

Sophie did not like Miriame's tone. "How so?"

"I know one of them of old. A sneak thief and bully from way back, turned informer and assassin for whoever will hire his arm. He likes the taste of blood better than the best Burgundian wine. Whoever has sent him after us means for us not to return."

"I shall take all three of them on in a fair fight," Courtney offered. "I'll hold the door so the pair of you can escape and make your way to England."

Sophie did not like the thought of leaving her friend in such danger, but the mission should not be jeopardized. Whatever Miriame said about his companions, she could not believe that Lamotte wished her and her companions evil. Courtney would be safe enough could she but hole herself up in the chamber until they tired of beating on the door. "But how shall we get out without them seeing us?"

Miriame spoke up with unusual determination. "That one I spoke of won't fight fair, you can be sure of that. He means to kill us all. Besides," she added, with an evil glint in her eye, "I have an old score to settle with him. I shall take him on, gutter rat to gutter rat, and may the smartest one win."

Courtney started to protest, but Miriame hushed her. "This is my fight. I shall not let you say me nay." She gestured to the high-set window. "Climb out there, the pair of you. I'll keep them busy for as long as I can. Our horses are rested and theirs blown, so they will be hard put to it to catch you again, once you get away."

Sophie looked down from the window, feeling sick to her stomach. The casement was not impossibly high, but to jump might well mean a broken ankle, which would spell disaster for her mission. A guttering ran around the edge of the roof, though. If she were to hang on to that and swing herself over to the roof of the stables, she might just make it.

"Follow me," she said to Courtney. "If I am hurt or taken, grab the nearest horse and ride for your life to England. Lamotte will see I do not come to any harm." She wished she could be as sure of that in her heart as her words made her seem to be.

Courtney nodded in understanding. "And you must do the same for me."

With one leg over the windowsill, Sophie turned back to Miriame, whose face was aglow with mischief. "Be careful of yourself. Keep the door locked and do not open it to them on any pretext. You shall be safe enough with the door locked. They cannot come at you then."

She looked down from the window, and then turned back again. "If it should come to a fight, do not hurt the count," she begged. Whether Lamotte had betrayed her or no, she could not bear have him hurt. He was her husband, after all, and her brother had loved him well. "He has suffered enough on my account already."

Miriame nodded. "I will delay him if I can, but I will take care not hurt him unless I cannot help it. My quarrel is with his companion."

Sophie had to be content with that. "Until we meet again in Paris."

Courtney jammed her hat down over her ears. *"Au revoir,* Madame thief. Until Paris."

Miriame grinned at the solemn farewell. "Don't worry about me. I'll come to no harm with the thought of all those golden pistoles waiting for me."

The way below was clear. Sophie swallowed hard as she looked down, summoning all her courage to make the leap. A bang on the chamber door behind her gave her the impetus she needed. She crossed herself hurriedly and swung out before she lost the moment, climbing hand over hand along the guttering. The roof creaked and groaned under her weight, but it did not break. Behind her she heard banging and cursing, but she didn't dare look back for fear of losing her grip and falling to the ground.

The guttering seemed endless, but at last, with a soft thud, she let go and landed on the gently pitched roof of the stables. She grabbed for a handhold, but her hands clutched at the empty air. Flailing wildly, she rolled off the roof, landing in a heap in the mud in the doorway. At least the mud was soft enough. She rose to her feet a trifle unsteadily and dusted herself down. Nothing seemed to be broken. So far, so good.

Courtney, following behind her, had better luck. She leaped down lightly and had the stable door open before Sophie had picked herself up off the ground.

There was no time to resaddle their mounts. Sophie grabbed her bridle and threw it over Seafoam's neck before leaping on bareback and tossing a couple of saddlebags in front of her. Courtney, her face pinched and white, did the same.

With a clatter of hooves on the stones of the courtyard, the pair of them rode out of the courtyard and onto the road to Calais—and England.

Lamotte pulled up his horse at the inn by the road. It was the first one he had seen for miles. He would lay a bet Sophie had stopped there to rest. She was no different from other women in that she liked a warm featherbed better than a cold piece of ground under a tree any day.

He signaled to the stable boy, who was lazily shoveling mucky straw out into the roadside. "Hey, boy. Have you had any strangers pass through your tavern this morning?"

The boy scratched his head. "We've got three fine horses in the stables. One of the soldiers told me to feed 'em good corn or he'd wrap my guts around the point of his sword, so I gave 'em the best I had."

"Three soldiers?"

"Aye. Fine soldiers dressed just like you."

The hired ruffians muttered together uneasily at this piece of news. "No one told me there was three of them," the rough-voiced one grumbled. "I thought we was just to deal to the boy and be home again in time for supper."

"Afraid, are you?" the cultured voice sneered.

"I ain't afraid of no man," the first man said belligerently, his hand closing threateningly on the hilt of his dagger. "Fair's fair is all, and I ain't been paid to deal to three."

His companion drew his dagger, shut one eye, and squinted critically at the edge of the blade with the other as he tested its sharpness with the ball of his thumb. "Shut your mouth and deal with the boy as you've been paid to do, and leave the others to better men than you."

Lamotte watched their squabbling with only half his attention. His wife had evidently obtained reinforcements from her fellow musketeers. All the more reason for him to stop her from carrying out this mad mission. Surely she could not hope to keep her sex hidden from the others in her party on such a long journey. Were they ever to find out she was a woman, he hated to think what her fate would be.

Whatever the reasons for which they had wed, she was his wife now and she owed him more duty than to go gallivanting around the countryside with two of her comrades. When he had hauled her back to Paris, he would renegotiate the terms of their deal and insist she be a proper wife to him. He could not live with such a runaway wife as she had proven to be.

The gruff-voiced killer turned his back on his companion and strode up to the door and bashed on it with his fist. "Open up in the name of the king."

The other man sneered as the landlord opened the door, his face looking like a frightened rabbit's. "So much for taking our quarry unawares, you fool."

Lamotte stepped up, shoving the others aside with little ceremony. "We are looking for a musketeer by the name of Gerard Delamanse. Have you seen him?"

The landlord nodded, his face clearing with relief that they were not looking for him. "Yes, sir. Three of them stopped by early this morning for a meal and a bed. I'm sure I heard one of them call the other Gerard, if I'm not mistaken, sir. I gave them a good meal, too, sir. Roasted rabbit and a good haunch of beef. Would you care to try some yourselves, sirs?"

The sneering killer fixed the landlord with a cold eye. "Where is the boy now?"

The landlord shuddered and made the sign of the cross. "Upstairs in his chamber."

"Show me."

The landlord led the way up the stairs and pointed to a door at the top. "That is their chamber, if it please you, sir."

The gruff-voiced killer shouldered the landlord aside and banged on the door. "Open up in there."

There was the sound of a scuffle inside and then a voice came through the door. "Who might you be that I should open my door for you?"

It was not Sophie who spoke, but the voice of a

man. Lamotte saw red to think of his wife closeted in a bedchamber with another soldier. "It doesn't matter who I am. Open the door, or I'll break you into pieces," he growled.

The man on the other side of the door laughed. "Temper, temper. Surely you gentlemen will not mind waiting until I put on my boots."

Lamotte waited, his soul bursting with impatience for what seemed long enough for someone to put on their boots five times over.

"Ah, that's better," the voice on the other side of the door finally said, stomping around the room in noisy satisfaction. "Now just let me put on my jacket."

The gruff-faced man banged furiously on the door. "Open up in the name of the king, you fool."

"You *do* like saying that, don't you? Does it make you feel big and important? I suppose a gutter rat like you must needs have something to make him feel his life has meaning. Still, I'm afraid you'll have to wait until I have attended to my hair before I let you in. A gentleman must never been seen, even by gutter rats, without his hair dressed."

The gruff-voiced man growled with fury at being insulted and drew out his dagger. "I shall kill you for that, you little weasel."

"You'll have to wait just a moment longer, I'm afraid, for the killing to start. Just let me button up my breeches, and I shall be right with you."

This last was too much for Lamotte. He rushed at the door, intending to batter it down and plant his fist straight into the face of the man who mocked him so.

The key turned in the lock, and a pretty-faced youth with dark curls tied up at his neck and a wicked-looking knife in his hand opened the door just as he reached it. Driven on by the force of his rage, he fell through it all in a heap. The gruff-faced man, swearing and cursing behind him, tripped over him and they fell on the floor together.

A dull thud marked the arrival of the third of their party.

Lamotte scrambled to his feet to see the door closing behind him and the sound of the key being turned in the lock from the outside. He knew the man who had caught them so neatly like rats in a trap. He would swear he had seen that face somewhere before.

Still, he had no time to worry about the identity of the stranger. The instant the door was locked behind him, his attention was grabbed by the bloody, violent death that lay before him.

On the floor in a rapidly widening pool of blood lay the sneering hired killer with the cultured voice, his sightless eyes staring at the ceiling, his bare, white throat slit from ear to ear.

They were caught in the most obvious of traps. Had he kept a cool head, he would have seen right through it. He had allowed the youth to rile him into forgetting all caution, and now one of his companions was dead. He was not sorry for the death, only for the manner of it. No man deserved to die like that. He hammered at the door in a fury. "Let me out."

"Can you not make up your mind?" came a taunting voice from the corridor. "When you were outside you begged to be let in. Now that you are in, you beg to be let out. I have no more time to play silly games with you."

The gruff-voiced man was shaking as he looked down at the body of his comrade. "Let me out, by God, or I will slit your throat as you have slit Andre's."

"I rather think *I* will do all the slitting of throats that is called for around here. I hope you were not over fond of your companion. He has received only what he has deserved for years.

"*Au revoir*, Monsieur le Comte," the youth continued. "And may I say that your wife is an exceptionally pleasant woman to share a chamber with. What a pity you came by too late to find all three of us abed together."

By all that is holy, what has he done to Sophie? Lamotte gave another roar of rage and shook the door until the hinges rattled. "I will kill you for that."

"You will have to find me first." The youth gave a merry giggle and clattered off down the stairs. "I doubt you will find it easy."

The large oaken door was stronger than it looked, and the heavy iron bolts held it together strongly. It took the best part of an hour before the two of them managed to break open the door.

"Ah," the landlord said with a jovial grin as Lamotte stomped down the stairs. "You have won the wager, I see."

He looked blankly at the landlord's smile. "The wager?"

"The wager you made with the merry young gentleman that you would be able to get out of the locked chamber within the hour. The hourglass I set has not yet run out. You'll find him in the stables seeing to his horse, if you want to collect your winnings."

Lamotte clenched his fists in frustration. There would be no point in chewing off the landlord's ears for not unlocking the door. He had been outfoxed well and truly. He turned toward the stables. First he would find Sophie and drag her home with him, and then he would deal to the youth who had so abused him.

The landlord stayed him with an outstretched hand. "My money for the door?"

"Your money?"

"Your young friend promised whoever won the wager would pay double the cost of a new door from his winnings."

Rigid with fury, he grabbed a handful of gold pistoles from his pocket and tossed them in the man's general direction. He had been utterly outwitted, and his defeat did not sit lightly on his shoulders.

The landlord protested his generosity. "This is far more than double what the door is worth."

"Keep them," Lamotte said, his face taut with rage. "Thanks to that young rascal and his quick knife, there's a corpse in the chamber overhead that needs burying. Use it to bribe the surgeon to swear he died in his sleep."

He threw a saddle on the best post horse in the stable. Sophie had at least an hour's start on him again. He would ride without stopping, changing horses as often as he could, until he caught up with her. He would not be tricked again.

Sophie turned her head to watch Courtney struggling up behind her, slipping and sliding on the back of her mare. She tried to stifle her impatience and not let it show in her manner that she was ready to scream with frustration at the slowness of their progress. Courtney could not help she never ridden bareback before and was finding it hard to keep upright.

Courtney was gripping her horse's mane with a death grip. "Go on ahead," she called as soon as Sophie was within earshot. "I am holding you back. You will be able to travel much faster alone."

"All for one and one for all," Sophie reminded her. "Two of us are stronger than one alone."

Courtney nodded with relief. Then the look on her face turned to dismay as, for the second time already that afternoon, she slid slowly off the back of her horse and onto the grassy bank by the side of the road.

She sat up with a groan, rubbing her backside. "Ouch. I cannot get the hang of riding those damned slippery beasts without a saddle."

Sophie wanted to laugh at the look on Courtney's face, but she resisted the temptation. "Hold on with your thighs and calves, not with your hands."

Courtney grunted as she heaved herself on to her mare's back for a third time. "I was trying to."

They rode on in silence for some time, until the light began to fail. Sophie cast a worried eye at the sky. They had not ridden as swiftly or gone as far as she would have liked. "We cannot afford to stop just yet. We'll ride on until we can swap our horses for fresh." How she hoped, and yet did not hope, that Lamotte was not far behind her.

Miriame will surely not have hurt him, she thought for the thousandth time that afternoon. *Not when she knows I did not want him harmed.* How she wished she had stayed behind to make sure no evil had befallen him. Her mission was important to her, but not as important as the lives of her husband and of her friend. She would disobey his orders and run from him to do her duty, but not even her conscience could make her harm him in earnest once more.

The air was starting to cool down noticeably. Courtney let go of her horse's mane for long enough to take her hat off and shake her hair down over her shoulders. "Anything you say, as long as they come with saddles."

Sophie liked the feeling of riding bareback with nothing to come in the way of her and the raw power of the horse between her legs, but even she was feeling the chafing on her thighs by now. "With saddles," she agreed.

Dusk was falling in earnest when they heard the hoofbeats behind them. In a few moments, they caught sight of their pursuers, riding hard toward them. Sophie felt her heart leap up into her chest with fear. Where there had been three before, now there were only two.

Courtney's face was set in a mask of determination. She nudged her horse into a trot. "Shall we try to outrun them?"

Sophie narrowed her eyes to see into the distance behind her. The gap between them and those who rode after them was closing slowly, but it was closing nonetheless. "We cannot outrun them all the way to England." She could not run before making sure Lamotte was one of the two. Besides, Courtney might well fall off again, and they would lose any advantage they had gained. "There's no point in making a race of it when we have little chance of winning."

She looked behind her once more. The foremost rider was Lamotte, she was sure of it. He was riding easily, with no sign of any wound. She felt a huge weight lift from her shoulders. Miriame had been true to her word and fought only the battle she had felt due her.

They were approaching a narrow part of road, where it wove a crooked path between a copse of trees. Their pursuers were so close now Sophie could see Lamotte's face clearly. His face was frozen in a look of fierce determination that made her quake in her boots. Never had she seen her husband look so wild.

Courtney pulled her horse to a standstill just before the path disappeared into the trees. "Ride as fast as your horse can carry you. I can hold the two of them off here for long enough to get you well away."

Sophie shook her head. "I will not leave you behind."

Courtney grinned. "Don't be daft. I cannot ride on this damned beast any longer. I will never make it all the way to Calais. With me alongside you, you will be caught for sure. Without me, you stand a chance of getting there. The least I can do for you is hold them off for long enough to get you safe away."

Lamotte wanted to shout with rage as he saw the hindmost rider stop in the narrowest part of the path and wheel about, sword raised in the air, as Sophie put her heels to her horse's flanks and urged her mount away into the gloom of the forest. He would have to fight his way through yet another of his wife's minions before he could reach her.

He spurred his horse on faster. God willing, he would dispatch this one in haste and catch his wife before she got into further trouble.

He yelled a battle cry, waved his sword around his head and pulled back tightly on the reins to make his horse rear up, her forelegs flailing in the air.

His opponent's horse, spooked by his noise and the motion of his sword, reared up as well. The musketeer on its back grabbed for its mane with his free hand and held on for dear life. With only one hand to hold on, he could not keep his grip. He slid unceremoniously off over its rump and landed with a thud on the ground, a look of utter consternation on his face.

Lamotte heard a thump as the hired thug behind him slid off his horse as well, intending no doubt to make short work of the fallen soldier. He wheeled around to protect him. He had no use for murder. If this musketeer deserved to die for debauching his wife, then die he would, but in a fair fight, and knowing what he died for.

The musketeer lay on his back on the ground, winded from his fall. Lamotte cantered up to his prone body and slipped off his horse just as the gruff-voiced assassin drew a wicked-looking knife from his belt and leaned over him with an attitude of menace.

"By God, it's woman, not a soldier at all." The face of the gruff-voiced assassin broke into an ugly leer. He ripped the musketeer's shirt open with the point of his knife and pawed at her breasts with greedy fingers. "I knew it," he crowed with evil delight. "What a piece of luck, huh? We can have a bit of fun with her before I stick her with my pretty little knife."

With his free hand, the killer fumbled with the lacings of his breeches, but they were knotted, and he could not get them free.

Lamotte saw a film of red appear before his eyes. His wife was a soldier, too. It could just as well be his wife that the killer was proposing to rape and then murder. "Let her go."

The hired assassin looked up at him in puzzlement. "Let her what? Have you gone mad? I'm just going to have a bit of fun with her. It won't take long, and then you can have your turn, too, afore I kill her nice and slow, like. We'll catch up with the other one later."

Lamotte's dagger was in his hand, trembling with the will to leap out and strike of its own accord. "I said, let her go, or I shall . . ."

He never got the chance to finish his threat. With a lethal swish, a feathered bolt came hurtling out of the woods to one side, hurtling past him mere inches from his chest, and burying itself deep in the killer's throat.

The killer's eyes grew wide and he gave just the

beginning of a strangled cry before it was cut off with a choke. Clawing uselessly at the bolt with desperate fingers, he fell to one side with a gurgle, the bright red blood spurting out of him in a ghoulish fountain. His body twitched and then lay still.

Lamotte looked around in the direction from which the arrow had come. He saw nothing stirring in the trees, but it had to have come from Sophie. She had mentioned once what a crack shot she was with a bow and arrow. He put his hand on his chest in a protective gesture. He owed his life to the fact she had not been making an idle boast.

The musketeer on the ground pushed the bleeding body off her with a shudder and got shakily to her feet, her face as white as milk and her left arm dangling uselessly at her side. She looked at the dagger in Lamotte's hand. "Ach, don't make me fight you, too," she said, her shoulders slumped and her voice weary. "I'm stiff as a board from falling off that damned horse all afternoon and I'd rather have a soak in a hot tub than a fight. Besides, it wouldn't be worth it. Sophie made me promise not to hurt you anyway."

Lamotte dropped his dagger arm. It seemed Sophie was not the only Amazon in France. Here was another, a regal blond beauty, for all that her face was smudged and her shirt torn and one of her hands hung limply from a broken wrist. "You're a woman. I do not need to kill you after all."

There was a crashing behind them in the bushes to the side of the path. He turned around and held out his hands as Sophie, his errant Sophie, appeared, a short bow in her hands and a look that mingled horror and relief in equal parts on her face.

* * *

Sophie peered through the leaves and took the most careful aim she had ever made with her bow. She forced her hands to stop shaking so her aim would be true. The only sounds she could hear were the pounding of her heart and the harsh rasp of her breath as she forced the air in and out of her chest. This was one time she could not afford to miss.

"Do not move," she whispered to herself, her eyes glued to her intended victim, willing him to stay steady with the force of her thoughts. Her eyes fixed on her target, she loosed her arrow with a twang. It flew through the air almost faster than her eye could follow it, and buried itself exactly where she had aimed.

People were harder to shoot than ducks, she thought, her arms wobbling with relief. Just a few inches off target and she would have buried the arrow in Lamotte's chest. She bowed her head for a moment, giving thanks to the Lord that he had guided her arrow swiftly and surely to its intended mark.

Her heart still pounding with the aftereffects of her fear, she ran to her husband, ignoring the hands he held out to her, and flung herself into his arms instead. "I didn't miss. I didn't miss," she babbled as she hugged him tightly to her. She looked at the corpse on the ground over his shoulder. She had killed a man.

Her stomach heaved at the sight of so much blood. She stepped back out of Lamotte's embrace and was promptly sick all over his boots. "I killed him."

"You saved me the trouble." Courtney and Lamotte both spoke at once, then grinned at each other.

Courtney handed her a flask of water and a clean handkerchief. "I wouldn't shed any tears over that beast. He was a vile worm, like all of his kind. He deserved to die."

Sophie rinsed her mouth out with the brackish water and spat it on to the ground. "Eugh," she said with feeling as she wiped her mouth and tossed the handkerchief onto the ground. Thank the Lord she had slipped off her horse and doubled back through the woods to help her friend. She looked searchingly into Courtney's face as she handed back the flask of water. "Are you all right?"

Courtney rubbed her buttocks a trifle gingerly with her good hand. "I'm not getting on any damned horse bareback again for as long as I live."

Sophie gasped as her friend held out a wrist that flopped at an unnatural angle.

"I don't know which pains me more—a broken wrist or a pair of very sore buttocks."

"I got the bastard who would've raped you," Sophie said, with grim satisfaction, now that her stomach had stopped heaving. "I'd rather shoot a villain like him than a brace of ducks any day." Still, she avoided looking at the body again. Knowing he deserved to die did not take away the horror of his death.

Courtney looked sideways at Lamotte. "You should have ridden off," she said to Sophie. "They never would have caught you."

Sophie was too relieved at Courtney's rescue to care she herself was caught. "I would not leave you to fight the pair of them alone. We are sisters, remember?"

Lamotte wrapped his arms around her from behind. "You are my wife. I will never fight you again, however much you provoke me."

Sophie sighed at his words even as she took comfort from the feeling of his arms wrapped around her body. "Can you please give that wife stuff a rest for now? Courtney needs a doctor to set her arm."

The three of them rode in silence back along the

path they had just come. Courtney perched on the pommel of Lamotte's saddle, in too much pain from the break in her arm to manage on her own. Lamotte guided his mare with one hand, while with the other he held her tightly against his chest.

Sophie felt a gnawing sensation in the pit of her belly at the sight of his arm wrapped around Courtney's middle. She knew he did it merely to keep her upright on the horse and to stop her from falling if she fainted with the pain, but she couldn't help wishing she was the one he was cradling in his arms. She wanted to be the one he held on to, his strong hand around her waist to clasp her closely to him. She wanted to be the one to whom he bent his head to whisper in her ear. She wanted to feel the touch of his body pressing against hers.

She had a moment of secret gladness that Courtney was in too much pain to enjoy her position, then chided herself for her mean spirit. She would spend no energy harboring jealous thoughts of her friend, or waste her spirit in delighting at her friend's misfortunes.

She had troubles enough of her own to deal with. Her husband had caught up with her and would no doubt try to drag her back to Paris by the ears as he had threatened. Once Courtney was safely settled, she would have to find some way of evading his guard and continuing on her quest to save Henrietta from the clutches of the Bastille.

She turned her head to look at Lamotte, and was absurdly gratified to see he was watching her, rather than looking at the woman he carried in his arms. *He is probably thinking only how he can keep hold of me now he has caught me,* she thought with a grimace, but it still made her happy. She caught his eye and smiled at him.

He looked startled for a moment, then smiled back. His smile softened the harsh angles of his face and eased the frown from his forehead. She felt as though she could go on looking at him forever.

Courtney's accusing voice suddenly broke the comfortable silence. "Why were you riding with such a scoundrel? Did you not care what manner of man he was?"

Lamotte gave a snort of disgust. "I was not so much riding with him as he was riding with me. We were both after my delightful wife—on the king's orders. I was to stop her from completing her mission to England, and he and his erstwhile companion were to kill her once I had caught her."

Sophie gasped, the smile well and truly wiped from her face with shock. "The king wants me dead?"

Suddenly her mission to England took on a new and desperate gravity. This was no mere adventure now to win her brother honor. It had well and truly ceased to be a game of outwitting her husband in the race for England and become a matter of life and death. Lamotte was in deadly earnest. Her life, along with Henrietta's, was at stake.

"So it would seem. He certainly sent a pair of thugs out to do the deed. He feared I lacked the stomach for it, so I believe."

The king of France, the fount of all honor, had sent a pair of desperadoes, killers of the night, to murder her? She never would have believed it. Philippe of Orleans was right—his brother was a monster who had to be stopped.

The king would murder her, who sought only to save a woman who had refused him? What worse deed would he do to Henrietta herself? She shuddered to think.

"A pair of thugs? What happened to the other one? Where is he now?"

Lamotte grunted. "Dead. Your companion took care of that with a slash of his knife from ear to ear."

Miriame. Sophie gave a sudden gasp. In the furor and sickness of killing a man, she had forgot about Miriame. "And he is unharmed?"

Lamotte's face was black and thunderous. "Why should you care? He is a scoundrel who deserves to be hanged from the yardarm."

Sophie would not bow before his anger. He was her husband, not her keeper. She knew not how Miriame had managed to make an enemy of her husband. His quarrels did not concern her. "I care greatly, as it happens."

"As do I," Courtney chimed in.

Lamotte glared down at her. "He is unhurt—as yet. Until I find him again, that is."

"So what are you going to do with us now?" Courtney asked wearily from her perch on the pommel of the saddle. "I doubt we can count on your manly honor to protect us. If you are going to dispose of us as your king intended, why not do it right here and save me the bother of riding any further? There's no point in getting my arm set if you intend to kill me a moment later."

Lamotte's face was set as if in stone. "The king may order me as he wishes, but I have honor enough not to harm either of you. I am a musketeer. I do not make war on women."

Sophie felt the heat of his gaze as he glared at her.

"Much as they might deserve it," he added under his breath, looking straight at her still.

She looked him straight in the eye. "I have done nothing but what my conscience demanded of me. I shall live in honor, or I shall not live."

He harrumphed at her, and they continued again through the fading light in silence.

Lamotte was relieved when they came to signs of habitation, a village big enough to boast at least a wise woman skilled in herbs, if not an apothecary. He directed his step to the wise woman's cottage, which lay on the outskirts of the hamlet, separated from the other shabby dwellings by several large fields.

He would prefer a barber surgeon at least, but beggars could not be choosers. The night was becoming dark and cloudy, his mare was tired to the bone, and the woman in his arms felt like a deadweight. His one concern was to get her off his horse before she fell off in a faint.

He and Sophie stood to one side while the wise woman poked and prodded at Courtney's arm, pronounced it a clean break, and proceeded to strap it to a board so it would heal straight and she would not pain herself by moving it.

Courtney acquiesced in the treatment with good grace for a woman, he supposed. At least she did not scream or cry out, but bit her lip until it bled. "You'll have to rest here for a bit, dearie," the woman said when she had done. "That arm of yours needs a good rest to let it heal. It will feel as weak as a newborn kitten when I unstrap it again in a few weeks, but with the grace of God, it will heal up and be as good as new."

Courtney made a face through her pain. "A month in this village with naught to wear but breeches?

Ugh—I wish I had broken my neck, not just my wrist. Or at least I wish I had not left my gowns in Paris."

The wise woman clucked her tongue. "Just a few days rest here, dearie, and you'll be up and about again as good as new. But there'll be no riding for you for a month or more."

Lamotte barely heard the words of the wise woman. His mind was ticking over at a furious rate. Gowns. In Paris. That was where he had seen her before—in a yellow gown at Sophie's side when they had joined hands in wedlock at the door of the church.

And the dark-haired youth at the tavern—now he remembered where he had seen her before, too. She was the second of Sophie's attendants and had worn a red dress with a bodice cut low enough that her womanhood could never be in doubt.

A woman. Of course. That explained her trickery and devious nature, and the way she had so outfoxed him. The devil take him if ever a man could match a woman for cunning tricks.

He shook his head in disbelief. "By God, there are three of you."

The youth at the tavern who had shared a chamber with Sophie was a woman. He should have guessed as much. She was simply taunting him for the love of it and to make him so blind with anger that he lost his cool head in a white-hot rage. He should have trusted Sophie's honor without question. He knew how much it meant to her.

Out of the corner of his eye he saw Sophie and her friend exchange a worried glance in the smoky yellow light of the rush tapers dotted sparsely around the tiny cottage.

"Three of us?" Sophie asked, her brow furrowed.

"Whatever are you talking about?" Courtney added with an air of nonchalance.

He grinned. Their false puzzlement could not fool him any longer. "Your comrade is a troublesome minx, but I am glad I shall not have to kill her after all."

Night had fallen in earnest while Courtney's arm was being set. Sophie looked as though she were about to collapse with exhaustion, and he felt little better. Whatever they were going to do, it would have to wait until the morn.

The wise woman made up a straw pallet for her patient on the floor of her cottage for the night, but there was no room for Sophie or him. Neither was there any barn or shelter from the elements close by. They would have to sleep out under the stars for the night.

He shouldered his bedroll and followed Sophie outside to the shelter of a pine tree, whose widespread branches and thick covering of needles would give them some protection from the night dew.

Without a murmur of complaint, Sophie lay down on the carpet of needles at the base of the tree to sleep, with naught but her clothes to cover her.

He shook his head at her staunchness, unrolled his blanket and spread it next to her. "Come and share my blanket. You'll freeze else."

She shook her head in the darkness, contrary to the last. "I have suffered worse."

He lay down on his blanket and drew her into his arms, their bodies sharing their warmth, the one blanket providing a covering for them both against the damp night air. Her body was stiff against his, but she did not protest.

He held her close as she gradually relaxed into the warmth of his chest. He liked her when she was like this, soft and pliant in his arms as a woman should be. "So now what, escaping wife of mine? Now that I have caught you, whatever shall I do with you?"

He felt her body turn rigid in his arms once more. "I go to England in the morning."

He tweaked one of her ears between his thumb and forefinger, wanting her to melt against him once more. He was almost sorry he had brought the topic up, but the air between them had to be cleared. He did not want to wake in the morning and find his arms empty and know she had fled from him again. "You deserve to be punished, wench. Have you forgotten I promised to drag you back to Paris by your ears did I ever catch you?"

"I will not come with you willingly."

He teased the soft back of her neck, winding her hair around his finger into curls and letting it go again. Her hair was as soft and sleek as the fur of a wildcat. "I did not think you would. Besides, I doubt you should return to Paris right now. The king is incensed against you. You would not live for long were you to return."

He felt her shudder in his arms. "Those men, they meant to kill me?"

He stroked her hair until she calmed down again and her tremors stopped. "They did, but I had no intention of letting them do so. You are my wife. I will always protect you."

"You would have saved Courtney, too, if I had not shot him first."

He thought of his blind rage when the villain had threatened the woman as she lay helpless on the ground. If Sophie's arrow hadn't separated the villain's soul from his body, his dagger would have done so in the next instant. "How could you doubt it? I would not see any woman brutalized by such a thug if I could prevent it."

"Even if she turned out to be a mere tavern wench?" she inquired, a little sharply.

He smacked the side of her rump with the flat of his hand. "None of your cheek, wife, or you will regret it."

She was silent for so long he thought she had fallen asleep. "I was so afeared I would miss him and shoot you instead." Her voice was small and soft and it trembled a little.

He hugged her close to him for comfort, warming her with his presence, his arms crossed over her chest. "You did not miss." He was feeling very much alive—more alive in certain parts of him than was quite comfortable. He shifted a little so his arousal did not press so obviously into her backside.

"I might have killed you by mistake."

He did not want her to dwell on the ifs and maybes of life. He was still here, and that was the important thing. He nudged her in the ribs with his elbow. "You would have been sorry to be made a widow then, my troublesome wife, who married me only so she could continue fighting with impunity?"

He felt her shake with suppressed laughter. "I suppose it would be one way of being rid of my troublesome husband who married me only for the sake of his duty, but it is not the way I would choose."

"I'm almost afraid to ask what way you would choose."

She shook her head and did not answer.

He hoped her silence boded well for his longevity. "The king may well have set more men on your tail," he said, after a short pause in which he tried unsuccessfully not to think about tumbling his virgin wife on the bed of pine needles on which they lay. "I cannot take you back to Paris."

"No, you cannot take me back to Paris. I will go to England when day breaks."

He considered his options aloud. "You would be safe enough in Burgundy. I doubt the king would feel secure enough to pursue you into the territory of the Duke of Burgundy." That assumed he would be able to get her and keep her there, of course, which was another matter altogether. Tying her to his bed appealed to him at the moment—with nice strong leather thongs she could not break away from, however much he teased and tormented her. And tease and torment her he would, until she cried out with pleasure again and again . . .

She squirmed in his grasp, trying to pull away from him as if she could read his licentious thoughts about her, but he held her tight. "I will go to England and ask King Charles to save his sister Henrietta, as Philippe of Orleans begged me to do. I will not go to Burgundy."

He was trying to concentrate on his thoughts rather than on the feeling of her backside wriggling against his aching groin. "I could tie your hands and feet and toss you across the back of my horse and take you to Burgundy that way."

"You cannot keep me tied up forever. One day I will escape, and then you will be sorry."

God, but he could keep her tied up for his pleasure for days and not be satisfied. He was unbelievably aroused by the little spitfire he held in his arms. She was soft and sweet on the outside, but with a core of steel that kept her together through the toughest of times. He had to admire her courage—it was beyond that of any other woman he had ever met—and thank the Lord as well for her steady hand with a bow.

If he did not want to spend the rest of his life chasing her from one end of Europe to the other, he would have to bend to her will once again. "I cannot let you go to England by yourself."

"There is no help for it now. Miriame was left behind at the first inn and Courtney will not be fit to ride for days. My message cannot wait that long."

Aha, so the third musketeer was called Miriame. A strange name, but one that suited her puckish nature. "I suppose I have no choice. I will have to go with you."

"But the king sent you to stop me."

The king did not know Sophie. He might as well have sent him to stop the wind. "No, the king sent me to kill you, and he may well have sent others besides the two who fell in with me. I will not take that risk with your life by leaving you unprotected for such a long journey."

"Why are you so concerned? You married me only for the sake of your word to my brother. Why should you care what happens to me?"

He could not dispute the truth of her words. He had only married her to keep his word, but since their wedding day he had come to respect her and like her for all that she was—loyal and strong and honorable to a fault. Besides, she was an eminently desirable woman, for all her contrariness.

He inched one hand under the edge of her jerkin, surreptitiously caressing her bound breasts through the fabric of her shirt. God, how he desired to strip all her layers of clothing away and clasp her naked breasts in his hands. One day he would make her melt for him, he promised himself. One day soon. "You are my wife. I owe you my protection."

She sighed as she settled down to sleep in his arms. "You may be my husband, but you owe me nothing. When will you ever learn that?"

He brushed her hair away from her face and kissed her lightly on the cheek. "Good night, Sophie," he whispered.

The pine needles rustled under her as she buried her head in her arms. "Good night, Monsieur le Comte."

The morning came too soon for Sophie's liking, bringing with it a nasty measure of wind and driving rain. She wrapped herself as well as she could in her greatcoat as she sat astride her horse, the rain dripping down inside the neck of her collar, making her back cold and clammy.

What with Courtney's horse she could no longer ride, and the horse of the dead assassin, they had four horses now between them, and two saddles. With double the number of mounts, they could make better time and not have to stop to haggle over a new pair of broken down, skinny-looking post horses at each stage. Their own four beasts were sleek and well-fed and made good time.

Despite her exhaustion, she had not had the most restful night. Sleeping in her husband's arms was torture. The warmth of his body close to hers and the touch of his hand holding her to him made her body burn with heat. His innocent touch of her breasts as they were settling down to sleep had almost undone her. How she had longed to turn over and kiss him wildly, passionately on the mouth as they lay together in their nest of pine needles under the tree.

No doubt he would have been horrified if she had done so. He had only married her for duty's sake, not because he desired her the way a man desired a woman. How she wished she possessed Courtney's slender, blond beauty, or Miriame's exotic dark hair and sloe eyes. If she was beautiful in his eyes, surely he would not be so cold to her.

He had threatened to seduce her into his bed once they were married. How she had longed last night for him to make good on his threat. Then she would not have been left this morning feeling hollow and empty, with a void only he could fill in her.

Her night had been passed in restless dreams and wild fantasies of her husband discovering just how beautiful he thought her. She had dreamed of him lying over her, parting her legs with a gentle hand and touching her softly between her thighs, driving her on to heights of passion she had not thought possible, making her restless and striving to reach a goal that remained forever out of reach. She regretted her inability to command her emotions now, as lack of sleep had dulled her wits and made her head ache.

Lamotte seemed as distracted as she was, too. He rode in silence, interrupting it only to bark out a terse command once in a while. She looked sideways at his stern face. How she hoped he was not regretting his decision to accompany her to England, or, worse still, plotting to abscond with her to his manor house in Burgundy as soon as might be.

She shook her head at her silly fears. She trusted her husband and his promise to help her. She should have been more pleased at their rate of progress, too, but all she could think of as she rode along was of how she could get close to Lamotte and force him to think of her as a woman, not just as an unfortunate duty he was saddled with.

How foolish she was. She was the one who had insisted on a platonic marriage, and he had accepted it only begrudgingly. He had been true to his word and had not attempted to force her. How she wished now she had never made such a devil's bargain.

She had not thought the touch of his hands on her body would rouse passions she never thought could exist. She had not thought her longing for him would surpass every other want or need of hers until she could think of nothing else. She had not thought she would give up even her quest for honor just for the sake of a kiss from his lips.

They stopped briefly under a tree at noon to eat a hunk of bread and cheese from their saddlebags. The drizzle in the air made Sophie shiver. She cut their pause as short as she could, wanting only to find a warm, dry place to stay and sleep.

It was getting on toward late afternoon by the time the road took them through several villages. Sophie looked longingly at the warm, dry taverns they rode by. She set her mouth in a line and passed them by without a murmur, though she was beginning to droop with wet and weariness. Henrietta, she reminded herself, as she was on the verge of begging Lamotte to stop for the night, was in a far worse place than she. How could she let a little bit of drizzle delay her, when Henrietta was immured in the cold, dank dungeons of the Bastille, slowly being driven mad by fear and deprivation?

Just as the last rays of the sun disappeared below the horizon, they came to another roadside inn. Miserable through and through, this time Sophie spoke up. "Can we not stop here?"

Lamotte wheeled his horse in without a word and headed for the welcoming light.

Sophie felt the need to explain. "It will soon be too dark to see where we are going, and it is raining too hard to sleep on the ground."

He slid off his horse and handed the reins of his mount and the horse he was leading to the post boy, who scurried out into the rain to take care of them. "I don't need any convincing to stop. I was disappointed you did not call a halt at either of the last two places we passed."

Maybe his face was drawn with weariness rather than with annoyance, Sophie thought with a flicker of hope. Maybe he had slept as badly as she had. "Why did you not stop, if you were weary?"

He gave a faint grin. "And have you accuse me of trying to sabotage your mission?" He shook his head. "I am not that brave a man."

Sophie slid off her horse in her turn. Her husband stood by to help her down, a small courtesy that pleased her. She leaned back slightly into his arms so it felt as though he was embracing her. "You think me such a dragon that I would begrudge you a rest?"

He set her firmly on her feet and stepped backward again, so their bodies were no longer touching. "I think you are a very single-minded young woman."

She wasn't sure that that was much of a compliment, she thought as she knocked on the door with her fist. He could have called her something more suited to her sex—beautiful, maybe, or desirable, or even strong. But single-minded?

The landlady welcomed them in with open arms. "What can I get the pair of you, your poor men?" she clucked as she bustled around them, taking their sodden greatcoats and hanging them up to dry in front of the fire and pressing mugs of hot mulled wine into their hands. "Food? Warm water? A nice soft featherbed warmed with a bedpan full of red hot coals?"

She was cold and wet through and through, not to mention stiff from climbing out a window, falling from the roof on to the ground, riding for an entire day, sleeping on the ground, and then riding all day again. Her body felt as though it had been rolled down a hill in a barrel of nails. She'd read once that the barbarous Germans used this nasty trick to punish wrongdoers. Whatever the wrongdoers had done, she was sure they didn't deserve such a punishment. She doubted she would ever feel quite the same again.

She stretched her arms out in front of her and rolled her shoulders around. "A whole tub full of steaming hot water," she said, as she pressed a gold coin into the woman's hands, "and a warm, dry bed, and I shall be quite content."

The tub of steaming water, brought up to her in pails by a sturdy serving man, looked better than anything she had seen in her life before. She glanced sideways at Lamotte as he lay sprawled out on the bed. They had been put together in the same chamber, and Sophie had not had the energy to ask that they be given separate rooms. Such a luxury for two single gentlemen traveling together would have taken more explanation that she felt up to giving.

She pulled off her boots and tossed them in the corner. "Shut your eyes," she said, as she pulled her shirt over her head and threw it on top of her boots. Not even the knowledge he was in the room with her could stop her from soaking herself in that steaming water until her skin was wrinkled and water-laden and the water had cooled. "I'm going to take a bath."

He grunted.

She took his grunt for consent and continued undressing, her back turned toward him.

Ah, how deliciously warm the water was as she stepped into it, lowering herself inch by inch into heaven. She lay back, her eyes closed, and sighed with pleasure.

"Move over, wife of mine."

At the sound of Lamotte's voice by her ear she opened her eyes with a start and instinctively drew up her knees to cover her chest.

What she saw made her gasp in earnest. Her husband stood before her, not a stitch of clothing on him from his head to his toe.

She spluttered, shock making her nearly incoherent. "You . . . you're naked."

Eight

She watched in dismay as he put one leg into the tub, gasping at the heat of the water. "You can't get in here," she said, balling her washcloth in her fist and throwing it at him. "You've got no clothes on."

The washcloth bounced off his chest and fell into the water with a splash. Without a word, he put his other leg in and sat down gingerly on the far side of the tub. The tub was plenty large enough for one, but not so generous for two. However tightly Sophie curled up on her end of the tub, he still took all the remaining room without even trying. Their knees were so close that they bumped together.

When he was settled nicely in the water, he leaned back and put his hands behind his head. "How perspicacious of you to notice, though I cannot see why this would surprise you. Did you expect me to bathe with my clothes on?"

She glared at him in disbelief. Things had gone from bad to worse before she had known what was happening. He was invading her privacy in a most shameful and shocking way, and she would not allow it. "You're in my bath."

He grinned at her discomfiture as he grabbed the soap and started to lather his chest. "Don't be selfish.

Did your mother never teach you that you must share?"

She stood up, the cold air making her overheated skin break out into goose bumps. She could not take so much naked man this close to her. In truth, she had never seen a naked man at all before. She supposed she should avert her eyes from his bare chest, from the triangle of hair that led down so invitingly to his male member, which stirred slightly under her gaze, but she couldn't bear to. He was quite glorious in his nakedness, and it was all too much for her. "I can't share my bath with you."

He pulled her down in to the water again. "Don't be a goose. You could always wait until I've done, but by then the water will be cooling, and not nearly so efficacious for easing your sore muscles."

She stood up again, though it hurt her to do so. She wanted that bath more than anything else she could think of right now. "I will ask for more hot water."

He lay back at his ease in the tub. "We can hardly expect the landlady to heat us up two such enormous tubs of water. She must have used a day's worth of firewood already."

No more hot water? She sat down again in the tub in such a hurry that at least a gallon of water slopped over the edge, and she glared at him with burgeoning determination. She was not going to be cheated out of her bath by any man under the sun. It was hers. She had a right to it and she would uphold that right with her last breath. "You are not stealing my bath from me. I will close my eyes and pretend you are not here."

"I had no intention of stealing your bath. I will even save your modesty so you do not need to shut your eyes." He put his soapy hands on her shoulders and turned her around so her back was turned to him. "Let me wash your back for you."

His fingers were slippery with soap as he kneaded the stiff muscles of her shoulders and back, probing every tight, sore spot with relentless fingers until every part of her loosened under his hands. He held pure heaven in his fingertips. She felt as though every ache and pain were being washed away under the touch of his hands. She never wanted him to stop.

"My arms?" she suggested, when he finished her back and washed the soap off with a sluicing of hot water. She held out one arm and looked at him over her shoulder with the most shamefully beseeching look she could muster. She wanted him to go on touching her forever, all over her body. "Please?"

He gave a small sigh as he took her arm in his hands and began to knead it with the same delicious torment, from the muscles in her shoulder blades down to the very tips of each finger. "Ah, the things I do for you, wife of mine."

When her first arm had been attended to, he took her other arm without a word and worked his magic on that one, too, pummeling it until every part of it felt as soft as butter.

Sophie wriggled her shoulders with a newfound sense of ease when he had finished. Her back and shoulders felt looser and freer than they had in a long while, and her arms felt like new.

She shifted uncomfortably on her bottom in the bath, feeling anew the muscles that hurt most from riding. Much as she would like her legs and backside to be pummeled and stroked into such delicious relaxation as her upper body, she did not dare to ask him to touch her there. Besides, he could not easily touch her legs, hidden as they were in the bath water.

She would make do with thanking him, keeping care to hold her tongue before she begged him never to take his hands off her body.

She turned her head around to smile at him. "Thank you." He had made her feel so wonderful she could even forgive him for stealing half her bath.

He lathered up his hands again. "Save your thanks for later. I have not yet finished." With lather dripping from his hands, he reached around from behind and began to wash her breasts and stomach.

His breath was in her ear, hot and sweet. At her back she could feel his manhood begin to rise and swell, pressing into her buttocks with an insistent touch. He wanted her. That much was quite clear. He wanted her as a man wanted his woman. She could feel his need for her, his desire for her, in every pore of her body. How she gloried in the feeling of being desired. How she gloried in the knowledge that she, and only she, could bring him to a state of quivering excitement and make his heart pound and his breath quicken from wanting her.

He was not kneading her sore muscles now. He was touching her as a man touched a woman, in gentleness and desire. After the first shock of his touch had worn off, Sophie arched her back, thrusting her breasts into his hands. She forgot his excitement and need in her own desire that was building relentlessly inside her. Her desire was a torrent of raging river water about to burst through the puny dam of her self-control. It was violent, ready to be unleashed to destroy everything in its path with the unstoppable force built up behind it.

She knew she was behaving shamelessly, like a true wanton, but she could not help it. Every fiber of her being was screaming at her, crying out for Lamotte's touch. Oh, how she had wanted this. How close she had come last night under the pine tree to begging for it. She could not say him nay. She could only luxuriate in the sensation of his hands rubbing the harsh washcloth over her body.

He soon abandoned the washcloth in favor of his bare hands. The touch of his fingers on her skin left trails of fire wherever he went. She felt her nipples harden and pucker into tight buds of desire as he kneaded her breasts in his hands, teasing the tips with gentle, flickering touches that left her weeping for more.

She moaned with desire for him, guiding his hands with her own to touch her body all over, wherever he desired to touch her. She had never guessed at the heaven a man's touch could bring to her body. His heat chased away the last lingering shreds of loneliness that lay buried deep in her heart.

His breathing quickened at her unspoken invitation and his soapy hands crept lower, over her belly, to the thatch of curls at the top of her thighs. She thrust her mound out to meet his questing hand, crying aloud at the pleasure of it, at the pleasure of opening her body and her soul for the very first time to the man she loved.

His fingers brushed a secret spot that left her quivering and aching for more. Again he brushed it, tantalizing her with a desperate desire.

The tip of his finger entered her secret passage, dipping in and out in a rhythm that made her gasp. She leaned back into his hard chest and grabbed hold of his knees with desperate fingers to steady herself as she held herself open to his explorations.

Relentlessly he teased her with his finger, now dipping it in and out of her, now flicking her sensitive spot so she screamed aloud at the pleasure of it, until she was completely under his spell, helpless in the throes of her desire.

Higher and higher he built up the tension in her body, until she thought she would never survive it. Just as she was sure she was going to die of wanting, she reached the peak she hadn't known she needed. She screamed aloud as the tension broke and waves of throbbing pleasure flooded her body, washing over and over her until she could take no more.

Limp and helpless as a newborn kitten, she lay back in the tub against his chest as little aftershocks of pleasure skittered through her body. "Mmmmm," she murmured, when she had regained enough of her breath to allow her to speak. "That was nice."

He snorted as he hugged her to him. "Nice? How insulting. Is that all?"

She felt as though she had been swept to faraway places she had only ever imagined in her dreams. "More than nice. I felt as though I had gone to heaven." She nuzzled her head into his chest, enjoying the tickling of his soft chest hairs against her heated cheek. "Does that mean we are married properly now?"

He wiggled his backside rather ruefully. "Not yet."

Sophie could feel that his erection had not faded, but was as huge and swollen as ever it had been. He had not been fulfilled, but was still full and aching with need. He must only have given her pleasure and not taken any for himself. She had not known such a thing was possible.

She suddenly felt ill at ease and embarrassed. What should she do now? What was he expecting of her? She did not know how to give him pleasure as he had given to her. She thought men took pleasure for themselves as they found it, not relying on the woman to help them in any way.

She ducked her head under the water, gave herself a final rinse, and clambered out of the tub. Her face burned as she thought of asking him how she could pleasure him. She could not ask him what he desired her to do. She could only hope that sooner or later the mystery would become clear without her saying a word.

What more can there be to marriage than that anyway? Sophie thought as she rubbed herself dry on a coarse towel, the bare floorboards sending shivers of cold into the soles of her feet. She was sure she could not feel more intensely without dying of it.

She tossed the damp towel at Lamotte and crept under the covers. She had no nightclothes nor any clean linen for the morrow, but she would worry about that when the time came. Right now, all she wanted to do was sleep.

By the time Lamotte had dried himself and crept in beside her, she was three-quarters asleep. She snuggled up to his warm body and fell into a deep, dreamless slumber.

She awoke to the sound of the dawn chorus, her husband's warm torso next to her. Her husband was abed with her, as naked as the day he was born. She shivered. Come to that, so was she.

His body burned against hers wherever it touched her. She turned over to escape the touch of his body against hers and lay still for a while, pretending to be dozing. The memory of the previous night made her feel sick to her stomach. How could she have forgotten herself so far as to behave like a perfect wanton in his arms?

He mumbled a sleepy good morning to her and

reached out to take her back into his embrace. She could not face his touch again. Not so soon as this. She sat up, threw off the covers, and swung her legs over the side of the bed, almost falling out in her hurry to escape him. She could not deal with him just yet. Her sense of shame was too great still. She would simply pretend to be in such a hurry to be moving again that she had no time to exchange early morning pleasantries with him.

She felt so vulnerable in the chill of the morning air with no clothes to cover her nakedness, as if she were laying not only her body but also her spirit bare to his searching gaze. She knew he was watching her every move. She could feel his eyes on her naked backside as she bent over to retrieve her clothes.

How she hated to put her travel-stained clothes onto her clean body. She held up her soiled linen with distaste, examining it critically in the dim light from the casement window. It looked worse this morning than it had the previous eve, but she had no choice other than to wear it or go without. She was tempted for a moment to go without, but she knew the leather of her breeches on her bare skin would chafe her unbearably. She shut her eyes to the sad state of her linen and struggled into it. Still damp from yesterday's rain, it stuck to her body with a cold, clammy feel.

Lamotte called at her to come back to bed, but she ignored him. With a grouch and a grumble, he got out of bed and started to dress himself in clean linen taken from his saddlebags.

She averted his eyes from his naked body as he rose from their bed. She would not watch the play of his muscles under his skin as he wandered around the chamber, taking an inordinately long time to find his clothes. She would not watch him dress. He was a distraction at a time when she could not afford to be distracted.

She would not look at him at all, or talk to him either, unless she had to, she decided, for the rest of the journey to England. She might be married to him, but she did not have to have aught to do with him, if she did not choose to.

This morning she wanted to forget the very fact of his existence.

They were on the road in short order. She refused to sit down for breakfast, but grabbed a hunk of cold meat wrapped in bread to eat on her way. Lamotte cast a look of longing at the bowls of steaming hot rabbit stew that the maid offered to them to break their fast, but he followed her suit without a word.

"Are you going to ignore me all day?" Lamotte inquired after some minutes of riding, when she had replied to his inconsequential chatter with a mere nod or shake of her head. She was too intent on schooling herself into not answering him to concentrate properly on what he was saying. "Are you upset at something, or are you just sulking?"

She could not open her mouth to talk to him without blushing for her behavior the previous evening. Still, he was not going get away with accusing her of sulking. "I was not ignoring you. I was thinking."

"You should leave thinking to the king's ministers. They can think up enough crackpot ideas for all the rest of France together."

"I was not thinking up crackpot schemes. I was merely . . ." Her voice trailed off into silence. She could not tell him what she was thinking about.

"Thinking?" he added helpfully.

"Exactly."

"Can I ask what you are thinking so hard about that you haven't heard a word I have said all morning?"

She was thinking about how she could possibly survive for the rest of the journey to England, being in her husband's company and sharing a chamber with him at night. How could she remain true to herself? How could she deny him, when her own body tried to make a traitor out of her? How could she tell him she was thinking of the touch of his hands on her body, and the gorgeous heaven of coming apart in his arms? "Nothing in particular."

"You think about nothing very hard."

She shrugged her shoulders and was silent.

After looking at her expectantly for an answer but receiving none, he rode on a few paces ahead and left her alone with her thoughts.

They were not comfortable ones.

She would have to exercise a far greater degree of self-control, Sophie decided. She would not think about the touch of Lamotte's hands on her body or the feel of his lips brushing hers. She would not think about that glorious moment when it seemed she was flying and would never come down to earth again. She would especially not think about how she could make Lamotte catch the same glimpse of heaven she had experienced. She would concentrate on her goal—to get to England—and distance herself from anything that would interfere with her plans.

Lamotte was the temptation she had to resist. The devil had put him in her way to distract her from her purpose. She would be strong and true and not allow herself to be distracted.

She looked sideways at him from under her lashes. He had been framed for distractions. His sight of his large, capable hands on the reins of his mare made her spine tingle with anticipation. She knew what the planes of his back looked like without their covering of linen and leather. She knew how the hairs grew in tight, golden curls on this chest and thighs. She knew how good he could make her feel.

She knew, and she must forget.

She forced herself to think of Henrietta, doomed to a cold dungeon and moldy bread. Henrietta must be saved, and by her alone. Philippe of Orleans had put all his trust in her, and she must not fail him. Despite all the temptations thrown in her path, she was determined not to forget the purpose of her mission.

The ride dragged on interminably. Torn between desire and duty, Sophie wrestled all day in her mind, determined to get the better of her desire. Long before nightfall, the effort had exhausted her.

She was thankful to stop at last at a humble tavern that boasted only one chamber for guests.

She washed briefly in a jug of cold water and climbed into the narrow bed with her soiled shirt and stockings still on. She dared not divest herself of all her clothing again, as she had the previous night. She would not be so foolhardy as to run headlong into temptation, but would rather seek to avoid it.

She lay on her back as far over on the edge of the bed as she could, clenched her fists into tight balls of determination, and stared at the ceiling. Tonight she would wrestle with the devil and she would win.

Out of the corner of her eye, she saw Lamotte take a look at her stiff posture and shrug his shoulders. Without a word, he blew out the candle and climbed in next to her. She tensed her body, waiting for him to reach out to her, but he stayed scrupulously on his side of the bed. "Good night." His voice, velvety and warm in the blackness, caressed her senses.

Sophie clenched her fists tighter together. She would not let herself be lulled into a false sense of security only to be surprised by an sudden attack from behind. "Good night."

His breathing soon deepened into the patterns of sleep, while her brain still tossed around in confusion. Did he desire her no longer? Why was he making no effort to touch her, to coax her into his arms again? Did he not care that she had determined to resist him?

She had been prepared for a battle to resist temptation, and the temptation was never even offered to her. She could not feel victorious over such a nonevent. Instead, she felt deflated, unfulfilled, almost insulted, by his lack of interest.

He started to snore lightly and she wanted to scream at him for being able to sleep when she could not. She turned over on to her side, her leg accidentally brushing his as she did so.

Startled, she jerked it away as if he had burned her with his touch. Her heart was still thudding with the sudden fright she had given herself when she heard another, more sinister thudding of soft shoes outside the chamber, and the muted creak of the door slowly and quietly being opened.

The flickering of a rush taper caught her eye, and the acrid smell of the smoke it gave off caught at the back of her throat.

She leaped out of bed in a flash, grabbed the dagger from its hiding place in her stocking where she had stashed in to ward off another kind of danger altogether, and shouted a warning to Lamotte.

Her eyes, accustomed to the darkness, made out a couple of stealthy figures creeping into their chamber. Damn it all. Did the king have an unending supply of assassins to send after her?

She leaped at the foremost of the intruders, striking him a glancing blow on the shoulder with her dagger. He gave a cry of pain and struck back at her weakly and wildly, evidently not expecting to meet with any resistance.

In that same instant Lamotte was beside her, his naked body large beside her, his sword flashing in the light of the rush taper.

Foiled in their attempt to take them by surprise, their attackers quickly turned tail, snuffed their lights, and fled into the darkness.

Sophie stood in the doorway, looking out into the blackness, searching for any sign of them. She was panting with the aftereffects of shock and fear. "Shall we go after them?"

"It could be an ambush. They could well try to trap us in the dark."

"Who do you think they were?"

He shut the door and secured it with a wooden chair shoved up against the handle. "I doubt they were looking simply to rob us. Ordinary robbers would normally give a pair of soldiers a wide berth."

She'd known it all along. "The king's men, then?"

"I fear so."

She scrunched her face up to aid her memory, but it did not help. "I did not see their faces. I would not recognize them again were I to bump into them."

"Nor I. We shall have to keep a far closer watch for the rest of the journey." He pulled on his breeches, threw on his jacket, and sat down on the edge of the bed. "Go back to sleep for now. I shall keep watch tonight."

She shivered in the chill of the night air. Suddenly conscious of her state of undress, she crawled back under the warm covers. She must not forget the other battle she had to fight. "Wake me in four hours and I shall do my turn."

She'd thought that after her scare she would never relax enough to sleep, but she was wrong. Her head had barely touched the pillow when her eyes drifted shut of their own accord, and she fell fast asleep.

She woke again in the darkness before early dawn. She turned over and was about to sink back into sleep again when she remembered Lamotte, still on guard duty. Trust him not to have awakened her, she thought with a grumble. He would have wakened any male companion to share the watch with him.

She rolled out of bed and threw on her clothes. "Get some sleep," she instructed Lamotte, whose head was drooping with weariness, "or you shall be no use at all."

He took her reproof meekly, lay down on the covers in his clothes, and was asleep in no time at all.

She undid the shutters and watched the pale dawn break over the horizon, resisting the temptation to watch him as he slept. Guard duty was a good time for thinking.

They would have to ride full speed ahead to England now. They could not afford to dally along the way, not with the king sending riders out after them to murder them in their beds. Three more days of hard riding would see them at Calais, from where they could find a boat to take them to England easily enough. The two countries, though always suspicious of each other, were not currently at war, so boats to take them across the Channel would be plentiful enough.

A smuggler's boat would be the best, if they could find one. That way they could make their way into

England quietly, without the king's spies able to track their movements so easily.

She glanced at Lamotte, lying outstretched on the bed, snoring softly in his sleep. There would be no more nights of sleeping in one bed together, curled up close to keep each other warm. One of them would always have to keep wakeful on watch, at least until they had delivered their message to the king of England and made a safe return to Paris.

Their enforced separation would be a relief in so many ways. She would no longer have to rely on her willpower to keep her away from distraction. The situation they were in would do that for them without her having to try.

She still could not face up to her own behavior with any degree of equanimity. Her own wantonness and her capitulation to her own desire had shocked her. She had no time or energy to deal with what that meant to her right now, not while she was in the middle of a mission that could not be delayed. There would be time enough to deal with her feelings when they had reached England and given their message to King Charles.

Still, a little voice whispered in her ear that her husband had not been shocked by her. Indeed, he had encouraged her and had seemed to enjoy her reaction to his caresses. Maybe this was how married couples were supposed to act. She did not know.

His chest was rising and falling with every breath he took, his eyelids fluttering as if he were having disturbing dreams. She could avoid being close to him for the rest of their journey, but she could not avoid him forever.

She watched the sun come up over the horizon, sending its pale yellow fingers out into the sky. Sooner or later their mission would be at an end, they would return to France, and she would have to work out what to do about her husband.

She had vowed to protect the honor of her family and win honor for the name of her brother. One thing at least was clear to her: she could not do that as Lamotte's wife.

If only, she thought to herself, as she gazed at his sleeping form, if only she had not fallen in love with her husband, deeply and helplessly in love with him, the path she should take at this crossroads in her life would be far more clear.

Calais was bustling with activity when they finally reached it, exhausted with their days of riding and their nights sharing the watch. They were not disturbed in the darkness again, nor were there any signs they were being followed, save for a prickly feeling in the back of Sophie's neck every so often that made her feel as though she was being watched. However often she turned her head at odd moments, she did not catch any glimpse of their pursuers, but she could not shake off her uneasy feeling.

The lack of obvious pursuit made her more, not less, edgy. Their pursuers must have some trick up their sleeve.

As they drew close to the wharf, they dismounted and made their way over the cobbles on foot, leading the horses behind them. They must look like a right pair of disreputable rogues, Sophie thought, as she followed in Lamotte's footsteps through the town. With hair unwashed and clothes stained with days of travel and so caked with mud they were unrecognizable as uniforms of the king's soldiers, they looked like a pair of not-so-prosperous horse traders.

At one point, a couple of fat merchants even stopped them in the streets and tried to buy one of Lamotte's steeds, offering him an absurdly paltry sum of money for his fine Arabian mare. They were hoping, no doubt, that the pair of them were foolish as well as poor. Taken by surprise, she merely stared stupidly at them. Lamotte growled at them so fiercely in a thick patois that they backed off again in a hurry.

The docks were busier than Sophie could have imagined, and the sea, when they finally reached it, was far vaster. She gazed in wonderment at the huge expanse of blueness that stretched out as far as the eye could see. At the horizon, the sea and the sky melted together until she could not see where one stopped and the other began. Gulls wheeled overhead, calling to each other with raucous voices. The air smelled of salt and fish and tar.

Lamotte tossed the reins over to her. She caught them and held them tight, unwilling to tear her eyes away from the blue-green ocean. "Look after the beasts," he said, as he strode off to find out which ships were sailing on the next tide, and to arrange their passage over to England.

She stayed where he had left her, holding the horses and gazing out at the water. This was the water she had to cross, the water that would take her to England. She shivered at the cold blueness of it, at the white-capped waves that broke against the pier, making the air hazy with showers of finely misted droplets that hung in the sunlight like fog.

She had never imagined what the sea would be like. She knew only the still ponds and marshes of the Camargue and the river that flowed swiftly through

Paris, dank and dirty with the refuse of a thousand city dwellers. They were deserts compared with the sight spread out before her eyes. She had not known there was this much water in the world.

For the first time since she had left Paris she was tempted to give up her mission, to turn back before she had completed it. The sea was so alien and strange to her. The thought of crossing it with only a few planks of wood to protect her from the cruelty of the water beneath her feet filled her with a sense of horror. She wanted to go back to Paris, shut her eyes and ears and pretend she had never heard of honor—or of Henrietta.

She could not do that. However much she feared the water, she was honor bound to complete her mission. Still, she could not help but hope as she stood watching the water, her unease growing by the moment, that Lamotte would not be able to find a captain who could be persuaded, cajoled, or bribed to take them over to England.

It seemed an age of water watching before he returned. She misliked the man he brought back with him, a burly seaman with a long, grizzled black beard and a nasty habit of spitting on the ground each time he said anything. Her dislike of crossing the water intensified and focused on this one man until she could believe quite readily he was the agent of the devil, come to doom her to destruction.

Lamotte and the Captain carried on their negotiations, unaware of the hatred from her eyes.

"Two of you to be carried over?"

"Two of us."

The seaman ran his hands over the legs of Sophie's precious Seafoam. "He's a mite skinny."

She glared at the captain, and then again at Lamotte.

She had plenty of pistoles for their passage. What was he doing promising her horse to this man? Seafoam had belonged to Gerard and he had served her well. She would never part with him. "My horse is not for sale."

Lamotte shook his head. "Not that one—the brown gelding."

The captain humphed and looked dismissively at the gelding Sophie led. "I'll take you both to England for the mare."

Sophie opened her mouth to protest, but Lamotte forestalled her. "The horse is not for sale," he said smoothly. "The gelding or nothing."

With a grunt, the captain slouched over to the gelding, ran his hands over its flanks and peered in his mouth. "He's too long in the tooth."

Lamotte crossed his arms over his chest and said nothing.

The captain lifted the gelding's foreleg and inspected the foot. "He's knock-kneed and he needs re-shoeing."

Sophie held tight to Seafoam's reins. There was no way she was letting this man get hold of her precious horse. She would go and find another captain herself who would not demand such an outrageous price for carrying them over the water.

The captain spat once more on the ground for emphasis. "He's fit for nothing but dog-tucker. He's not worth passage for two."

Lamotte shrugged his shoulders. "If you're not interested . . ."

"But I suppose I'll do you a favor, seeing as I've got a kind heart," the captain hastily interjected. "As long as you throw in the saddle with the horse."

Lamotte spat in his hand and held it out to be

shaken. Sophie could see he was well pleased with the bargain he had struck. "Done."

"We leave this evening on the turn of the tide," the captain said, giving a toothless smile. "Don't be late. My boat and I wait for no man, however much he may offer me to stay or however urgent his business may be. If you're late, you won't be coming with me. And I won't be givin' back your horse, neither."

"We have plenty of gold pistoles to pay for our passage," Sophie hissed in his ear as they walked off to find food and a stable for their remaining horses. "Why did you not just pay him what he asked?"

"Would you have me wave a bag of gold under his nose, whetting his appetite and putting us in danger of being tossed overboard a few miles out to sea so he can safely abscond with the lot? Far better that he think we are poor and have to sell one of our horses for passage. We are more likely to make it to England alive."

Put that way, it was hard to argue with.

"Besides," he added, "I do not like to keep the horse of the man you killed so neatly with an arrow in the neck. Inconspicuous as it is, someone may yet recognize it and have us hanged for horse thieves and murderers."

She rubbed her neck thoughtfully. That was even harder to argue with. She had no desire to have her neck stretched on the end of the hangman's rope.

By the time they had concluded all their business ashore, there was scarce an hour left till the turn of the tide. Sophie wandered along the docks, a feeling of nervous excitement building in the pit of her belly. She was about to leave the shores of France for the first time in her life, and travel over the wide blue sea to a new land where they even spoke in a whole new tongue. Once upon a time, not so long ago, a visit to Paris had been the height of her ambition. A visit to London had been so far out her reach that it was utterly unthinkable. Now, thanks to her life as Gerard, to her life as a musketeer, the unthinkable was about to become a reality.

Just as they approached the boat that was to take them across the water and her excitement was reaching a fever pitch, Lamotte stopped her with a hand on her arm. "What do you make of that?"

Two men, obviously not seamen, dressed in dark clothes, were huddled with the captain in a dark corner of the pier. As they watched, the two men raised their heads, looked around them with a secretive air, and slunk away out of sight. The captain, now left alone on the pier, tucked a heavy-looking pouch into his shirt with an air of satisfaction.

She stood stock-still, her excitement turned into apprehension. "I don't like the look of that."

"Maybe I am too suspicious. They could have been having an innocent conversation about the price of fish."

Sophie shook her head. It paid to be suspicious in this day and age. Those who were too trusting ended up dead. "They were paying him—probably for doing their dirty work for them. If we sail with him, we shall be feeding the fishes before morning."

They backtracked their steps, keeping a wary eye out for the two spies.

Lamotte's face was drawn with worry. "Damn. We can't sail with him now. I sold that horse for nothing and nearly got us killed into the bargain."

She felt only relief that she would not have to share a boat with the man she had distrusted from the beginning. "Look on the bright side. He may yet be hanged for horse stealing."

He rubbed his hand slowly over his forehead. "We have to get on that boat."

Surely he was not going to risk their lives on such a small thing as a sea captain's honesty? "What?"

"If the spies think we are taken care of, we shall be safe all the way to England, and back again. Otherwise they will come after us again and again, until they finally succeed."

She was not convinced. "How shall we escape once we are on the boat? There will be half a dozen seamen against the pair of us."

"Can you swim?"

"A little."

"Good. The water is calm enough. A little is all we need. Come, we don't have much time."

They were panting hard as they raced up the wharf again, just moments after the turn of the tide. The captain was already on board, standing on the prow of the boat keeping a lookout, a watchful frown on his face.

His expression relaxed when he caught sight of them. "You're just in time," he said, and he gave a twisted smile. "I thought we would have to leave without you."

Sophie shot a quick look at Lamotte. The fact that he had stayed for them even moments past the turning of the tide spoke volumes. It confirmed all their suspicions that he was counting on something other than simple trade to make his money on this voyage.

They clambered aboard, holding tight to the side stays as they made their way into the tiny cabin. Their heavy riding boots slipped and skidded on the wet deck. "Cast off," the captain ordered as soon as their feet left the dock, and a couple of wiry-looking seamen cast off the mooring lines.

The cabin reeked so badly of fish that Sophie gagged as soon as she put one foot into it. She immediately thrust her head out again into the fresh salt air. "I can't stay down there," she said with a shudder. "I will die before I reach England."

Lamotte's face was green already. Without a word, he nodded to Sophie and climbed out on to the deck again.

The captain gave them a scowl as they came back up on deck. "Passengers stay below decks."

The ship was rolling up and down on the waves as if it were a cork, bobbing around in the middle of the sea. Sophie grabbed on to a side rail and looked at the white caps of the waves as they broke against the side of the ship. She'd never been on a boat before. The motion was unusual, and it made her feet feel unsteady beneath her, but she didn't find it too unpleasant. It was a bit like the feeling of riding a horse, only more so—like riding a wild sea horse that jumped and bucked and tossed and turned this way and that beneath her as it ran with the wind in its sails and the current beneath its keel.

Lamotte staggered to the rail and vomited over the side.

The captain's scowl became even more pronounced. "Stinking landlubber," he muttered under his breath as he scuttled past, as agile as a monkey on the pitching deck, slippery now with salt spray. "I won't have you fouling up my cabin. Stay up here, but don't get in the way or I'll toss you overboard myself."

Lamotte just groaned and heaved over the side again.

"Look at the horizon," one of the seamen said with

an unpleasant grin, and he spat a wad of tobacco juice over the side. "It might stop you puking your guts out like a girl."

Sophie raised her eyes to the horizon. Despite the nasty tone of his voice, the seaman's advice held good. Looking far out to sea made her notice the pitching of the boat beneath her feet less.

Out of the corner of her eye she saw Lamotte raise his head to look out to sea, only to lower it again with a groan as he retched again and again over the side.

Despite all her sympathy for his misery, she could not help laughing to herself just a little at his predicament. All it took to unman such a brave soldier was to put him in a boat and set him out to sea. She would have to remember that in future. It would be a good threat to hold against him. If he proved a bad husband to her, she would simply run off to England again, or to the Americas, and he would not be able to face following her.

The land was fast disappearing behind them. Once they had left the shelter of the harbor, the wind had freshened against her face and the waves had picked up noticeably in strength. Sophie made her way to the stern of the boat, found herself a spot out of the way of the sailors, and scanned the sea behind them with a watchful eye. Lamotte staggered over to stand beside her, his hip touching hers as if by accident. She took comfort from his presence. They were well out into the channel now. If they had been right in their conjectures, the seamen would move against them at any time.

She could make out a couple of sails in the distance, but they were too far away to make out what boats they belonged to. She grasped the railing with nervous fingers. What if all their preparation had been in vain?

What if they had no hope of rescue and were doomed to die out here, in the middle of the sea?

One of the sails changed tack, veering away from them. All her attention was concentrated on the other sail she could see. It was moving in their direction, but it did not seem to be drawing any closer. If anything, it was falling further behind.

She swore under her breath. She did not like the look of things. Even assuming the boat was willing to pick them up, she would drown before she would be able to swim half that distance. Their best bet would be to stay where they were and hope they had been mistaken in the honesty of their captain.

She turned her head to check over her shoulder at the captain. It was just as well she did so. Three of the sailors were sidling up behind them, knives in their hand. She nudged Lamotte hard with her elbow and he whirled around to face them.

She could not fight off three of them by herself on the deck of a ship that rolled under her feet. She was in a sailor's territory, and they had the advantage over her. Neither was Lamotte much use. His face green and his hands shaking, he looked as though he would not care if he were to die.

She looked first at the sailors, who had stopped a few feet away, their knives held in front of them, and then down at the white-tipped green of the water. She had to choose her doom, it would seem—death by the knife or death by drowning. She was unwilling to stand by the rails and offer up her throat as calmly as a sacrificial lamb. She would take her fate into her own hands if she could, and make one last choice. The water looked cold but it not menacing. It lacked the deliberate evil of the filthy grins on the sailors' faces. "Shall we jump?"

One of the sailors laughed an ugly laugh. "Jumping will do as well for us. It'll save us dirtying our knives on you."

The three of them moved another step closer. "So what'll it be?" one of them asked, showing his dirty yellowed teeth in a vicious grin. "The water or the knife?"

Sophie looked toward the closest sail, noting its position as well as she could. She took a deep breath and climbed the railing, moving awkwardly in her landlubber's clothing, Lamotte beside her.

Sophie thought for a moment about using her height and leaping down on to the sailors. She would sell her life dearly were she to get among them. More than one of them would go with her into the oblivion of death.

The sailors rushed at them, knives held high. Death at their hand would be certain. At least in the water she had a chance to live.

She closed her eyes and held tight to Lamotte's fingers. Hand in hand they jumped off the railing and into the cold, rushing waters of the channel.

Nine

She hit the water with a vicious smack that tore Lamotte's fingers from her grasp and forced all the air out of her at once. The waves closed over her head as she plummeted down into the cold, green depths.

She had been wrong about the water. It was worse than cold. It was evil and terrifying, remorseless in its hunt for living prey. It was sucking at her with long, green tentacles of death, clawing at her, dragging her down into the depths of the ocean where fishes would feast on her body and golden-haired mermaids make harps of her bones.

She failed her arms and legs desperately, fighting to get her head above water and take a breath of life-giving air. She felt a hand grab at her and try to drag her down. A sea monster, she thought, panic invading every fiber of her being, taking its chance to drag her down to its watery lair and feast on her drowned body. Desperately she fought it off, with no thought in her head but to find air and to breathe again.

It was too strong for her. Relentlessly the grasp on her shoulder pulled her down, down, down, toward a watery death at the bottom of the sea.

Her head broke the surface. Air!

She grabbed a mouthful of it with such greed that she inhaled half water. Coughing and spluttering, she forced the water out of her lungs again. Air—pure and sweet. How good it was to breathe again.

Lamotte was treading water beside her, his hand still grasping her shoulder. Lamotte, not a sea monster. He had saved her, not pulled her down to drown her.

Her panic subsided enough for her to breathe without choking this time.

"Kick off your boots," he barked at her.

She looked at him stupidly. She was trying to survive in the tossing ocean. Why was he worrying about her feet at a time like this? She would hardly get more blisters trying to tread water.

"Kick off your boots. They will fill with water and drag you down."

Ah, that made sense to her. Her fingers aching with the cold, she reached down to unbuckle her boots. Immediately, the water closed over her head and she flailed to the surface again, terrified she would sink and drown.

He slapped her face. Hard. "Take a deep breath. Take a deep breath and kick off your boots."

She stopped her flailing and looked at him in surprise, the shock of the slap overpowering her fear of drowning for the moment. He had never struck her before.

"You are a soldier and you must obey orders. Take a deep breath and kick off your boots."

He was right. She was a musketeer, and she must follow his orders even if it mean that she drowned. Every soldier had to be prepared to die in the line of duty. She took a deep breath and doubled over to unfasten her boots. The water closed over her head and she fought to control her fear. She must unfasten her boot as she had been ordered.

One boot was off. She returned to the surface and took a gulp of air.

"Good work. Now take a deep breath and unfasten the other boot."

Her commanding officer was pleased with her. She glowed with the praise he bestowed on her. She took another deep breath and bent over to unfasten her other boot. It was easier this time to control her fear. The boot came off without a struggle. Her head was above water before she was desperate for a breath again.

It was easier to stay afloat now without the weight on her ankles pulling her down. She kicked with her legs, keeping her head above water, and her breathing started to slow. She could stay afloat for some time, she thought. If another boat came along to pick them up again, they might yet have a chance to stay alive.

She looked around her. All she could see was the white caps of the waves and Lamotte's head bobbing beside her. There was no sign of any boat save the one they had jumped from, already sailing off into the distance. Her eyes widened, and she began to beat at the water with her fists. They had to find a boat or they would drown. They had to find a boat.

Lamotte grabbed one of her hands and held it tight between his. "Calm down, Sophie. Tell me what ails you."

She pulled her hand away. All she could think about was the boat. "We have to find the boat." Her voice was dangerously high as she felt panic overwhelm her once more. "We have to find the boat, or we'll both drown."

* * *

Lamotte drew his hand back and slapped Sophie on the cheek with as much force as he could muster. This was the second time in as many minutes he had hit her as hard as he was able. He hated raising his hand to a woman, but he had no choice. Her eyes were glazing over. If he let her be overtaken with panic again, she could well drown them both.

His hand left a red imprint on her cheek that clutched at his heart. She would hurt for days. She blinked her eyes, tears running down her red cheeks. When she opened them again, her panic had subsided and her soul was back.

"Lie on your back," he instructed her, making his voice stern so she would follow his orders without questioning them. "You will float well like that."

Meekly she did as she was told. They floated there in the water for some minutes, not speaking.

He hated to disturb her newfound sense of calm, but he had to do something to get them out of this mess if he could. He kicked up with his feet as hard as he could to lift himself up out of the water and see if he could see any other boats nearby. He managed to lift his shoulders and chest out of the water, but it was not far enough. The waves were too high to let him see far in front of him. He tried again, but it was no use. He had best stop before he exhausted himself.

He turned himself over on to his back and waited until he had regained his breath before speaking. "Was the fishing smack following us, as he had promised to do? I was too ill on the boat to take any notice as I ought to have done."

He could have kicked himself now for failing to search the seas for sails before he jumped. Standing on the rails, he had not cared if there were other sails in sight or not. He had wanted only to die just so he would stop feeling as though his stomach was being pounded into knots.

Sophie gave a brief nod. "I saw two sails behind us. One of them seemed to be following the same course as us, though it was too far away to be certain. I took a bearing on it before I jumped, so we could swim to it if we could. But it was too far away. We will never make it." She was no longer panicking. On the contrary, she sounded as though she simply didn't care any more, that she would be happy floating on her back until her eyes closed in weariness and she sank to the bottom.

Despair was just as dangerous as panic, though it would kill less quickly. "Kick up as far as you can and see if you can take a bearing so we know which way to swim." He injected as much urgency in his tone as he could.

She did not move. "What's the point?"

He needed to get through to her and break the grip despair had on her soul. "You're a soldier, Sophie. You cannot give up."

"I'm not a soldier. I'm a woman. Women can't be soldiers."

"You are a soldier until such time as the king releases you from his service. Now, give me the best bearings you can. That is an order."

With a sigh, she heaved herself upright in the water, gave a few kicks and turned over on to her back again. "I couldn't see anything."

He knew how much Sophie prided herself on being a fighter. He would have to work on her sense of honor to give her the will to keep on trying to survive, the will not to give up and allow herself to die. "That is not adequate. I ordered you to give me the best bearings you can. Get back in that water and tell me which way to swim, or, by God, I'll drown you myself for insubordination."

This time she turned herself up in the water and kicked a little harder. She rose head and shoulders above the water, her eyes straining to see above the waves. With a small sigh, she sank down in the water to regain her breath and then kicked up again as high as she could. He could see the effort she was making to hold herself high in the water.

Finally she sank back down again. "That way," she said, indicating the direction with her arm. "I lined the boat up with a hill on the shore before I jumped. If it really was the fishing smack following us, it should be in that direction."

She seemed sure enough. That was a good sign. "We'll swim for it." There was naught else they could do.

The chance of rescue, small though it was, gave Sophie a new lease of life. She paddled gallantly in the direction where they hoped the boat would be. Up and over waves, and down again the other side they paddled, swimming with all the intensity of the desperate, who have nothing else to lose but their lives. The wind was against them, and their progress was slow.

Every so often, Sophie kicked herself high in the water to check the direction they were traveling in.

They swam for what seemed like forever. His body had grown numb with cold. He did not think he could hold out for much longer when Sophie kicked herself high out of the water for the fourth or fifth time. To his surprise, she started to scream and wave her arms about.

"Save your energy," he muttered. "There is no one to hear your cry." He could feel himself slipping away.

Only the vow he had made to Gerard Delamanse kept his mind focused. He had promised to look after Sophie. He would not leave her here to drown if there was even the slimmest chance of rescue.

"The boat," Sophie screamed in his ear. "I can see the boat."

He shook his head to clear out his fuzzy thoughts. He was finding it hard to concentrate. His mind wanted to wander off into odd thoughts of his childhood, at home in the peach orchard with the sound of bees buzzing in the sweet grasses and the mellow scent of ripe peaches in the air. "Can they see us?"

"They saw me wave and changed course toward us."

A large wave rolled over them, and in the lull before the next swell, he saw the boat. It was coming right for them. He closed his eyes. Sophie would be rescued. He had kept his word to Gerard. He could die in peace.

He felt a sharp sting on his face, breaking in on his dream of the orchard. "Go away," he muttered without so much as opening his eyes. He could almost feel the warm summer sun on his face and the taste of ripe peaches on his tongue.

The sting came again, and then again. He opened his eyes. Sophie was hitting him. He brushed her away with the back of her hand. "Leave me be."

"I need you."

He tried to kick away from her, but he was so tired and he could no longer feel his feet. "Don't worry. You will be rescued and they will take you to England. You will save Henrietta and win all the honor you could ever want."

She slapped his face again. It was funny how his cheek could still hurt even though he would have sworn that his entire body was numb from the cold. "I need you."

"What for?"

"You are my husband, you dolt. Besides, I need you to help me climb up."

"Up where?"

She gave an impatient gesture. "Up on to the boat."

She was right. The fishing smack was nearly on top of them and one of the fishermen was clambering down a rope to haul them in.

With a small sigh he said good-bye to his vision of the peach orchard. It was not yet time for him to be called home again. The fisherman tied a rope around his chest, under his arms. He tried to shake it off again. "Save Sophie first. Save my wife."

The rope was knotted tightly around his chest. The fisherman tested it, and then called for the others in the boat to pull him up. "She's in the boat already."

He didn't make another protest as the fishermen hauled him in, for all the world as if he were just another part of their catch.

His body was blue and shivering uncontrollably. He did not think he would ever be warm again. One of the fishermen tossed him a dry blanket. "Get down below with your lady and get your wet things off, or you'll freeze to death."

He made his way with shaking legs to the cabin below, his wet stocking feet slipping on the deck. Sophie was there before him, stripping off her clothes with fumbling fingers and dropping them where she stood. Her arms were covered with goose bumps and she was shivering.

He stripped his own wet gear off him as fast as he could with fingers he could scarcely feel. If anything, he was colder with them off.

Sophie was shivering in her blanket. He clasped her in his cold arms and threw his own blanket over the pair of them. "We'll warm up faster this way."

The ship climbed another swell and nosedived over the side, making the bottom drop out of his stomach. He almost wished he was back in the water again as he retched salt water and bile on to the floor of the cabin at his feet. At least in the water he would be able to die in peace and with his dignity intact.

Sophie nudged him over to the side where a narrow bunk was set into the wall. "Lie down. You might feel better."

They lay together on a narrow bunk in the cabin as the boat pitched and tossed its way over the channel. If anything, this cabin smelled worse than that of the other boat—of rotten fish and sweat and misery.

He had nothing left in his stomach to throw up but bile, but he could not stop his heaving.

His body began to tingle all over as if it were being pierced with a thousand pins. At least he was no longer numb with cold. He could feel his feet again, and the tips of his fingers.

Through the long hours of the passage, Sophie stayed glued to his side, warming his body with hers and keeping the blankets tucked around their bodies as he dozed and retched all the way to England.

Their clothes were drying stiff with salt by the time they set anchor off the coast of England and the owner of the boat came to rouse them. "We're but a few hundred yards off the south coast. I daren't go any further in daylight. The excise men know me a little too well for me to poke my nose in to shore any closer."

Sophie shook some salt crystals from her damp

jacket and pulled it over her shoulders. "You saved our lives. We are very grateful to you."

He chuckled. "Ye paid me well enough to save your skins, so I reckon we're even. Now, do you want to swim the last wee bit, or would you be wanting to buy me dinghy to row yourselves there?"

He never wanted to swim anywhere in his life again. He took a couple of gold pistoles out from the bag concealed next to his skin. "One gold pistole for your boat. Two if one of your men will row us to shore."

A crafty look came into the fisherman's eyes. "Can I keep the dinghy then, and row it back again?"

"You may do with it as you will. We shall have no further need of it."

"Tom," the fisherman called to one of the younger of the crew. "Row our passengers to shore and look sharp about it, me lad."

Two more gold pistoles seemed little enough when set against Sophie's life—not to mention his own. He poured a handful of pistoles onto his hand and gave them to the fisherman, who accepted them with delighted surprise. "The gold I gave you before was a fee. This is a reward that I give you out of gratitude. We owe you our lives."

"Its been a pleasure doing business with you, monsieur," the fisherman said with a toothless grin. He doffed his cap deferentially as they climbed into the little dinghy and were rowed to shore.

Sophie wanted to scream with delight when they came across the first sign of life on the desolate coast of England they had landed upon. The stolid farmer at work in his field looked askance at their bare feet covered only with the tattered remnants of their stockings and their ruined finery, but when she explained in her halting English that they needed food and rest and new clothes, and were prepared to pay for them with good French gold, his face brightened considerably. He led them off over the fields to a farmhouse and left them with his wife, a bustling woman whose kitchen smelled of good broth and onions.

At the sight of the gold coin they offered her, she disappeared for a moment, returning with a selection of clean woolen undergarments and rough woolen clothes like those she and her husband wore.

Sophie pounced on the homespun dress with glee. The farmer's wife gave her a bucket of cold water, with a bit of hot from the kettle thrown in, and she sluiced herself down out the back of the house, removing all the dried salt from her body. Wrapped in the clean woolen clothes, coarse and scratchy though they were, she felt reborn.

"To the king in the morning," she said as they lay on a pallet in front of the kitchen fire that evening, toasting their whole bodies with warmth. She had never before appreciated a fire so well. Tossing and turning in the boat, huddling up to Lamotte for the scrap of warmth his body had afforded her, she had felt as if she would never be warm again. With the embers of the well-banked fire at one side of her, and Lamotte at the other holding her in his arms, she was baking in warmth. "And then our task is done."

Lamotte plucked at the coarse woolen undergarments she was wearing for warmth and laughed. "We cannot go to the king as we are. The most lowly of his footmen would have us thrown out on the street as beggars and rogues. We will have to have some fresh clothes made first so we can appear in style."

She did not like the thought of yet more delay.

"Must we spend the time? We look like very sober farmers in this gear, honest and respectable. Surely he will listen to us."

"Clothes maketh the man. If we look like farmers, we will be treated as farmers. If we look like soldiers, we shall be treated that way, too."

She was silent for a while, thinking of the truth in his words. When she was dressed as a musketeer, Lamotte treated her as a musketeer. Let her but once put on a dress, and her husband had treated her as a woman. He was not alone in this. Kings and their courts were notoriously prone to judge on appearances. "And if I look like a fine French lady?"

"Then you will be treated royally, as a fine French lady ought to be."

She could not argue with this. She knew the truth of it only too well. "New clothes then, the best we can afford. We shall go to the court of the English king in style—as ambassadors, not as petitioners."

"And when we have seen the king—what then?"

She did not know. She had purposely put off thinking about it until she was out of danger. She shrugged her shoulders and was silent.

"The king of France wanted to kill Gerard Delamanse. Gerard is now dead. He drowned in the sea between France and England. I think it would be wise for him to remain there."

She had feared this, but had not wanted to accept it. She did not know what else she could do. "I can no longer be Gerard, then? I can no longer be a musketeer?"

"You chose to give up your service to the king in favor of saving an innocent woman whom the king had declared a traitor. From that moment on, you ceased to be a musketeer."

She could not regret her decision. "I had to follow the path of honor."

"If Gerard comes back to life again, I doubt not the king will have him killed. Sooner or later, you will not be able to escape your fate."

She did not doubt that, either. The king of France was quite ruthless enough to have her murdered for the sake of revenge.

"It seems to me that you face a choice—death as Gerard or life as Sophie."

She knew he spoke the truth, but she could not accept it. She would not accept it. She lay in silence in front of the fire, feeling the warmth seep into her bones.

There had to be another way. There just had to be. Somehow or other, she would find it.

Lamotte raised Sophie's hand to his lips and kissed it. "I promised you new shoes if you married me. See how well I have kept my promise."

She looked down at her feet, distaste wrinkling her nose. "You promised me new boots. These are high-heeled silk slippers. They do not count."

"They are the same color as your eyes."

"God forbid I should ever have to fight in them. I would lose my balance and go sprawling head over heels."

"Even sprawled out on the floor, you would be the most beautiful woman in the room."

She pulled her hand away, feeling unaccountably vexed with his foolishness. "There's no need to play the courtier with me. Save your meaningless flattery for when we have reached the side of the English king."

"Even if King Louis has sent men to reach the ear of the English king first, he will be bound to listen to you. He is supposed to have an eye for a pretty face."

She scowled. She wished he would not call her pretty in that mocking tone of voice. It made her feel like less of a woman than ever. "I do not care what he thinks of my looks. He may think me an old hag, for all I care. While I am in England, I am still a soldier on a mission, not a decoration."

He patted her hand. "I know that, my dear wife, but King Charles of England does not."

Dressed as they were in silks and satins, and bearing a message for the English king from his sister in France, they had little trouble securing an immediate audience.

King Charles of England beamed genially at Sophie as they were ushered into his presence. "A message from my dear sister, Henrietta?" he asked. "I'm sure such a beautiful messenger can carry only a joyous message. Come, come, let me know what it is. I am all ears."

Sophie looked nervously around her at the courtiers all crowding close around the King. She could not announce the imprisonment of the king's sister to the whole English court. "Henrietta told me it was for your ears alone," she prevaricated.

The smile on the king's face faded slightly. "She did? Come now, I am sure everyone here will be as delighted as I am to hear her news."

Sophie shuffled her feet. "May I not tell you in private the news from your sister, sire?" she begged in her halting English. "I do not feel easy speaking before so many people."

He chucked her under the chin. "Ah, I do believe

our young French friend is shy of crowds. You do not need to be, my sweet. Your accent is quite charming.

"Come, Rochester and Saville, let us to our closet where we can hear the minx's news in as much solitude as she could wish for. Some woman's news it may be that Henrietta would not have all the world know just yet."

The king and his two chosen attendants led the way into a narrow room off the Great Hall. Sophie and Lamotte followed close behind.

"So what is your news then?" the king asked, his face now devoid of any smile. "I trust I will find it worth the interruption."

She did not mince her words now they were apart from the crowd. As soon as the door to the chamber was shut behind them, she spoke up loud and clear. "Your sister Henrietta, the Duchesse of Orleans, has been imprisoned in the Bastille. Her husband, Philippe of Orleans, cannot free her. He sent me to ask you for your help."

Ten

One of the English lords took a step forward. "Is this some kind of a sick jest?"

Lamotte stepped forward in his turn, his face taut with rage. "My wife speaks true."

The king tapped his fingernails against the arm of his chair. "You know this for a fact?"

"I arrested her myself on the orders of the French king and took her to the Bastille."

"You? A woman?" The king looked incredulous and one of the English lords laughed out loud.

"I may be a woman, but I am also a musketeer in the King's Guard."

"You are jesting."

Sophie had been prepared for such an eventuality. She reached in her pocket for the small dagger she had placed there, withdrew it in a fluid movement and flung it with a sudden flick of her wrist. The dagger flew through the air, knocking off the curled wig of the doubting lord and pinning it to the wall behind him. There was a collective intake of breath from all present.

The doubting lord's face grew gray and he looked as if he were about to be sick.

"I do not jest."

She had been prepared for anger, but the king gave

a snort of laughter instead. "I see not. Saville, retrieve your wig. The sight of your bald pate will give me palpitations."

Saville pulled the blade out of his wig and placed his hairpiece firmly back on his head. He tested the sharpness of the dagger and tossed it back at Sophie with rather more force than he needed to. She grabbed it by the handle as it somersaulted through the air and tucked it back into her pocket again.

"She is even better with a bow and arrow."

The king raised his eyebrows at Lamotte's comment.

"Only passable with a sword as yet, though she is proving an apt student. She has more agility than most. She just needs to work on her strength more. And her concentration. She may lose sight of the end goal in the immediate press of the battle."

The king looked long and hard at him before turning his attention back to Sophie. "So, what of my sister?"

"Monsieur, Philippe of Orleans, found her missing and suspected her arrest. His brother, King Louis, claimed she had run off with her lover, the Comte de Guiche."

The King nodded. "I had heard rumors little Hetty had found a man to console her. I can hardly blame her for indulging in what I so enjoy myself, especially with the husband she has. Pah. He is only half a man."

"Monsieur did not believe she would run off without telling him. They are fond of each other, though not in the usual manner of married couples, I do believe."

Rochester chortled. "You're in England now. You've no need to be so damned tactful. Philippe of Orleans is well known as a buggerer of young boys."

"Monsieur asked me to come to you. He knew you would help her if you could."

"Why did he come to you? Because you were a woman and would take pity on his wife?"

Sophie thought of monsieur's hand on her knee and felt the tips of her ears burning. "Somehow or another he found out I had arrested her, and so he sought me out. He does not know I am a woman."

Rochester burst out laughing at her confusion and even Saville broke into a grin. "I can see how monsieur would find it difficult to resist you in your guise as a musketeer. You would make a very pretty boy. How mortified he would be, though, were he ever to find out he was trying to seduce a woman."

The king ignored his councillor. "So why did you agree to come?"

Her sense of honor and her sense of pity, she supposed, and because she could not bear to see another woman hurt for protecting the man she loved. "He asked me to save her on my honor as a soldier. I accepted the mission because I am a woman."

Rochester turned to Lamotte. "You are the husband of this delightful Amazon?"

Lamotte bowed. "I have that honor."

"You came along to guard her on the way?"

"Not at all. King Louis was not happy when his spies discovered her mission. He sent me to stop her by any means possible." He took Sophie's hand in his and squeezed it to give her reassurance. "He would have me murder her. Little did he guess he had asked me to kill my own wife."

"I take it my French brother does not know you are a woman, either?"

Sophie shook her head. "Few know the truth of my sex. My husband here, and two of my sisters in arms."

"You are not the only woman musketeer in my French brother's army?"

"There are three I know of, and maybe more."

King Charles of England gave a great guffaw of laughter. "My French brother is guarded by women and he does not even know of it? The jest is too good to be believed."

Sophie bowed her head. "What answer shall I carry back to monsieur?"

The king lost his mirth all of a sudden. "Tell him you have faithfully delivered your message. Poor, poor Hetty. I wish I had not agreed to the match. I will have to get her out of there by some means or another."

Saville scratched his chin. "We can hardly declare war on our neighbor. France is too powerful, and the Scots would be sure to harass our northern border were we to go to war over the channel."

"The Dutch might well join us," Rochester suggested. "They have no love for our Catholic neighbors."

Saville shook his head. "After the latest hostilities, I would think not. Their trading interests are diametrically opposed to ours. They would watch us batter ourselves to death against France and raise no finger to help us. Their intent would be only to take command of the trade routes when we are soundly beaten. Spain, maybe, would be interested in a war against France, for reasons of their own. That might not be the wisest course for us to take. An even stronger Spain would skew the balance of power too much in the continent. A later war against Spain would take the combined effort of all her neighbors . . ."

King Charles silenced them both with a wave of his bejeweled fingers. "There will be no war."

Rochester made a noise of protest. "You cannot ignore the insult to a daughter of England."

Even the phlegmatic Saville seemed disturbed. "The king of France has offered an insult to your own sister, to the sister of the king of England. He cannot be allowed to do so with impunity."

The king rubbed the end of his nose. "I do not know yet of Henrietta's imprisonment. My French brother has not informed me of the fact, so no insult can be taken over the matter. Even were I to go to war, Henrietta would long be dead ere the English army could reach Paris. No, that is not the answer. I do not need to go to war."

Sophie gasped. Had her journey been all for nothing then? "So you will leave Madame Henrietta to languish in the Bastille?"

King Charles drew his brows together at her incautious words. "I will do no such thing. She is my sister, and I will protect her. As King Louis has seen fit to imprison her by stealth, I shall see fit to rescue her by stealth."

"You will bring her back to England?"

"I should never have agreed to the match with Philippe of Orleans. He is no husband at all for any woman, let alone a woman such as my sister. Let her but set foot back on good English soil, and I will get the Pope to annul her marriage to that buggering French fool. Then I shall find a good English husband for her, let my brother in France storm as he will."

"She is in the Bastille. It is impregnable."

"No fortress is impregnable for those who wish to escape and have skilled enough friends on the outside to help them. She has the will to escape, no doubt. All I need to do is send her the skill."

Rochester grinned. "Are you thinking what I think you're thinking?"

The King raised his eyebrows. "What may that be?"

"Hugh of Coventry."

"Who else? Arrange to have him brought here as soon as possible."

Rochester bowed. "I am at your service, sire, as always."

The King turned to Sophie and Lamotte. "Rochester will have Hugh fetched right away and told to prepare for a journey to Paris. I would take it well if you would accompany him."

What could one say to a king but yes? Sophie bowed her head in acceptance of this last task.

"Please, do not hurt him or misplace him. He is worth more than his weight in gold to me, and I would be seriously angry if he did not come home again. If I did not love my little sister so dearly and fear for her treatment at the hands of my brother of France, I would not send him away."

The King of England made this Hugh of Coventry sound like the right hand of God. "Who is he, this Hugh?"

The King smiled into his sleeve. "He is my secret weapon—silent, stealthy, and deadly. I have never known him to fail in any task I have seen fit to give him. As long as he is by my side, I know I shall be safe. He is Henrietta's best—and only—hope."

Hugh of Coventry turned out to be a slight, pale man with a shock of dark brown hair.

Sophie wiggled her toes in her new English boots

and eyed him warily. What was so special about him that the king of England could not do without him?

She nudged her horse with her toe to spur on her gait a little. The King had arranged horses for them to take them as far as the coast, where a boat was waiting for them. Lamotte had groaned at the thought of another crossing, but she could not wait to get her feet on to good French soil once more.

Lamotte had been right. English food was barely edible. How she longed for a good ragout, seasoned with plenty of fresh herbs, instead of endless slabs of beef boiled until it was gray as a corpse and as tough as leather to chew.

She came up alongside Hugh and slowed down a fraction so they could ride side by side. She wanted to know more about this mysterious stranger. "Why did the king send you?"

He did not take offense at her directness. "I am the king's thief. He sends me on errands that call for a light touch and a complete absence of morals."

"You steal for him?"

"All the time. Secrets, mostly. They are easy to store and hard to prove against you if you are caught."

"You think you could rescue madame from the Bastille?"

He grinned, showing a set of fine, white teeth. "Prisons are easy game. They are built, you see, to keep people in, not to keep them out. Once you have found a way in, all you need to do is to retrace your steps again, and voilà, you are free."

"You have broken many people out of prison?"

He gave her another easy grin. "All the time. Myself, mostly."

Lamotte chose this moment to come riding up to them. The path was too narrow for three to ride alongside one another. Sophie dropped back to leave the men together. She was happy enough to be alone with her thoughts for the moment.

Indeed, she had much to sort out in her mind. Her mission was over. Hugh of Coventry would rescue the Princesse Henrietta and spirit her back to England, with no one the wiser. The king would not be pleased that Lamotte had failed in his mission to stop her, but no doubt his misdemeanor would be overlooked. The king would not know why he had not carried out his mission, and he could not be punished for mere failure.

Now that King Charles knew of his sister's imprisonment, she felt relieved of the burden she had been carrying ever since monsieur had begged for her help. She was no longer the guardian of a dire political secret. She had done her duty and satisfied her conscience. The force that had kept her on her feet for the past days of relentless journeying toward her goal was dissipated. She was a free agent once more.

What was she to do now, though?

She could not return to Paris as Gerard Delamanse if she did not want her life to be cut short. Lamotte was right about that. If nothing else, she had learned that those who disobeyed the orders of their king were doomed to a hasty death.

She was not ready to die. She had too much to live for.

Nor did she want to serve her king any longer. She had become a musketeer to win honor in the name of her brother. There was no honor in serving a lecher who invested himself with the dignity of a Sun King, then misused his power by imprisoning his own brother's wife. She had no pride in being a king's man anymore. The king was corrupt and evil. She would not be his servant.

Loyalty in and of itself held no virtue. Loyalty was only a merit when the obedience served some higher purpose. Corrupting one's sister was no virtue. She no longer owed any loyalty to her king.

Her mind was made up. She would be a musketeer no longer. But if not a soldier, then what?

She could hire her arm out as a mercenary, she supposed, fighting for whoever would pay her wages. She would be free to wander where she pleased, fighting all over Europe if she chose to, wherever the winds of war blew and a strong arm could find a willing master.

That was no answer to her dilemma, though. She would simply be changing one bad master for another. She had no desire to fight for the sake of fighting. She needed to fight on the side of righteousness, for a purpose, for honor and glory and justice.

She would have to cease soldiering and return home in defeat, foiled in her efforts. Turn farmer and look after her land, she supposed, though she had no one to look after it for, no future generations to pass it down to.

Why should she bother to practice good husbandry when on her death the land would be gone, sold to strangers? She might as well be a mercenary than lead a life of such pointless toil.

The thought of going home to the Camargue was no sanctuary, either. She shuddered as she remembered the winter she had spent there, alone and afraid. The manor house she had grown up in was haunted with the spirits of her family. She would never live there in peace again.

Mayhap she would have to give up being a man

and be a woman again. She turned the thought over in her mind. The more she thought about it, the more practical it seemed to be. As Sophie Delamanse she would never be in high favor with the king, but neither would her life be in danger.

She would not go to Paris as Sophie Delamanse. Now that she had decided to give up her commission in the musketeers, Lamotte would have little interest in her. There would be no need for her to live with him, and Paris held no other attractions for her. She would rather die than molder away her life living in a garret in the city, of use to no one and for nothing, living only for the rare, chance sighting of her husband in the streets she had once walked down with him.

She wondered if he would offer once more to send her to his home in Burgundy to live with his widowed mother. She shuddered to herself at the prospect. Such a fate would be worse than death. She would rather toil on her own land, with the ghosts of her family to keep her company, than to be buried alive, alone and unloved, in a strange county.

She shook her skirts with an irritable hand. She detested riding in skirts now that she was so used to the far more practical garb of breeches. To make matters worse, she had no one to blame but herself for her discomfort. She herself had suggested she remain a woman for the time being to put any of King Louis's remaining spies off the scent, if indeed they were still searching for her. Somehow, having no one else to blame made her discomfort seem all the worse.

The disguise should serve its purpose. With any luck the king's spies would believe her drowned at the bottom of the channel, and Lamotte alongside her. She would attract no attention as a woman. Hugh of Coventry would have a better chance of rescuing Henrietta if they could slip into Paris unnoticed, rather than having to fight their way back.

Lamotte staggered off the boat, fell to his knees, and kissed the ground beneath his feet, his heart full of thankfulness. "Ah, French soil. I swear I shall never leave the shores of beautiful France again as long as I live."

"Does that mean I shall have to journey to the Americas by myself then?"

He stared in horror at Sophie. "You cannot want to go to the Americas. I will not allow it."

Her face dimpled into a smile.

He had never noticed before how her right cheek held a merry dimple in it. He wanted to kiss his fingers and place them on the spot.

"I was jesting, milord."

He heaved a sigh of relief. "Thank the good Lord for that. It was an ill jest to torment me with, lady wife of mine, while my guts are still heaving from the last crossing."

She looked down her nose at him with a haughty expression on her face. "The water was as smooth as silk, and calmer than a nun's nature."

She was irrepressible, and how he loved her for it. "Do not count on your pretty blue gown saving you from my just and righteous wrath, wife."

She wrinkled her nose at him. He knew how much she hated being called his wife, but he could not forebear reminding her of it. She had married him. They belonged to each other. He would not let her go easily.

"I may be wearing a gown, but I still have my knife tucked into my bodice."

"Ouch. Be careful where you aim it. I am not wearing a wig."

She laughed and held out her arm to him. "If you have finished spilling your guts on the ground, please be a gentleman and escort me to the place where we are to stay the night."

Lamotte put on his haughtiest air for the proprietor of the tavern. "A chamber for me and my lady wife, and another for my friend. We are traveling incognito, without our entourage, so two chambers will be sufficient."

Sophie watched him in amusement. She had never seen him play the wealthy lord before. He did it to perfection, with just the right mix of imperious demand and friendly condescension. At any rate, he soon had the innkeeper and maidservants bustling around to serve them both.

Hugh of Coventry stayed in the background, merging into the scenery and not opening his mouth unless he had to. He spoke French with only the merest trace of an English accent, but even that could prove dangerous in the wrong company.

They met for a council of war in the larger chamber Sophie and Lamotte were to share as husband and wife. Lamotte stretched his legs out in front of him, his hands clasped behind his back. "I shall hire a coach to take us to Paris. We shall move more slowly than on horseback, but we shall seem less suspicious. Two men and a woman on horseback would raise eyebrows wherever we passed through."

Sophie shrugged. Horseback or coach made little difference to her. "Once we are in Paris, what then?"

Hugh steepled his fingers together. "I have been considering the best way of rescuing Madame Henrietta. I will need your help, Comtesse."

Lamotte growled. "Sophie's job is done. She has taken the message to the king. Her life is in danger were she to stay in Paris."

Hugh raised his eyebrows. "And mine is not? Or yours, too, for that matter, if your part in this escapade should ever be known?"

"My safety is my own affair. You are not a woman. Or my wife. Let us rescue the woman on our own."

"We may well need Sophie to aid us."

"Leave her out of it."

Sophie shook her head. "This was my mission to start with, not yours. I may as well see it through to the end." She might as well make the most of her life while it still had some meaning to it. She would be exiled from Paris again soon enough.

Hugh nodded approvingly. "You are a brave woman. Had the count not claimed you already, I would carry you off back to England with me."

Sophie smiled. At least one man in the world could appreciate her for what she was without desiring to turn her into a delicate porcelain figurine, to be protected from the world. "Thank you for your offer. Were I not already married to the count, I might be able to be persuaded to accompany you willingly."

Lamotte placed one arm around her shoulders and scowled at Hugh. "Sophie is my wife."

Hugh shrugged as he turned to leave for his own chamber. "Unfortunately for me that is so. If you ever get tired of your husband, madame, come to Coventry. I will always be glad to see you."

She could not ever imagine getting tired of Lamotte. "I will."

Lamotte glared at the door as it shut behind Hugh's departing back. "He is an Englishman and a thief. He is not worthy of you."

Sophie kicked off her riding boots and tossed her cloak on the end of the bed. Her husband deserved to be teased a little for his rudeness to their companion. "He is in high favor with his master."

He snorted as he tossed his own boots aside.

She turned her back on her husband. "Help me with these buttons, will you? I cannot reach them all myself."

He undid her buttons one by one, his large fingers surprisingly deft. When he had done, she laid her dress by on a chair. She eyed the bed longingly. How she longed to have her husband join her in it.

Whatever path she chose to take, he would not be walking beside her for much longer. He was a musketeer still, and in high favor with the king. All he needed to do was keep his part in this affair secret from the world and he would continue in this favor. He had no need to share her exile.

Until they reached Paris, though, he was hers. She needed to feel his arms around her again.

She fiddled with the ties of her petticoats until they dropped to the floor. She stepped out of them and laid them over her gown. "And he is quite handsome really. I could do worse than go to Coventry with him."

She could not sleep comfortably in her bodice. "Unlace me now, if you would."

His fingers were warm on her cold back. "You seem to have forgotten something, wife."

She slid the straps of her bodice down her shoulders, tossed the garment aside and turned to face him. "I have?"

He took her breasts in his hands—as she had hoped he would, as she had been longing for him to do. His hands burned her with their touch and she felt ripples of pleasure shimmer though her body. "You cannot go to Coventry with Hugh. You are my wife."

God, how she wanted him. How foolish of her to admit this to herself only as she was on the eve of losing him forever. She took his shoulders in her hands, feeling the hardness of his muscles under his jacket. She would make the most of the time they had left to them, clinging to him while she still could. "I could have the marriage annulled in England."

A slow smile spread over his face. "You could, could you?"

She nodded, her mouth dry.

He held her naked body to him with a strong arm. "Then I will have to put it out of your power to do so, won't I? I will have to make you my wife tonight in deed, as well as in word."

Her eager fingers helped him out of his jacket and undid the buttons of his linen shirt. In no time at all he was standing before her as naked as she was, the candlelight glowing on the golden muscles of his body. His manhood stood up proudly, a drop of moisture beading its tip.

She brushed it gently with her fingertips and he groaned. "Come to bed with me, wife of mine."

They slid in between the crisp, white sheet, hugging together for warmth. He took her breasts into his hands again and bent down to suck tenderly at her nipples. "You have the most beautiful breasts in the world," he murmured against her skin. Shafts of desire shot up her spine at the touch of his lips. She wanted him as she had never wanted anything before.

She felt the hardness of his proud manhood against her stomach and she squirmed against him, wanting to feel him closer.

His hand reached in between their bodies and

touched her in between her legs, in the secret spot that made her cry out with wanting him.

She writhed against him as he tormented her with his touch, thrusting first one finger, then two, into her in a gentle rhythm that drove her to a frenzy.

His eyes were dark with desire. He lifted himself over her body, his manhood at the entry to her channel. Slowly he guided himself into her until he was sheathed inside her, his sword in her warm, wet scabbard, welcoming him home.

She felt full. Filled to the brim with her husband. She wanted him to stay there forever, filling her with his presence, loving her with his body.

He withdrew a little and she ached for his presence again, but he had withdrawn only to thrust into her again. She arched her body to meet his thrust, urging him into her.

She was breathless now, gasping for air as he filled her again and again.

The tension in her body was unbearable. As he moved in her, she could feel herself coiling ever tighter, until, with a cry, the coil inside her snapped and her body was flooded with waves of release.

His body on top of hers went rigid and he cried out as spasms shook his body.

She felt the warm fluid of his essence flood into the core of her being. She lay back, exhausted with happiness. She would never be lonely again.

"You would go to Coventry after this, wife of mine?" His voice was thick with sleepy satisfaction.

She snuffed the candles and snuggled down to sleep in his arms, feeling loved and protected as she never had before. "Never."

* * *

They reached Paris too soon for Sophie's liking. Though she slept next to her husband every night, curled up against his warm body like a cat, she had not got enough of him. Every time he touched her she wanted to weep, thinking how few were the nights they had left for showing each other a glimpse of heaven.

Her desire for him was like a fever in her blood that could not be quenched. Every sight of him made the fever in her soul burn hotter and brighter. She would never tire of him, not ever. She loved him so well her heart was nigh to bursting with it.

Now they were in Paris, near the end of their journey. Very soon now she would have to summon up the courage to bid him good-bye.

First she would rescue Henrietta. She would not allow herself to be distracted. She would not think of their final parting until her mission was done.

The Bastille loomed out of the night in front of them, gloomy and forbidding. Its walls were so high they reached almost to the clouds. Sophie shuddered as she looked at it. She could not imagine rescuing someone from this place of death and horror. It was indeed impregnable.

Hugh was unaffected by her fears. He simply stood there and looked at it for some minutes without speaking, his chin on his hands as if deep in thought.

Finally Sophie could stand it no longer. "Well?" she demanded in a whisper. "What do you think? Can you get her out?"

His teeth gleamed white in the darkness. "Have faith, madame. I have never failed yet."

"So what will you do? How will you rescue her?"

"Go to my chamber in the house of the delightful Widow Poussin, eat my supper, and sleep and think."

***

King Louis kneeled before her in the filth of the dungeon and took her hand in his. "Henrietta, I beg of you to stop this foolishness. Just one word from you and I can release you from this hellhole. Just one word and you will be a princess again, living in all the luxury that the might and wealth of France can acquire for you."

So now he was trying to blame her for her imprisonment. Naturally, since he was the king, his actions had to be infallible, and all the blame had to lie with her. She had no patience for him or his deluded, self-seeking arguments. She would rather be left alone in the dark than listen to his nonsense any longer. "You could release me any time you pleased, if you had a mind to."

He got up from his uncomfortable perch on the floor and paced up and down her narrow cell. "Say you will be my mistress, the idol of my heart, and I will release you gladly."

She eyed the guard standing over by the door with interest. He was new to his post, younger than the others she had seen before, with a look of youthful fervor rather than the stolid cynicism of the older guards. He seemed to look on her with an eye of pity. She hated to think what she looked like after a fortnight in the Bastille with little food and no water for washing. She felt gaunt and thin already and her velvet dress, once so grand and gay, now hung on her weakened frame in dirty folds. She felt the grime of the prison cell in every pore of her body. What wouldn't she give just to wash her hands, even just her fingertips, in a bowl of clean, sweetly scented water?

She did not even have a comb to brush her hair.

She had always been so proud of her hair. Unlike other women, she had never had to spend hours with heated tongs and curling papers to give her coiffure a fashionable look. Her hair had always hung naturally in perfect corkscrew curls around her white neck. She had tried to comb it through with her fingers for the first few days she had been imprisoned, but the effort had made so little difference she had given it up. Her once prized hair now lay in matted tangles over her shoulders. Even if she were to get out of prison, it would never be the same.

With a little bit of luck, maybe she could turn her bedraggled state to her advantage. The young guard seemed to be her best chance yet of escaping this putrid dungeon.

She waited for the king to leave with more impatience than usual. As self-absorbed as was his wont, he did not notice her distraction. He trod up and down her tiny cell, blathering on at her until she thought she would scream.

"I have been waiting for many weeks for you to give up this foolishness. I am running out of patience, Henrietta."

"What do I care for your lack of patience?" she spat at him, suddenly sick unto death of the torment of his presence. "I care naught for you, you foolish old lecher. You disgust me. Even if I did not love the Comte de Guiche with all my heart, I would never take you to my bed."

The king stopped his ranting and looked at her as if seeing her face for the first time. "Beware the words you speak to your king. I am slow to anger, but when roused, my ire is terrible to behold."

She laughed in his face. "What else can you do to me? You have torn me out of the arms of my lover, locked me up away from the sunlight and the air, and starved me half to death. What more can you do to me save take my life? Even death would be preferable to a life wasting away in this cell. Do your worst. I care not."

"That is your last word?"

She spat at his feet. "That is my last word. I will die rather than become your lover."

The King shook his head as if he were truly saddened by her words. "I am sorry for it, Henrietta. I have ever loved you dearly and would have made you mistress of the world. If I cannot have you, then no one else shall, either." With these words he left and took the guard with him, shooting home the bolts on the other side of the door behind him. One pair of feet clumped loudly down the stone corridor.

Henrietta stood close to the door and sighed loudly. She would work on the youthful guard without delay. She feared her time was running out. "Ah, me. How much is wrong with the world when a poor young woman is imprisoned in a freezing dungeon and fed on bread and water only for refusing to give in to the base desires of her king."

The sound of a faint cough came from the other side of the door, a signal the guard had heard and understood her complaint, though he dared not answer her.

Henrietta put her arms around herself and hugged her tattered velvet dress close to her body, smiling. With any luck, her guard would have the religious fervor of the very young and have been disturbed by the corruption of the king. She only hoped her first sally in her fight for her life had fallen on fertile ground.

* * *

Ricard Lamotte bowed low before the king. "Gerard Delamanse is dead, sire." It was no lie he told. A stretching of the truth, mayhap, and an omission of certain rather pertinent facts, but not exactly a lie.

"Where did you catch up with him? In France or England?"

"He never reached England. He died in France."

The King drummed his fingers on the arm of his chair. "You are sure of this?"

He thought of Sophie's grief for her brother. Yes, he was sure Gerard was dead. "As sure as I am of my own life, your majesty."

The King nodded and fell silent. "You are a good soldier, Lamotte, and a loyal one."

Lamotte felt his insides cramp with guilt. He was a good soldier, and loyal to his sense of right, but these did not always coincide with the desires of his king. "Yes, sire."

The king toyed with a heavy gold ring on his finger. "Would you also like to be a rich one?"

"You have been royally munificent to my family already," he murmured, feeling as though he were skirting a patch of quicksand that stood ready to swallow him whole if he made a false step.

The king brushed his answer aside with a wave of one puffy hand, weighed down with rings laden with precious stones on every finger. "Pah, a county in Burgundy is nothing. No one lives there but farmers and villeins, rooting together like pigs in the stinking mud. Would you not rather have a post at court? A rich post that would keep you always at my side, in Paris?"

He would rather hang himself from the rafters than become a sycophant at court, fawning over the king's very word and maneuvering others aside for the honor of wiping the royal arse or emptying the royal chamber pot of the royal shit. "I am already in your service as a member of your guard, and ready to obey your every order. Command me as you will." *And I will obey you if it does not go against my conscience,* he added to himself.

The king tapped one finger up and down on the arm of the chair and cleared his throat several times.

Lamotte waited, a sick feeling starting to grow in the pit of his stomach. Whatever task the king had for him, it was important enough for the king to offer him a coveted position in court. That in itself spoke eloquently of its seriousness.

The king's hesitation in giving voice to the task made him suspicious that the bribe might well be needed—that the task was onerous and unpleasant in the extreme.

"I have heard some disturbing news." The king's voice was heavy when he finally opened his mouth to speak. "There is an Englishman come to Paris."

He hoped against hope that the king was not referring to Hugh of Coventry. Surely Englishmen must come to Paris all the time. "Sire?"

"A particular Englishman, a known spy in the pay of my English cousin, Charles II."

Things were not looking good for Hugh. He felt his bowels cramp with fear for his beautiful, fierce wife. He had left her in Hugh's care while he answered the summons from his king. How he wanted to rush off and take her into a place of safety where the king and his minions could not touch her.

He mastered his discomfort as best he could, hoping it did not show on his face. He could not give the game away. He had too much to lose.

"I suspect he may have been sent to rescue a particular prisoner in the Bastille, one traitor to France." He stopped and looked directly into Lamotte's eyes. "I would not have this traitor escape."

The king was definitely talking about Hugh and his quest to rescue Henrietta. He needed to warn Hugh right away that his presence in Paris had been noted and the purpose of his visit guessed at.

More to the point, he needed to make sure Sophie was kept well away from Hugh from now on and did not share in the danger to him by association. Hugh had been sent by the king of England to rescue his sister. He and Sophie had played their part and should now retire before they were further compromised. "You would have me find and kill the Englishman?"

The king shook his head. "That would be worth little. My English cousin would simply send another spy, and then another, and another. Eventually, one of them might be successful, and the traitor would walk free. I cannot allow this to happen."

He could breathe easier now he knew that Hugh, and Sophie with him, was in no immediate danger. His legs still trembled with the desire to race to his Sophie's side and protect her from whatever force the king could muster against her. By God, once he had her in his arms, he would never let her go again. "You will allow the Englishman to walk free?"

"Pah. What do I care for one English spy? Once the traitor is dead, there will be no more need for spies."

A thought lit up in his brain. Mayhap this could be the way into the Bastille they had been looking for. The sooner Hugh performed his rescue, the easier it would be to send him packing where he could no longer endanger them both by his presence. "If it please you, sire, to give me the order for the execution of this traitor, I will have it carried to the governor of the Bastille at once and see the order is carried out immediately. Then you need fear no English spies." He liked the plan. Once he was inside the Bastille, instead of carrying out an execution, he would plan to stage a rescue.

The king heaved a sigh. "If only it were that simple."

Lamotte stood silently. Far be it from him outwardly to question to motives of his king. Inside, his mind was turning over every possibility.

"I cannot sign an order for the execution of the traitor. There are reasons of state that forbid it."

Knowing the identity of the traitor as he did, he could guess only too well what those reasons of state were. What, then, did he intend to do? Let her go free? Exile her away from France? Leave her in her dungeon in the Bastille until she died of jail fever or was rescued by a sympathizer? "Yes, sire."

"The traitor is none other than the English princess, Madame Henrietta. I cannot allow her to live and to spread her treasons, but I cannot try her and execute her as she deserves. Her brother, Charles of England, would be incensed against me and would league with the Dutch or the Spaniards against me. France would be drawn into a war over the fate of a traitor. I cannot risk such a state of affairs. I need her to die quietly and quickly, with no order and no publicity."

He would never have believed it possible of the king of France if he had not heard those words with his own ears. The King had sent rascals after Sophie to have her killed. Now he wanted Henrietta murdered on the sly, killed off quickly and quietly with no trial and no chance of defending herself from the accusations made against her. Was nothing sacred to him? Was there no depths to which he would not stoop?

"You are a soldier. You must know a thousand ways to kill someone without leaving a trace."

Lamotte half closed his eyes to hide the disgust he could feel burning in his face. He was a soldier, not an assassin. He would not turn murderer for any man in Christendom—or out of it.

"Kill the traitor in such a way that no one knows she has been murdered and I shall make you an earl. You have my solemn word on this."

What worth was the word of a king who sought to dishonor and then to murder his own brother's wife? He would more likely find himself imprisoned deep in an oubliette, where all knowledge of the crimes of the king would languish away into obscurity along with his soul.

He could no longer serve his king with honor. With a snap that felt as though his heart was breaking within his breast, he unbuckled his sword and knelt down before the king. "Your Majesty," he said, as he laid the sword in its scabbard at the feet of the King, "I hereby relinquish my commission. As of this moment, I am no longer a musketeer in the King's Guard."

The king's beady eyes bulged out of his head with disappointed rage. "What do you mean by this?"

He stood up and saluted smartly, feeling as though he were free once more. "I cannot carry out this task you have demanded of me. Were I to do so, I would not be able to live with my conscience. I must therefore quit your service."

The king half rose in his chair, his fingers gripping the armrests so tightly his knuckles had gone white. "You, too, Count Lamotte? You would turn traitor to your king?"

He would probably be punished for it, but he could not hold his tongue. "No, sire. I am as loyal as ever I was, when my king is worth serving. It is you who have turned traitor to your own good name."

He snapped his heels together and left without another word, the king's sputters of rage burning in his ears. He had burned his bridges behind him. He knew the king's implacable temperament well enough to know he would never be forgiven as long as the king as alive. Never again would he be admitted at court. Never again would he hold a post as a musketeer, or any other position of importance.

Whatever the consequences, he could not regret a single word he had spoken. The king of France had shamed himself this day, and he had borne witness to it.

He found Hugh and Sophie sitting together, poring over their maps and diagrams. The sight of their heads bent in mutual comradeship and cooperation over the papers bothered him more than he cared to admit. He had not forgotten—or forgiven—Hugh's invitation to his wife. The damned Englishman should learn to keep his hands away from other men's wives. He would teach him the lesson himself, did Hugh make the slightest move on his wife again.

His mood was not improved when he saw the third person in the room, the woman dressed as a youth who had so taunted him at the inn. She sketched him a mocking bow. "Your servant, Monsieur le Comte. I did not expect to meet you again so soon."

He leaned on his elbow against the wall, crowding her into a corner with the largeness of his presence. "If I had not found out your secret, Madame Assassin," he muttered in her ear, "you would not be alive by now."

She gave him a feral smile. "You are twice my size and strength and full of brave and boastful words, Monsieur musketeer, but you will never win a single round against me. Honesty has no defense against trickery, at which I am an expert. You were lucky Sophie begged me to save you. I was nigh to slitting your throat too, merely for the company you were keeping."

"That company was none of my choosing. They would have died by my hand if you and my dear wife had not gotten to them before I could."

She raised her eyebrows. "Outdone by a woman? Twice? Shame upon you, Monsieur musketeer."

She was too quick and slippery for him for sure. He turned away, swallowing his rage with some difficulty. He would not demean himself by trading insults with a mere woman, for all that she had the viciousness and dexterity of a venomous snake. Sophie, his Amazonian Sophie, was a positive haven of softness and sweetness compared with her sisters in arms. "If you would rescue the sister of your king," he barked at Hugh, "you had best hurry before it is too late."

Hugh ignored the interruption. "Once you are inside . . ." he said to Sophie.

"Once *you* are inside," he corrected the arrogant Englishman, his fingers itching to teach the pup a lesson in manners he would not soon forget. "My wife will not be going anywhere with you. As I said, you had best hurry, or once *you* are inside, all you will find will be the duchesse's corpse."

Sophie at least took heed of him. She looked up, her eyes wide and shining with excitement and determination. "Have you news from the king?"

"Yes, what news from your lord and master, Monsieur musketeer?" chimed in the venomous snake.

He took off his hat and tossed it on the ground. "I am no longer a musketeer in the King's employ. He asked me to kill the English princess: garrotte her or poison her or anything that could make it look like it had been an accident. He wants her dead without seeming to be responsible for her death. Even now he may have found some one else to do his dirty work for him. As you sit here talking, she could already be dead."

"We cannot afford to wait. We must go straightway."

Hugh finally dragged his eyes away from Sophie. "I have not made arrangements yet for the princess's carriage out of Paris. Getting her out of the Bastille is the easy part. Getting her out of France will require more time."

The snake shrugged one shoulder. "We have no more time if she is to be rescued."

Lamotte shot her an evil look. "As if you care aught for her."

"True. I care more for the good French gold I have been promised for her rescue. Why else would I risk my skin on a fool's errand?"

Sophie shushed her with one hand and talked urgently to Hugh. "Miriame and I will go into the Bastille alone on the plan you have made for us. We have no need of you. While we are inside, you make all the arrangements you can."

His wife was surely not thinking of going into the Bastille to rescue a prisoner with only a single companion to help her. "I will not let you go alone."

"Sophie will be safe enough inside the Bastille."

He glared at the Englishman. "She is not your wife. I will go with her or she will not go."

"She has no need of an escort to help her get inside, but both of them will need help to escape the guards once they are out again. I will take Henrietta away. Let you look to the safety of your wife and her companion.

"It seems we do not have a second to lose. Ladies, your costumes, please."

Sophie and the snake grabbed a collection of tattered garments and began to disrobe as Hugh pored over his chicken scratchings once more.

He watched, scandalized, as Sophie and her friend transformed themselves in seconds to women of the street, tattered, ragged, and world-weary. "What are you intending?"

Hugh walked around them, inspecting with the eye of a true connoisseur. "Take your neckline a little lower," he said, as he tugged on Sophie's bodice until her breasts were nearly ready to spill out. "Try not to appear nervous. You're a tart now, a cheap streetwalker. You've seen it all, done it all before. You're after the money—remember that. A gold coin that will pay the rent and put food in your belly for another day."

He looked appraisingly at the snake. "Perfect. You've got the look exactly right. Greed and distrust in equal parts. Just try not to look as though you will bite the man's head off if he gets too close. It will put off your potential customers like nothing else could."

They had not answered his question. He stood in front of Sophie, blocking out her light. "What are you intending to do dressed in that garb?"

She looked up at him with those blue, blue eyes, and his heart turned over in his chest. When had she become so dear to him? How had she pierced through to the innermost core of his heart, this unlikely woman with her fierce ways and her determined will?

"To rescue Henrietta—the best way I know how."

"That is the task of a soldier. You are dressed as a woman."

She smiled into his face. "The better to put them off their guard. They will not expect any tricks from a woman. Women do not fight, do they?"

She was throwing his own words back in his face, the minx. He would kiss her if they were not in such a confounded hurry.

Hugh buckled on a knife under his jacket. "Don't waste your breath arguing. Time is too short to think of another plan."

Sophie smiled at him and his heart turned over in his breast at her brave beauty. "My job is only half done. There will be little danger in it for Miriame and me. You cannot come with us, or you will spoil our charade."

He did not like to leave Sophie to break into the prison without his aid, but she was a soldier and a musketeer. He had trained her as best he could. Whether or not he liked the idea, he had no right to stop her from doing her duty as she saw fit.

Miriame gave a mocking smile. "If you are afraid, Monsieur musketeer, leave it to others who are not."

No one would ever call him a coward. He would not leave Sophie to endanger herself alone, but he would protect her, even in the shadow of the Bastille. "What would you have me do to help?"

Hugh grinned at him, showing a row of even white teeth. "You can hold the horses outside and be ready for when we need you for the escape. Come with me and I will explain the plan to you on the way."

* * *

Sophie's insides were achurn with nervous excitement as the cheap hired coach trundled along in the deepening twilight, the poor tired horse clopping over the cobbles with weary legs. She was about to face a battle of a different kind, where her wits and not her strength with a sword would be her best ally.

Miriame looked as calm and detached as ever. "No need to be nervous," she advised. "Men are ruled by what lies between their legs. Pull your bodice a little lower, show them some more bosom and a bit of leg and they won't have a drop of blood left in their head to think with."

They passed Lamotte, pulling along a street barrow. She hardly recognized him in the failing light with his hair matted and filthy, his face smudged with dirt and wearing Hugh's tattered clothes and thick peasant's boots. It gave her some measure of comfort to know he would be waiting for them outside, ready to whisk them off and out of danger as soon as they had rescued Henrietta.

She had put her life in his hands before, and he had saved her. She felt secure and protected whenever he was around. She only hoped he would not run into any trouble as he watched and waited for them.

She clutched Miriame's hand tightly as they alighted in front of the Bastille. "You don't have to do this, you know," she said to Miriame as she looked up at the forbidding gray walls in front of her. They were enough to send a chill though the bones of even the most stouthearted person. "I will think none the worse of you if you pull out now."

"And give up the reward Hugh has promised me if we are successful? Enough money to keep my belly full for a year or more?" Miriame shook her head. "I think not. If you knew me better, you would not waste your breath suggesting such a thing."

The guards leered at them through the darkness with greedy eyes as they banged on the door.

"We wos sent for," whined Miriame in a voice Sophie had never heard her use before. "The guv wants us."

One of the guards sniggered as he held his lantern so the light shone right into their eyes. "What could he want with a pair of dirty slatterns like you?"

Sophie tugged her bodice down a little lower. Miriame was right about the power of naked flesh. The eyes of both guards were fixated on her now. "We have special talents, if you know what I mean."

Miriame cackled. "Naughty boys like to be punished, and the guv's been a very naughty boy lately."

The guards sniggered again, but they unbolted the gate and let them in.

Sophie felt her breathing quicken as the gate slammed shut behind them. They were trapped inside the most evil prison in France, and of their own free will, too. There was no turning back now. She would rescue Henrietta or die trying.

After a short but vicious argument, one of the guards left the gate to escort them to the governor's apartments. The other stayed at the gate with bad grace, spitting on the ground and muttering curses at their departing backs.

Their escort dawdled his way through the passages. "Is the guv in a hurry to see you?"

Sophie wiped the sweat off her palms surreptitiously on her tattered dress. If worse came to worst, they both had daggers within easy reach and there were two of them against one of him. Stringing along a lecherous guard had seemed easy enough while they were simply sitting around a table talking about it. It was a lot harder to do for real, when the stone walls of the prison were all around her and the scent of prison misery corrupted the very air she was breathing.

"You wanna quickie afore we go in to him, eh, soldier?" Miriame sidled up to him, took his arm in hers and ran her free hand over the bulge in his groin with an appreciative coo. "I ain't never been in here before. Show us where you keep all the prisoners and Polly 'n me, we'll give you one for free, right Poll?"

He licked his lips with greedy anticipation. "What about the governor? Won't he be expecting you?"

Sophie sidled up to him on the other side and took hold of his other arm. "He can wait on us for a bit. Won't do him no harm."

With a woman on each side, the guard led them through the passages, opening peepholes in every dungeon they passed to show them the human misery that lay behind each door. Sophie felt her heart sink with every chamber she looked into. Human misery she saw aplenty, but there was no sign of the woman she had come to rescue.

"Ain't you got no one famous in here?" Miriame whined after they'd gone through a half dozen corridors with no sight nor sign of the imprisoned duchesse. "We wanna see the famous prisoners, don't we, Poll?"

The guard hesitated.

"Show us the famous ones you got, and Poll and me will do you both together, just like the guv likes, eh, Poll? A special favor for a special favor."

He scratched his belly with a thoughtful air. "I got one real famous prisoner I could show you. But you'd better not tell a word of it to no one else, or tell who showed you, or I'll be strung up by me neck."

Sophie held her breath with excitement. Maybe their plan was going to work. "We won't breathe a word of it. Not a word, we promise."

Still he hesitated. "I'm risking my neck for you," he grumbled. "You sure you'll make it worth my while?"

Miriame gave an evil grin that made Sophie shudder as she rubbed up against him like a cat. "You'll die a happy man."

Another guard was stationed outside the door, a young guard with a pale face and a guilty cast to his countenance. He did not look happy to see them as they rounded the corner. "What brings you here?"

Their guard gave an awkward grin. "Visitors for the princesse."

The princesse. Sophie wanted to shout with joy. They had the right cell. Now they just had to get her out of it, and she would be free. Well, almost free. They still had to get her out of the Bastille, out of Paris, and out of France. At any rate, they were making good progress.

Henrietta's guard did not look convinced. "Harlots come to mock at their betters, more like it. Be off with ye. I have orders to let no one near her."

Miriame sidled up to him and put one grubby hand on his chest. "We just wants to take a peep."

Had she not been listening for it with all her night, Sophie would have missed the telltale clink that signified success. Miriame had lifted the keys to the dungeon right off the guard's belt, and without him suspecting a thing.

He pushed her hand off him with a look of distaste.

"Be off with ye, ye slatternly drabtails, or I'll beat ye off with the flat of my sword."

Voices. Sophie heard voices from the other side of the door. There was a cry as if a woman was in pain, and then silence. They had to act now—if they were not already too late. There was no time to lose.

With a quick flick, she drew her knife from beneath her skirts and slashed at the guard's right knee. She had had enough of killing. She wanted only to immobilize him, not kill him.

He gave a bellow of rage as he fell to the floor, unable to stand.

"Hush your mouth," Sophie barked at him, no longer needing to play the seductress, "or I'll slit your throat instead."

His noise stopped abruptly in mid bellow as if by magic.

Miriame had her guard on the floor, bleeding from a wound in his side. "Who is in there with Madame Henrietta?" she demanded, her knife at his neck.

"Priests," Henrietta's guard babbled, his face white with fear and guilt. "I felt sorry for her. They said she had called for them and they were there to comfort her in her distress."

"Fool," Sophie said, as she caught the keys Miriame tossed at her. She was deadly afraid they had come too late to be of any use. "You have let in her assassins."

The guard groaned with fear and pain. "Do not kill me, I beg of you. I was only trying to help a soul in need."

She unlocked the door with shaking fingers, fearing what she would find on the other side.

Two black-robed figures rushed at them as soon as the door swung open. Sophie had no qualms about killing hired assassins. She plunged her dagger deep into the belly of one and he fell with a gurgle of blood in his throat. Miriame, on her feet again with an agile leap, slit the throat of the other before he knew what had hit him.

The body of a woman dressed in tattered red velvet lay on the cold stone floor. Sophie ran to her side. "Madame," she said urgently, shaking the woman's shoulder gently. "We have come to deliver you from this place."

Henrietta opened her eyes just a slit. Her face was pale and contorted with pain. "Those false priests have already freed me. I am on my way to heaven."

Miriame wiped the blood off her dagger and stuck in back into her bodice. "What ails you? You are not wounded that I can see."

Henrietta closed her eyes again as if the effort of keeping them open was too much for her. "Not wounded. Poisoned."

"Your brother sent us to free you and bring you back to England. You must not disappoint him."

A smile spread across her white, anguished face. "Charles did not forget me, then? He sent someone for me?"

"He did."

"Tell him I love him and am sorry to leave him so. And tell the comte . . ." Her voice faded away.

"Tell the comte what?" Sophie bent her head down to the dying woman.

The words were a mere flicker of sound in the dying air. "Tell the Comte de Guiche I loved him to my very last breath, and beyond."

"I will tell him."

"You promise?"

"I swear it, on my word on honor."

"I am not sorry I loved him." Her hand fluttered for a moment in the air and then lay still. "I am sorry only that our love had to end."

Her throat rattled, a twist of pain crossed her features, and then she lay still.

Too still.

Eleven

Sophie bowed her head for a moment. There was nothing more they could do for her.

"Dead?"

Sophie nodded.

Miriame swore. "Let's get out of here."

They had no need of their disguise now, and voluminous skirts would only slow them down. With hasty fingers, they ripped off their skirts and tossed them to one side. Clad once again in the breeches of their more familiar disguise, they leaped over the bodies of the false priests and the fallen guards and took to their heels as fast as they could go.

To the courtyard they raced, as if they wings on their heels. Behind them they could hear a hue and cry start up. They had mere moments up their sleeve.

The courtyard was deserted, with only a few smoky torches casting a flickering light onto the blackness that surrounded them. So far their luck was holding up. They ran to the wall where the rope should be waiting for them. They searched the wall on either side with desperate eyes.

No rope.

Behind them, a dozen guards with drawn swords rushed into the courtyard.

Miriame swore again, worse than before. "I should

have slit Lamotte's throat, too, while I had the chance. He has failed us."

Sophie took her dagger in her hand. They stood no chance against a bevy of well-armed guards, but she would not simply give in. "We'll have to fight our way out and hope to slip by them in the dark."

A whistling noise made her look up. An arrow attached to a length of line hurtled down mere inches from where she was standing. She stuck her dagger in her teeth and grabbed the line. Lamotte had not failed them after all. "Hold off the guards," she cried as she pulled on the thin rope.

Attached to the thin rope in her hands would be a length of thick rope. That rope was their ticket to freedom.

The thin rope seemed endless as she pulled and pulled on it, looping lengths and lengths of it at her feet. Miriame danced around her, her sword flashing, keeping her from harm.

Ah, there it was. Finally she could see it. With another burst of energy she pulled in the last lengths of thin line, until she felt the thickness of their savior in her hand.

A grapnel was attached to the end. She gave three swift sharp tugs on the rope, followed by another three. "Jump on," she yelled to Miriame, as she felt the rope start to move.

The sharp ends of the grapnel bored into the soles of her boots as she balanced on it, holding on to the rope for dear life. With a leap, Miriame joined her.

The guards stared in openmouthed wonder as the rope was pulled higher and higher into the air, away from them on the ground and out of their sight into the darkness above, until they were standing on the topmost battlements of the Bastille's outer wall.

Below them, the guards were running for the gate to catch them on the other side.

Sophie hooked the grapnel over the edge of the battlement and tugged on it firmly. It held tight.

She unbuckled the belt from her waist and swallowed nervously. "Ready?"

Miriame grinned. "This looks like fun."

The rope was stretched taut all the way from the topmost battlements to the street barrow on the road below, where Lamotte waited with the horses who had so bravely hauled them to the topmost tower of the Bastille.

Sophie flung her belt over the rope, wrapped the ends of the belt around her wrists, said a brief but heartfelt prayer, and flung herself over the battlements into the air below.

It was almost like flying, she thought, as she plummeted toward the ground at an alarming speed.

A hay wagon loomed out of the darkness in front of her. Her landing would be softer than she had hoped. She let go of the belt and slammed into the hay with such force that it knocked the breath from her body.

A moment later, Miriame fell beside her. "Whee, that was fun," she spluttered. "Let's go up and do it again."

Sophie shuddered as she reached overhead and cut their lifeline. The cut end whipped back like a snake and hung twitching against the prison wall. "Let's get the hell out of here."

Lamotte, waiting with their horses, had seen their wild ride down from the battlements.

He vaulted down from his horse and gathered Sophie into his arms.

She ran there willingly, feeling as if she had come home.

"You are not hurt?"

She shook her head. A little breathless maybe, and her arms would surely ache in the morn from her wild ride, but that was little enough. "No."

He brushed hay out of her hair with a hand so tender it brought tears to her eyes. "Henrietta?"

"Dead. Murdered a mere instant before we could get to her."

He hugged her closer. "I care not, so long as you are safe."

Just then, a huge commotion broke out behind them. Sophie turned her head to see the cause.

A barrow cart had broken an axle and overturned just before the gates of the Bastille. The owner of the barrow was wringing his hands and wailing at the top of his voice. Apples were rolling everywhere, to the delight of the street kids who scavenged a meager living under the shadow of the Bastille. With cries of glee they dashed in among the guards and horses to gather such an unforeseen treat into their grubby hands and pockets.

The rolling apples under their hooves and the squealing children darting around their legs were too much for the horses. One by one they whinnied in panic and fear and reared up, depositing their riders on the ground. Those who managed to retain their seats were too busy trying to get their scared mounts under control to give chase.

Lamotte hugged her to his side. "Hugh. It seems he has his uses after all."

They put the spurs to their horses, dodging the crowds who had come to witness the fun. Several guards who had escaped the melee caused by Hugh's cartload of apples gave chase.

Miriame lifted her hat off her head and whirled it around her head as they rode at top speed through the narrow streets. "Wheeee," she shouted at them above the noise of the galloping hooves. "This is almost as much as flying down the rope."

Sophie looked back at their pursuers. There were half a dozen of them now, riding after them as fast as they could go, caring little for the innocents who might get caught up in their furious path. "Shall we split up and divide the pursuit?" she shouted at her companions.

Lamotte shook his head vehemently as he galloped along. "I will not let you out of my sight, wife. You seem to get into trouble the instant I turn my back on you."

Miriame waved her hand in a gesture of farewell. "I'll leave you two lovebirds alone then," she called with a grin on her face. "Until later. Don't worry if you get yourselves caught. I'd come to your rescue just for the sake of another wild ride down that rope."

With a quick twist of her reins, she disappeared down a side street. Two of the guards wheeled around to follow her. The other four kept up their dogged pursuit.

Through the streets they went, their sole aim to lose the guards so they could make their way unmolested to their nominated meeting place. Sophie started to get worried as the chase went on through the darkness until the sky was pinkening with the approaching dawn, with no sign that the guards were flagging.

One of their pursuers gave a cry and went down, felled by a missile thrown at his head. It looked suspiciously like an apple. Hugh must still be on the case, Sophie thought with glee.

Through the streets they went, making their way slowly toward the marketplace. The market was thronged with early morning shoppers. They picked their way among them as fast as they were able.

There was a crash behind them as another pursuer went down, felled by a barrow stand accidentally kicked over by his comrade's horse. Only two were left now.

The day was breaking and the sky becoming dangerously light. They could not allow their pursuers to see their faces in the clear light of day or they would be doomed. Sophie looked at Lamotte. "Now?"

He reached into the saddle bags behind him and drew out two large gourds. Sophie reached behind her and drew out two of her own. They were heavy in her hands. Gripping her horse tightly with her knees, she unplugged the stoppers and threw the leaking gourds over her shoulder. Within moments, a thick, slippery, treacherous oil slick covered the ground behind her.

A barrow cart trundled by its owner slid out of control into the path of the guards. Seeing their quarry escaping them, they took a desperate chance and tried to leap over the impediment. The horses's hooves could get no purchase of the slippery ground. The lead horse slid on the oil and its legs went from under him with a sickening crunch of broken bone.

The last guard left on their tail saw the disaster that had befallen his comrade and tried to pull his horse up short from the jump, but he was too late. Pulled down at the last minute from the jump, the second horse, too, lost its footing on the treacherous cobblestones and crashed in a heap.

As Sophie and Lamotte turned the corner out of the

marketplace, all they could hear behind them was the screaming of the horses and the cursing of their pursuers at their double loss.

The sky was bright and blue when they reached the house of the Widow Poussin, where they had arranged to meet. Sophie had no love for her avaricious old landlady, but her old attic chamber had proven a perfect bolt-hole for Hugh of Coventry to hide in. As a lodger in a respectable boarding house, he would attract no undue attention to himself.

Wiping her hands on her greasy apron, the Widow Poussin herself shuffled outside to meet them as they dismounted, greeting them with an unpleasant grin that showed her teeth rotted down to the yellow stumps. "The others are waiting for you upstairs, if you please."

Sophie did not like the way the woman's eyes gleamed with a fearful gold fever as she watched them with her beady eyes or the way she wrung her hands together under the pretext of wiping them. She felt a cold shiver run down her back as the widow bobbed a curtsey at them and held the door open for them to enter. Old Widow Poussin was not usually so welcoming.

She stopped Lamotte with one hand on his arm as he strode toward the stairs. All was not right here. She could smell fear and lust together on the old woman's breath.

"Go upstairs and fetch them for me, would you," she said to the widow, tossing a small silver coin at her. "My legs are too stiff from riding to manage the stairs."

Lamotte looked at her with a curious eye and opened his mouth to speak. She silenced him with a finger laid to her lips. "All is not right," she whispered soft in his ear. "I suspect a trap."

As she had suspected, the widow's face grew black at her request. "Step inside and fetch them yourself," she grumbled, as she tucked the coin into her skinny bodice and scuttled back into the doorway. "I am no maidservant to a couple of traitors."

So that was the way the wind blew, Sophie thought as she reached wearily for her dagger. Their quest was over, they had failed in their mission, and they had been betrayed at the last. She was tired to the bottom of her soul, but there was no help for it. They would have to fight their way out once more and hope they could win through one last time.

Lamotte was on the widow before she had taken more than a couple of steps. "Where are my friends?" he said, his dagger at her neck.

The widow stood stock-still, her face white and shaking. "Don't kill me, monsieur," she gabbled, spittle forming at the corners of her mouth in her agitation to get the words out fast enough to avoid the blade of his knife. "Don't kill me and I'll tell you everything I know."

He took the edge of the knife away from her throat so she would calm down enough to answer him. "I'm listening."

"They're upstairs, just like I told you. Both of them." Removed from immediate danger, her voice had regained its truculence.

He gave Sophie an exasperated look and pressed the knife back against the hag's neck. "Who is up there with them?"

She shivered. "I don't know who they are, honest to God I don't. I've never seen them afore in all me life."

"Try a little harder." His voice held a silky menace. "You can do better than that."

Sophie turned away. She did not like to see the poor old woman bullied, even though she had blithely tried to send them to their deaths. Only the thought of Miriame and Hugh in danger prevented her from putting a stop to the interrogation. A few moments of fear might enable them to save two lives.

The old woman's shoulders slumped, her resistance finally broken. "Guards. Sent by the king."

"How many?"

"Five."

"Who are they after?"

"They wanted the English spy—and anyone who helped him."

"How did they know where to come?"

She gave a convulsive swallow and was silent.

He pressed a little harder with his knife so the blade just nicked her skin.

"Me," the hag shrieked at the feel of the knife. "I told them to come here."

"Ah, I thought as much."

"Word on the street was that the king would pay royally for news of an English spy. I'm a poor old woman, monsieur," she whined, "with nobody to take care of me in my old age. I have to look after myself because no one else will. I needed the money, and he was only an Englishman. They paid me two whole pistoles in gold to know where he was hiding."

"Two pistoles for betraying a man's life?" Having gotten what he needed from her, Lamotte took his knife away with a shrug. She was no danger to him anymore. "You were robbed. The king would have paid two thousand for such news."

"Two thousand?" The old woman's voice was laced

with abject misery. She didn't even seem to notice that the knife had gone from her neck. "He would have paid me two thousand gold pistoles?" She held her hands out beseechingly. "Tell me you are mocking me. Tell me you are making fun of a poor old woman with one foot in her grave. He would have paid me two thousand pistoles?"

"Or more."

They left the hag in the doorway wringing her hands with a look of despair on her face. "Two thousand pistoles or more?" she was repeating over to herself in accents of deepest grief. "How could I throw away such riches?"

Up the stairs they ran as quietly as they could, the soles of their boots making a muffled thwack on the wooden stairs.

The door to Sophie's old chamber was shut, with only the soft shuffle of anxious feet and the noise of breathing to give away the presence of the soldiers inside.

Sophie drew her sword, hefting it lightly in her hand. Lamotte looked at her and she nodded.

With a rush, they burst in at the door.

Hugh was tied to a chair in a corner, his hands behind his back. Five guards surrounded him, weapons in their hands.

The sudden attack took them by surprise. Two of them were disarmed and wounded in the first charge before they knew what was happening, and lay groaning on the floor, but the other three had time enough to collect their wits before Sophie and Lamotte were on them.

"Where is Miriame?" Sophie called to Hugh, as she fought off one of her attackers with desperate sword strokes.

Hugh shrugged his shoulders. "I haven't seen her."

There was a crash from up above them, and through the skylight in the roof jumped Miriame, her face aglow with the light of battle. "Was somebody looking for me?"

All five combatants stopped for a second to stare at the apparition. A second was all she needed to leap to Hugh and cut his bonds with a slash of her dagger. He jumped to his feet, a knife magically appearing in his hand.

The odds were now tipped the other way, in favor of the conspirators. There were four of them against three guards, and they were fighting for their lives.

With a frightened squeal, the guard nearest the door jumped through and ran off down the stairs, his boots clattering noisily as he ran. The remaining two guards looked at the fierce faces in front of them, and threw down their weapons. "We surrender."

Miriame looked disappointed at the cessation of hostilities. "Can I kill them?"

The guards looked pale. The younger of them started to tremble and opened his mouth to beg for mercy. The older guard jabbed him sharply in the stomach with his elbow, and the younger one shut his mouth again, a look of abject misery on his face.

Sophie shook her head. "No more killing."

Miriame grumbled in her sleeve and glared at the prisoners, but she put her sword back in its scabbard.

"Tie 'em up," Lamotte ordered Hugh. "I've no wish to see them dead, but they can stay here until we are well out of their reach."

Hugh gathered up the loose pieces of rope that had recently been on his wrists and tied their hands behind their backs and their ankles together. He rubbed his wrists together with a grimace as he did so. "I'll tie them as tightly as they tied me, the whoremongering French bastards," he said, as he pulled the knots tight. "I hope to God they won't be able to lift a sword for three days together once they win free again."

The two wounded guards lay on the floor, still groaning, one of them with a nasty cut to his thigh which was bleeding all over the floor. Sophie did not like to leave them there untended. She bent down over the badly wounded guard and hastily tied up his wound so it no longer bled. He mumbled his thanks. "I will send a leech to you anon," she said. "You will live."

Half an hour later, they reined in their horses and came to a stop outside the gates of Paris. The countryside stretched before them, an open land.

"Where to now?" Sophie asked. Where indeed could she go? Paris was no longer safe for her. She had nowhere to go but to the Camargue, to live among the ghosts of her family. Reluctantly she turned to face the south, to admit her defeat and desolation. She had failed in her quest. Her brother's name would die an undeserved death, and she would live a woman again.

Hugh sniffed the breeze from the west. "If I close my eyes, I can almost imagine I can smell the sea. I am to England by the shortest way to tell the king the sad news of his sister. You may all come with me, if you have a mind to. France may be too hot to hold you now, but King Charles will welcome you in England for your efforts to save the princess."

Settle in England and serve the English king instead of king of France? Sophie shot a sideways glance at Lamotte, who was frowning slightly. She did not think she could bear to leave beautiful France for a cold, remote island kingdom. Besides, she could not leave

Lamotte behind without the hope ever of seeing him again. She loved him too well for that.

Miriame turned her horse around to face back the way she had come. "I am French through and through. England is not the place for me. I am back to Paris."

Her friend was brave as well as foolish. "You are not scared of the king? That he will put you under sentence of death?"

"I've been under sentence of death for as long as I can remember—for picking pockets mostly. I'm not going to let a little thing like that stop me from being a musketeer. Besides, the king does not know my name, and his guards barely caught the merest glimpse of my face. I shall be perfectly safe. And you, Sophie? What shall you do?"

She looked at her husband in misery. How could she bear to leave him now that the time had come for them to part? "I do not know."

Lamotte shook his reins and his mare flicked her ears in acknowledgement. "I have nothing left to hold me in Paris. I have resigned my commission and angered the king so he will never forgive or forget."

"To England then?" suggested Hugh.

He shook his head. "I have long wanted to show my new wife my estates in Burgundy. It would be a good time to visit, I feel. The peaches in the orchard will be nicely ripe. Besides, the Duke of Burgundy is an honorable man, and I wager he will not say nay to a couple of king's guards joining his household. Will you come with me, Sophie, and serve the duke? Come with me as my companion? And as the wife of my heart?"

He was offering her the third way when she had least expected it. He was offering her life—the life she wanted to live. "You would stay married to a soldier, then?"

"I would stay married to you, Sophie, whether you be a soldier or no. I love you."

Sophie looked into his eyes and saw what she had never hoped or expected to see—the love he carried for her in his heart. A love that mirrored her own. "I love you, too, Ricard Lamotte, husband of my heart. Yes, I will come with you to Burgundy, be your wife, and serve the duke, with all my heart."

If you liked ON MY LADY'S HONOR, be sure to look for Kate Silver's next release in the passionate . . . *And One for All* series, A LADY BETRAYED, available wherever books are sold in October 2002.

Courtney Ruthgard may have been spoiled by her wealthy father, but she never considered herself foolish. Not until she gave her heart—and much more—to a dashing musketeer in the service of the king. Breaking her heart would have been one thing, but Pierre de Tournay stole papers incriminating Courtney's father in an illegal scheme. Suddenly penniless and alone, Courtney's only desire was to take revenge on the man who had betrayed her . . . and infiltrating the King's Guard was the perfect method. For Pierre, the arrival of Courtney's young male cousin in the guard was a godsend. Finally he had a sympathetic friend who would listen to his guilty outpourings about what the king had forced him to do and the painful regret he felt for hurting Courtney. But when a dangerous rebellion threw them into the fray together, he learned his new comrade in arms was none other than the woman he loved—and that his greatest battle would be proving to her his heart has always been true.

COMING IN SEPTEMBER 2002 FROM ZEBRA BALLAD ROMANCES

__AFTER THE STORM: Haven
by Jo Ann Ferguson   0-8217-7377-1 $5.99US/$7.99CAN
Cailin Rafferty will stop at nothing to find her children. Her journey brings her to the sleepy town of Haven, Ohio, where gentle Samuel Jennings had rescued them from the orphan train. For Cailin, wrenching them from the peaceful comfort of Sam's home is hard—almost as difficult as admitting her feelings for the quiet, warm-hearted man.

__EXPLORER: The Vikings
by Kathryn Hockett   0-8217-7259-7 $5.99US/$7.99CAN
Unaware that he is the son of a Viking jarl, Sean was raised in an Irish monastery. But then he offers shelter to a lovely young slave—and changes his life forever. For when Natasha is recaptured and dispatched aboard a Viking ship, Sean knows that he must rescue her. He ventures out on the high seas—seeking his heritage, his family, and his lady love.

__THE HEALING: Men of Honor
by Kathryn Fox   0-8217-7244-9 $5.99US/$7.99CAN
On the run after killing her violent lover in self-defense, Jenny Hanson needs a safe haven. She heads for Dawson City—only to hitch a ride with the very man sent to bring her to justice. Northwest Mounted Policeman Mike Finnegan is a man who left behind a troubled past to serve the law. He's also a man offering her protection and love . . .

__TO TOUCH THE SKY: The MacInness Legacy
by Julie Moffett   0-8217-7271-6 $5.99US/$7.99CAN
Gillian Saunders is content with her simple life, until it is turned upside down by handsome physician Spencer Reeves, who's been badly injured in a shipwreck. She never expects to be swept into an irresistible passion . . . or that an ancient curse which haunts her family will soon threaten her newfound love with him.

Call toll free **1-888-345-BOOK** to order by phone or use this coupon to order by mail. *ALL BOOKS AVAILABLE SEPTEMBER 1, 2002.*

Name _____
Address _____
City_____ State _____ Zip _____
Please send me the books that I checked above.
I am enclosing $_____
Plus postage and handling* $_____
Sales tax (in NY and TN) $_____
Total amount enclosed $_____
*Add $2.50 for the first book and $.50 for each additional book.
Send check or money order (no cash or CODs) to: **Kensington Publishing Corp., Dept. C.O., 850 Third Avenue, New York, NY 10022**
Prices and numbers subject to change without notice. Valid only in the U.S. All orders subject to availability. **NO ADVANCE ORDERS.**
Visit our website at **www.kensingtonbooks.com**